SHANE'S FALL

The Escort Series #2

SLOANE KENNEDY

CONTENTS

Copyright v
Shane's Fall vii
Trademark Acknowledgements ix
Series Reading Order xi
Series Crossover Chart xv
Trigger Warning xvii

Chapter 1 1
Chapter 2 10
Chapter 3 19
Chapter 4 27
Chapter 5 33
Chapter 6 43
Chapter 7 53
Chapter 8 65
Chapter 9 78
Chapter 10 89
Chapter 11 99
Chapter 12 112
Chapter 13 128
Chapter 14 145
Chapter 15 159
Chapter 16 181
Chapter 17 189
Chapter 18 198
Epilogue 204

About the Author 209
Also by Sloane Kennedy 211

Shane's Fall is a work of fiction. Names, characters, businesses, places, events and incidents are either the products of the author's imagination or used in a fictitious manner. Any resemblance to actual persons, living or dead, or actual events is purely coincidental.

Published in the United States by Sloane Kennedy

Cover Image: © artem_furman

Cover By: Jay Aheer, Simply Defined Art

ISBN-13:
978-1511789776

ISBN-10:
1511789778

SHANE'S FALL

Sloane Kennedy

TRADEMARK ACKNOWLEDGEMENTS

The author acknowledges the trademarked status and trademark owners of the following trademarks mentioned in this work of fiction:

Armani
http://www.armani.com/us
BMW
www.bmwusa.com
Rolex
www.rolex.com
Boy Scouts Club of America
www.scouting.org
YouTube
http://www.youtube.com/
Valentino
www.valentino.com/us

SERIES READING ORDER

All of my series cross over with one another so I've provided a couple of recommended reading orders for you. If you want to start with the Protectors books, use the first list. If you want to follow the books according to timing, use the second list. Note that you can skip any of the books (including M/F) as each was written to be a standalone story.

Note that some books may not be readily available on all retail sites

Recommended Reading Order (Use this list if you want to start with "The Protectors" series)

1. Absolution (m/m/m) (The Protectors, #1)
2. Salvation (m/m) (The Protectors, #2)
3. Retribution (m/m) (The Protectors, #3)
4. Gabriel's Rule (m/f) (The Escort Series, #1)
5. Shane's Fall (m/f) (The Escort Series, #2)
6. Logan's Need (m/m) (The Escort Series, #3)
7. Finding Home (m/m/m) (Finding Series, #1)
8. Finding Trust (m/m) (Finding Series, #2)
9. Loving Vin (m/f) (Barretti Security Series, #1)

10. Redeeming Rafe (m/m) (Barretti Security Series, #2)
11. Saving Ren (m/m/m) (Barretti Security Series, #3)
12. Freeing Zane (m/m) (Barretti Security Series, #4)
13. Finding Peace (m/m) (Finding Series, #3)
14. Finding Forgiveness (m/m) (Finding Series, #4)
15. Forsaken (m/m) (The Protectors, #4)
16. Vengeance (m/m/m) (The Protectors, #5)
17. A Protectors Family Christmas (The Protectors, #5.5)
18. Atonement (m/m) (The Protectors, #6)
19. Revelation (m/m) (The Protectors, #7)
20. Redemption (m/m) (The Protectors, #8)
21. Finding Hope (m/m/m) (Finding Series, #5)
22. Defiance (m/m) (The Protectors #9)

Recommended Reading Order (Use this list if you want to follow according to timing)

1. Gabriel's Rule (m/f) (The Escort Series, #1)
2. Shane's Fall (m/f) (The Escort Series, #2)
3. Logan's Need (m/m) (The Escort Series, #3)
4. Finding Home (m/m/m) (Finding Series, #1)
5. Finding Trust (m/m) (Finding Series, #2)
6. Loving Vin (m/f) (Barretti Security Series, #1)
7. Redeeming Rafe (m/m) (Barretti Security Series, #2)
8. Saving Ren (m/m/m) (Barretti Security Series, #3)
9. Freeing Zane (m/m) (Barretti Security Series, #4)
10. Finding Peace (m/m) (Finding Series, #3)
11. Finding Forgiveness (m/m) (Finding Series, #4)
12. Absolution (m/m/m) (The Protectors, #1)
13. Salvation (m/m) (The Protectors, #2)
14. Retribution (m/m) (The Protectors, #3)
15. Forsaken (m/m) (The Protectors, #4)
16. Vengeance (m/m/m) (The Protectors, #5)
17. A Protectors Family Christmas (The Protectors, #5.5)
18. Atonement (m/m) (The Protectors, #6)
19. Revelation (m/m) (The Protectors, #7)

20. Redemption (m/m) (The Protectors, #8)
21. Finding Hope (m/m/m) (Finding Series, #5)
22. Defiance (m/m) (The Protectors #9)

SERIES CROSSOVER CHART

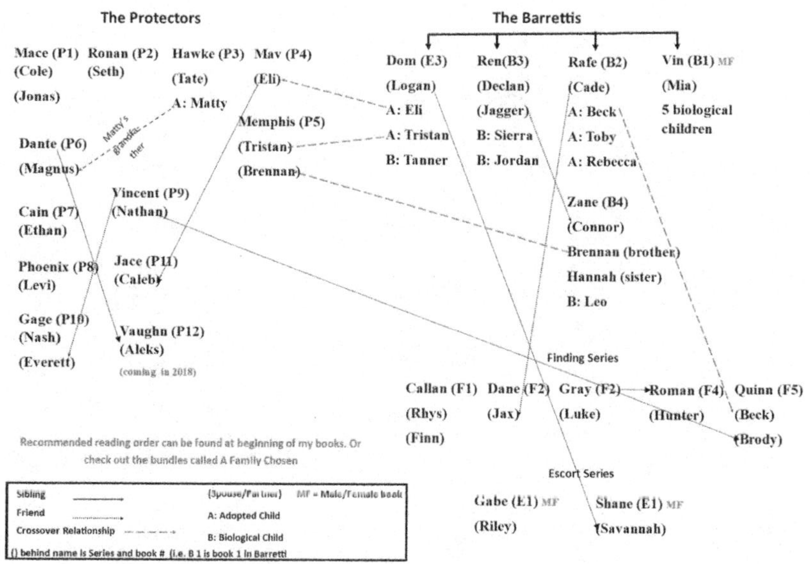

TRIGGER WARNING

Listed below are the trigger warnings for this book. Reading them may cause spoilers:

This book contains references to sexual assault and self-injuring.

CHAPTER 1

THE HOTEL ROOM WASN'T EXACTLY A DUMP, BUT IT WASN'T WHAT HE was used to either. Shane Matthews looked around the room as he worked the buttons of his dress shirt free. Most of his clients typically spared no expense when fulfilling their fantasies, which wasn't surprising. With the amount of money they were paying for his services, it made sense to go all out and get the whole package. The hotel was located just north of the city and the view sucked – he liked it when he could fuck the woman while she was pressed up against a huge window with the busy Seattle streets just below, tourists and residents alike completely oblivious as they hurried down the sidewalk. Every once in a while a customer would balk at his demand, but a little dirty talk and the forbidden threat of being discovered had them plastered up against that glass in no time, their hot breath steaming up the window as he brought them the pleasure they had bought and paid for.

Escorting had become a way of life for him, as easy and straightforward as eating or going to the store. After all, he'd been at it for more than seven years. The fact that it no longer fueled his adrenaline to be paid to fuck a woman senseless was something he didn't spend a lot of time dwelling on. As the thrill had started to wane, he had tried experimenting with more risqué excursions including some S&M crap that he still didn't get and the occasional "fuck me while my husband watches" kink. There was always an initial rush at trying something different, but it never lasted. So he'd gone back to his roots and focused on doing what he did best; becoming whoever his clients wanted him to be.

He toed off his shoes and went to work on his pants. His customer still hadn't made an appearance, but he could see a light under the closed bathroom door so he assumed that was where she was hiding. He could hear water running but nothing else. He'd been given pretty specific instructions so he didn't call out or knock on the door. A quick glance around the room indicated a woman's jacket thrown over the back of the desk chair so he felt a little better knowing that the chances that his customer really was a woman were good. He didn't usually accept new clients via email but, this one's request had interested him and the fact that she had his email address at all meant she either knew one of his other customers or he had given her his card at some point because he had been intrigued by her – a rare occurrence, but not unheard of.

She had only referred to herself as "S" in the email and had indicated she wanted to play out a control fantasy. The unusual part was that she wanted to be the one in control. While that part had caught his attention, her insistence that he be tied up as well as blindfolded for the duration of their time together had been what had made him hit the reply button. He'd agreed to everything she asked for except the tying up part because as much as his body had hardened at the idea of a woman temporarily taking his control from him, he wasn't stupid enough to put himself in a complete stranger's hands with no way to defend himself. He was probably pushing it with the blindfold part, but he figured his instincts were well-honed enough that he'd be able to sense if she wasn't on the up and up. And truthfully, when he had felt that little prick of excitement that came with the unknown, he'd felt something he hadn't felt in a while. Sure, things could go really wrong really fast, but he was willing to risk it if it meant he could just escape the darkness that seemed to be wrapping its fingers around every part of his soul these days.

Shane pulled a couple of condom packets from his pants and tossed them on the nightstand before he removed the pants and kicked them aside. *'Always be prepared'* – wasn't that the Boy Scout motto? Probably not what they had in mind, but a good lesson all the same. Grabbing the dark red blindfold - which actually appeared to just be a generic sleep mask - from the nightstand, Shane got up on the bed and positioned himself so that he was lying flat with his hands folded behind his head. While his customer had finally agreed to him not being bound, she'd been insistent that he couldn't touch her. It was strange, he thought, but his entire career was built on strange so who was he to judge? The woman obviously had some need to be in control of everything that went on and if it got her off, then all the power to her – that's what he was here for, after all.

As he waited, he ran through the rest of his week in his mind. Classes started in a few weeks so he could fit in a few more client sessions each week until then, but then he would have to start paring it down to one or two a week. Just thinking about getting through his final year of law school had the pressure building in his chest. Less than a year left of freedom and then he'd be joining his dad's firm in Chicago as planned. It had all been worked out years ago and like the good son he was, he'd made it to the finish line. Didn't matter how he got there, as long as he crossed it.

The sound of a door opening snapped him from his thoughts and his ears honed in on the sound of someone approaching. A single set of footsteps, light and soft. Some of the tension eased as he confirmed that whoever it was was alone. So far so good. As the steps grew closer, he detected a light floral scent, perfume or body wash probably. Very feminine. Another sigh of relief. He couldn't see through the blindfold, but knew he could have it off in a millisecond if he needed to. He clasped his hands together tightly so that he wouldn't be tempted to do just that and waited. He could hear her - at least he was 99 percent sure it was a her - breathing softly as she stopped next to him. Sensing her gaze running the length of his body, he felt his dick start to harden. He knew she probably liked what she saw – he'd been fortunate to inherit his father's tall, muscular frame but his mother's golden looks. He wasn't a muscle head like his buddy Gabe, but he took care of himself and women always seemed to appreciate it. Gabe's girlfriend,

Riley, was always commenting on his shaggy, blonde hair and had offered to trim it more than once for him, but he also caught her admiring it on more than one occasion and he knew it was good just the way it was.

A good minute passed, but Shane kept his mouth shut and let the woman have her fill of him. He was surprised to feel her fingers briefly brush against his lips, almost reverently. He was tempted to suck the tip of one into his mouth, but held himself back – this was her game. A moment later the fingers were gone and he heard her move around to the other side of the bed. The bed barely dipped under her weight as she climbed onto it so he was guessing she had a lighter frame. He felt her knees press against his outer thigh and he pictured her kneeling next to him as she examined him, like he was a buffet laid out for her enjoyment – in reality, that's what he was.

For all the times had had done a similar perusal to a woman, it felt strange to be the one being looked at. The woman's fingertips drifted over his chest and down to his abdomen before coming to a stop. Sensation shot through him and he forced back a curse. She'd barely touched him and he had felt it everywhere. She might as well have used a live wire on him. He tensed, silently begging her hand to move further down his body to the part that needed to feel her the most, but she stroked back up his abdomen and circled one of his nipples, then the other. And even though her touch wasn't sensual at this point, more curious than anything else, he felt like he was going to explode. What the hell was happening to him? Seconds passed and then her hand was stroking up one of his bent arms, stopping just short of where his hand lay under his head.

Shane let out a sigh of relief when her hand disappeared, but then nearly shot off the bed when he felt her lips brush his chest. He forced himself to remain still, but when he felt her hair brush his nipple he nearly came on the spot. An image of long, black hair flashed through his mind followed by a set of wide, pale blue eyes. No, he wouldn't do that – he wouldn't picture *her* while he was working. He felt a hand put pressure on his chest and then suddenly her lips were on his, a fleeting touch. He hadn't expected kissing at all and he guessed she hadn't planned on it either because he could sense her hovering just above him, her lips just inches from his, her breathing now heavy. If he lifted his head just a little bit, he'd be able to get that lush mouth back on his. Before he could even tell himself why it was a bad idea, her lips were back and brushing his with feather light kisses, one right after the other. After a few seconds he returned each soft kiss and a warning light went on in his head that this was getting way too heavy; too emotionally charged. But his body wasn't listening because his tongue skated across her plump lips and she gasped and stilled.

He waited for what seemed like forever and then her mouth was pressed back against his, more demanding this time, but still not sure what it was actually seeking. The word 'inexperienced' was flashing through his head like a set of hazard lights warning of dangerous conditions ahead, but he didn't care as he opened to her in silent invitation. When her tongue finally slipped inside, his was there to meet it, to welcome it. He sealed their mouths together and sucked on her tongue and then followed it back into her mouth so he could search every surface. The fingers of one of his hands bit into the wrist of the other and he briefly wondered if he would have bruises tomorrow. But he knew if he didn't keep a death grip on his arm, it would rip free of its moorings and snake around to grab her by the head so he could plunder her mouth the way he really wanted to.

She finally pulled back from the kiss so she could catch her breath and that's when he noticed the fabric rubbing over his chest as she leaned across him. She was still wearing a shirt, but he was sure her legs had been bare when she had shimmied up against him earlier. It took everything in him not to rip the blindfold off so he could see her. He'd never been affected this much, this fast and he had no idea what she even looked like. Fingers drifted down his chin, along his neck and then down his chest. He held his breath when her hand continued down to his pelvis and skittered to a stop near the base of his cock, the tips of her fingers testing the light, rough hair surrounding his hard length. She shifted her weight and he instantly missed the warmth of her body pressed against his. But then her hand was moving again and she trailed her thumb against his base as her fingers gently closed around him. His cock was aching now, almost painful, and he heard her breathing increase as she began slowly stroking him. As pre-cum leaked from his top, she smeared it with her fingers around the head.

On her next down stroke he instinctively lifted his hips up and she hesitated for a moment before stroking him again. "Tighter," he muttered harshly, his voice sounding loud in the quiet room. She stilled for several seconds, probably caught off guard by his voice and his guttural command, and then tightened her grip as she dragged her hand up and down his length. Heat rushed through his body and he began reciting criminal codes in his head to try to keep his raging body under control. But when he felt her tongue explore the head of his dick, he let out a harsh moan and started to reach for her. Luckily she was too busy to notice and he caught himself and forced his hands back under his head.

She licked him up and down several times as her hands explored his balls and then she took his length into her mouth. He instinctively thrust further down her throat and instantly felt bad when she started to gag. She was clearly a novice at this, but his body didn't care and for once, he couldn't control his responses. Even now his hips were pushing back up to try and seek out as much of her warm mouth as it could. She used her hand at his base to keep him from choking her but didn't pull off. When she added suction he yelled out, "Stop or I'm gonna come!"

She seemed startled by his words, but gently released him. He was glad he had the blindfold on or she'd be able to see how humiliated he was that he couldn't control his reaction to her. He was supposed to be this Sex God who could last for hours, but she had him ready to come like some horny teenager in the back of a beat up old car with the older and much more experienced captain of the cheerleading squad. He sucked in several deep breaths and waited to see what she would do next. When a minute passed, and then another, he started to worry that she was done – that he'd fucked this up so bad that he'd turned her off. But then he felt the silky skin of her inner thigh brush his leg as she shifted her weight so she could sit astride him. At some point, she had grabbed one of the condoms off the night stand or she had her own because she was trying to get it down his length, her hands fumbling at the task. He could tell she was still wearing the shirt, but her lower half was bare, evidenced by the heat radiating from her core against his thighs.

After several torturous starts and stops, the condom finally sheathed him and he felt her hesitate for a moment as if wondering what to do next. She finally leaned forward over him and he felt the brush of her breasts against his chest through the fabric of her shirt. He imagined what they would taste like, but the thought was short-lived as he felt her hand fumble between them before closing around his dick. It took her several tries, but she finally got it positioned against her opening and then lowered her weight down. He felt the tip press inside her but knew instantly what the problem was. He heard her harsh breathing grow more rapid as frustration kicked in. She was bearing down on him, but there was little progress and he heard her whimpers of frustration turn to tears. As she grew more desperate, she tried to force herself farther down on him and he knew it had to be causing her some discomfort, if not downright pain.

"Sweetheart, your body isn't ready for me yet," he said softly. She choked back the sad little cries that had been escaping her throat and eased off of him a little bit, unsure what to do next. He sensed she was on the verge of giving up and he really didn't want that, although he refused to wonder why it mattered so much to him either way. She was braced on her knees over him, her hand pressed against his chest for support, the tip of his cock still pressed to her entrance.

"I can help you but I need to use my hand," he began. At the mention of his hand, he felt her tense up further so he said, "Or I can use my mouth." She gasped at that and he felt a little bit of moisture coat the head of his cock. As much as he wanted her to choose the latter, he'd be glad for any chance to touch her. When she didn't respond, he was sure he'd lost her, but then he felt her hand reach up to touch his arm. He released the vise-like grip he had on his wrist and slowly moved his arm down, wincing when he felt blood rushing into it. He almost laughed because at this point he'd been sure that all the blood in his body had rushed to his dick the second she'd touched him.

He settled his hand on her leg and slowly caressed her thigh – it was as silky smooth as he had hoped it would be. When he felt her tense under his touch, he decided not to push his luck and moved his hand to where their bodies were still joined. She had to be uncomfortable in the position, but he suspected that she was still desperate to make this happen and if she pulled off him now, she might not have the courage to finish what she'd started. With that in mind, his fingers sought out the bud between her folds and gently stroked it once. He couldn't see her reaction but he heard it – shocked surprise. He circled her clit with his thumb a few times before allowing the rough pad to press over the hard nub of flesh. Heat engulfed him as he felt the tip of his cock slide into her and she moaned. He suspected she had dropped her head forward too because he felt her hair brush his abdomen. He continued to circle and stroke her, applying a little bit more pressure each time. Every time her body rippled with pleasure as he hit her clit, he felt her sink further down on him.

Within minutes she had pulled her body upright to accommodate the angle she needed to move further down his shaft. When he felt her ass touch up against his balls, he slowed his strokes so she could just enjoy the feel of him deep inside her. She was like liquid fire around him and the lust was quickly taking over him, telling him to thrust into her tight body as hard and as fast as he could. His brain reminded him that this was her show and he started to pull his hand back, but stopped when she grabbed it and held it tight. He rewarded her with another hard stroke of her clit and then bit back a rush of pleasure as she forced herself further down on his cock. She whimpered and then lifted herself up just a fraction before dropping down again. He could feel her moisture seeping out of her now and each time she moved he was able to glide more easily in and out. Stroking her as she raised herself higher each time, he nearly bit his tongue when he felt her long hair brush over the tops of his thighs. That meant her hair was super long or she had her head angled back in her desire, or both. God, he hoped it was both.

She continued to ride him, her hand gripping his wrist, trying to control how he stroked her. He began to meet her thrusts with an upward motion of his hips and she was forced to release his wrist so she could drop both her hands to his chest in order to support herself as she countered his powerful lunges. When her hair brushed against his chest and her small nails raked his skin, he lost the battle and grabbed both her hips with his hands. He raised himself up in one quick motion and had her pinned beneath him a second later, his body pushing into hers as far as it could go. Another powerful thrust and he reached up to pull the blindfold off, his control shattered. Several long seconds passed before he realized two horrifying things – one, she was no longer writhing in pleasure around him but was in fact pushing against him in terror and two, he recognized the beautiful, pale blue eyes staring back at his in fear.

CHAPTER 2

Holy Shit.

Shane couldn't believe it. He was balls deep inside of Savannah Bradshaw, his best friend Logan's little sister, and she was scared to death and trying to get away from him. She hadn't made any sound as she squeezed her eyes closed and pushed at his chest. Tears began to stream from her eyes. Her abject fear had obliterated all his lust instantly, but his brain was still confused by what was happening so he hadn't been able to pull himself from her yet. She started crying these hoarse, harsh sobs as she fought him and that was when reality finally kicked in.

"Savannah, honey, it's me Shane. Open your eyes." He gently pinned her flailing wrists so she wouldn't hurt herself or him in her struggles. "Open your eyes Savannah!" His voice was harsher than he intended it to be, but it seemed to knock her out of the daze she had been in and she finally stilled, tears spilling down her face and disappearing under the collar of the white, button up blouse she was wearing. "I'm going to pull out now but I need you to be still so I don't hurt you, okay," he said quietly, carefully, his heart ripped to shreds as he saw the pain and fear in her eyes. She nodded slowly, her hands still fisted in his grip. He gently pulled free of her body and lifted his weight off of her, his hands releasing hers as he positioned himself next to her on the edge of the bed. The second she was free of him she curled onto her side away from him and cried, her tormented sobs clawing at his insides. He covered her lower body carefully with the bedspread and went to the bathroom to dispose of the condom, grabbing his pants off the floor on his way there. He returned with a wet washcloth and a glass of water. He'd managed to pull his pants on but was still shirtless.

Her cries had slowed so he lowered himself to sit back down on the bed. "Sweetheart, can you sit up for me please?" he asked softly. She wiped at her tears and pulled herself into a sitting position, her back pressed against the headboard, her arms wrapped protectively around her pulled up knees. He gently cleaned her red face with the washcloth and then handed her the water and waited as she took a long drink. He put the glass on the nightstand and then turned to look at her. She looked young and innocent and his insides knotted as he realized what he'd done – she was his best friend's baby sister. He'd know her since she was fifteen years old, had lusted after her almost as long and now he'd actually gone and fucked her. And it had ended with him hurting her, even if that hadn't been his intention. From her violent reaction the moment he took control, he knew something bad had happened to her at some point and he had triggered a memory of it.

"Did I hurt you?" he asked brokenly, afraid to hear the truth, but needing to know all the same. She shook her head.

"I'm sorry Shane," she said, fresh tears welling in her eyes. She snatched the washcloth off the night stand and wiped at her face. She was a mess, but God, she was the most beautiful thing he'd ever seen. It was her pale, luminous eyes he'd envisioned when she'd first touched him, her long, sleek black hair he'd imagine brushing over him. And it *was* long, down to the small of her back, and he'd always wondered what it would feel like against his skin. And now he knew. *Shit.*

"I don't understand what's going on here Savannah," he admitted. Never in his wildest dreams could he have imagined this happening. He'd promised himself he would never touch her and yet here they were.

"I just..." she paused and shook her head. "I just needed to know if it would be possible to be with someone like this someday." He could see the shame in her eyes. "I picked you because I knew I could trust you. I used you," she cried, as the harsh reality of her words seemed to sink in even to her own ears.

"Start at the beginning," he said, surprised at his even tone despite the knot of anxiety in his gut. He knew this situation could only get worse as she revealed more.

"I found your card in Riley's purse last week when we were having lunch and she said I could borrow some tissues from it while she ran to the bathroom."

"So you know what I am?" he asked, ashamed that she knew his secret. It wasn't that he was exactly proud of what he did, but it wasn't something you flaunted in front of an innocent young girl.

"And Logan too," she said quietly. "I overheard you guys talking about it one night when you thought I'd gone to bed. You were all a bit drunk," she said sheepishly.

"When?"

"A few years ago. Gabe was there too." She was talking about Gabe Maddox, his other best friend who had just recently managed to get out of the life after meeting Riley. And she knew about her brother, something Shane knew Logan would be horrified to learn.

"So you found my card," he pressed.

"I thought with the blindfold you wouldn't figure out it was me and I could have this one time to see if I could go through with it. I thought if I was in control-" Her voice dropped off.

"Why did you need to be in control Savannah?"

She was quiet for a really long time. It clearly hurt her to have to tell him, but he needed to know, even if he already suspected what she was going to say.

"Because I didn't have any last time," she whispered, the words barely audible.

Shane tensed, his hands fisting. "Did someone hurt you?" His world fell apart when she nodded and he sucked in a breath and bit back tears. He hadn't seen it – how could he not have known? Yes, he'd avoided her as much as possible, but something like that would have shown, right?

"Does Logan know?" When she shook her head, Shane had to get up and move. He was about to put his hand through a wall when he realized that would scare the hell out of her and she was already freaked out as it was. He paced back and forth, but the room was too small and his rage was too big. They'd failed her and she had gone through it all alone. She hadn't trusted any one of them to tell them the truth.

"When?" was all he could get out. When she didn't answer, he looked at her. She had her chin resting on her knees, her eyes on the bed. He got the message – she wasn't going to tell him anymore specifics.

"Please don't tell Logan. It would kill him," she said softly. She was right. Her brother had given up everything to raise her when their parents had died in a car crash shortly after she had turned fourteen. Logan was barely nineteen and in his first year of school with Gabe. Shane was younger, just sixteen at the time. He and Gabe had been friends since childhood, along with Shane's older brother Michael. Gabe and Michael had befriended Logan in college and it was only natural for Shane to be part of the group, even after his brother's death later that year. He'd even followed Logan and Gabe into the escorting business, but their reasons had been so different. Shane knew that Logan had needed the money to keep Savannah out of the hands of child services and he would be horrified to learn that not only did his sister know what he did for extra cash, but that she'd been hurt, presumably while under his care.

"Please Shane," Savannah pleaded and Shane realized he'd been silent for a long time, giving her the impression he was contemplating telling Logan her secret. He wouldn't, not now anyway, not until he knew more about what had happened.

"I won't tell him," he assured her and she visibly relaxed. "Help me understand this," he said, motioning to the room. She was quiet for so long that he thought she wouldn't answer but then she finally spoke.

"After," she began before swallowing hard. "After, it was hard to be around men. It got worse at school."

Shane realized she'd just slipped up by indicating she'd been assaulted before leaving for college. Jesus, she'd barely been eighteen when she left.

"I just felt like I was suffocating – it was a coed dorm, the classes were coed. I tried to just keep to myself, but they'd approach me and ask me out and I would just freeze up." She choked back a harsh laugh. "They started calling me a freak around campus, but at least they stopped asking me on dates." She wiped at a stray tear so he grabbed a tissue from the dispenser on the nightstand and handed it to her. He was glad to see she didn't flinch away from him.

"Did you talk to anyone about it?"

She shook her head. "Not at first – I thought it would go away, the fear. But I started spending more and more time in my room, took online classes. But things got really dark so I went and saw a counselor." She fell silent and took several long breaths to calm herself. "None of what she said made any sense to me – it just seemed like a lot of psychobabble so I stopped going."

"What happened then?" He was reeling at the knowledge that she'd been going through all this and no one had known, no one had stepped up to help her.

"Nothing. I just focused on finishing school. A guy asked me out just before graduation a few months ago – he must have been new to campus because he didn't seem to know I was the freak..."

"Don't," he said quietly, firmly. "Don't call yourself that." He hoped the anger in his voice didn't shut her down, but he couldn't hear that word used in reference to her again and keep his sanity.

She nodded at him before continuing. "I agreed to go to get coffee with him. I managed to keep it together but I was a mess inside and when he tried to kiss me good night I lost it – the dorm's RA had to help me back to my room because I couldn't remember where I was. She wanted to call someone but I begged her not to. I convinced her I was just really tired and hadn't slept well because of finals."

"Why didn't you tell Logan? Or me?" He saw her flinch at the accusation in his voice and he cursed himself.

"I'm sorry I did this to you Shane. I know it was wrong."

"Savannah, look at me." When she lifted her eyes, he moved back to the bed and sat down on the edge so he was facing her. "I don't blame you and I understand why you did it. I just wish you had come to me-"

"I couldn't," she said roughly. "I knew what you would say – you only see me as Logan's little sister. I knew you could never want me that way." When she dropped her eyes again, he placed his fingers under her chin and forced her eyes up to meet his.

"You're right – I would have said no, but not because I don't want you." He leaned over and kissed her gently, his lips barely brushing hers. He pulled back so that there was just a sliver of space between them. "I've wanted you from the moment I met you." He sealed his lips back over hers and licked the seam of her closed mouth until she opened on a gasp, then thrust his tongue into the warm depths. A few more seconds, he promised himself as he twined his tongue around hers. He just needed a few more seconds to memorize her taste. When he finally pulled back she followed him, her hand closing around the back of his neck to stop his departure. He allowed himself another few moments of pleasure and then put his hand on her cheek as he separated their mouths. They were both breathing heavy and he rested his forehead against hers for a moment.

"I'm not saying no because you're my best friend's sister," he began and he saw her squeeze her eyes closed because she knew he was going to walk away from her. "I'm saying no because I still have enough sense to know that you deserve better." He brushed another kiss over her lips and then stood. He forced himself not to look back as he grabbed his shirt and shoes and disappeared out the door. He thought he heard a sob as the door clicked shut, but he wasn't sure and it didn't matter anyway.

THE SUN WAS JUST STARTING TO SET AND THE ROOM HAD GROWN DIM when Savannah finally forced herself to move. She hated that she was cold again – in those few brief moments when Shane had been inside her, she'd felt nothing but warmth. The noise in her head was back too – that annoying white noise that always seemed to be taunting her, reminding her that the control she had over her life was an illusion.

The knot began forming in her stomach and she felt the tingling underneath her skin – it was nothing like the sparks she had felt when Shane had grazed her thigh or the overwhelming tightness she had felt when he stroked her as her body welcomed him deep inside her.

When she'd first seen him on the bed, his nudity had overwhelmed her and it had taken everything in her not to grab her clothes and run. She hadn't been sure what she was thinking when she had come up with the idea that someone like her could control a man like him. He was strong, beautiful, confident, experienced – she was none of those things. But when he hadn't moved or made any effort to break the rules she had set, her curiosity had gotten the better of her and she'd approached him. He'd warned her that he wouldn't allow himself to be tied up, but when she saw his muscular arms raised in submission, she'd been humbled. He was giving her as much as he could. His good looks had been what her initial fifteen-year-old crush had been based on, but as the years passed and she'd gotten to know him, she'd starting losing her heart to his charm and kindness. But he'd been different when she'd returned home just a couple of months ago – harder, darker. Whenever she had spoken to him, he'd replied with short, clipped answers and rarely tried to draw her into any further conversation.

The impulse to hire him had been just that. She'd had many years to ponder what he, her brother and Gabe did for extra money and her young mind hadn't really comprehended it at first. The word "prostitute" had kept flashing in her mind when she looked at her brother after overhearing that brief, drunken conversation. But then she would see how tired he looked and she remembered how hard he worked to keep up with his studies, work full-time and still take care of her so that they could stay together. As a teenager, he hadn't dated much so she figured he hadn't been into the whole thing just for the thrill of having sex with strangers for money. He had done it purely out of need so he could take care of her.

In his younger years, Shane definitely seemed the most likely of the three men to enjoy what they were doing. He had always had a girl on his arm though she couldn't remember anyone serious, or even seeing the same girl more than once for that matter. But whatever his motives might have been, he wasn't the same, charismatic boy next door that he'd once been. He seemed haunted. It was probably foolish to think of him that way; she was probably just over dramatizing the whole thing. The man was incredibly successful – top of his class in law school with plans to join his father's high-powered, criminal defense law firm in Chicago next year. He even had a gorgeous, rich girlfriend that he often escorted to fancy parties and functions – she'd never actually met the woman but every once in a while her face would be in the society pages of the paper as she arrived via limo in a fancy dress to some important event, a beautiful but bored looking Shane on her arm. Bile rose in her throat as she realized that not only had she used Shane for her own selfish needs, she had been a part of him cheating on his own girlfriend. How had she fallen this far, this fast?

Savannah made her way to the bathroom and turned the shower on. She took the blouse off, her eyes carefully avoiding the mirror. She was glad he hadn't asked why she'd left the shirt on – lying to Shane was hard, but there was no way she could have shared that part of her life with him. She climbed into the shower and let the water warm her. She ran her fingers over her body and allowed her mind to drift back to how she'd been able to explore Shane's naked body. The initial fear she had had when she first touched his chest had evaporated when she felt how warm and hard he was, all at the same time. She hadn't meant to kiss him, but his lips had been too tempting – she'd never actually kissed a man before - and when he had opened his mouth to hers, she'd been stunned at the desire that had flashed through her body. She had nothing to compare the kiss to, but she couldn't imagine it got much better than that. She also hadn't meant to explore his body either – her plan had been to get him inside of her as quickly as possible so she wouldn't have time to overthink things and freak out.

His hardness had been too difficult to resist though. And his moans of pleasure as she touched his length with her tongue had made her bold. She'd read about oral sex and had even snuck a peek at some porn online, but it wasn't something that had overly appealed to her. But his taste, the feel of him in her mouth...it had been hard to stop when he had called out his warning. If she hadn't been so desperate to complete the act to prove that she could, she'd have kept going for sure. And then it had all gone to hell.

She didn't even know her own body well enough to realize that she wasn't physically ready to take him. When she'd felt that burning pain as she tried to force his length inside her, dark memories had assailed her and threatened to pull her under. Her humiliation was complete when he called her on it and she had wanted to die on the spot. But he had given her a choice to continue, no pressure, no condemnation – just a choice. And then it had felt amazing, like someone had set fire to her from the inside. She had felt so full when he finally slid all the way into her depths and something inside of her just kept winding tighter and tighter. At that point, her instincts had taken over and all she could do was feel.

And just like that, it was gone and she was back under a heavy weight, a heaving, sweaty body ripping her apart as a thick hand covered her mouth to muffle her cries. She'd closed her eyes so she could escape and go to her quiet place, but then Shane's voice had called to her through the darkness. He'd sounded worried and she had to see what was going on, to make sure he was okay. And when she opened her eyes, he was there and she knew she'd lost time again. It was happening more often now and she was starting to worry that one day she might not be able to find her way back.

As the water turned cold, she climbed out of the shower and dried off, suddenly eager to get out of this room. It was almost worse now because she had had those few minutes of pure pleasure with Shane so she knew it was possible, but it could also turn on a dime and plunge her into darkness. And worst of all, she'd used someone she loved in the most horrific way – she had been selfish and unthinking. She pulled her clothes on and grabbed her stuff. As she passed the bed and grabbed her jacket, she realized that it hadn't been worth it because she'd lost the one person she'd hope to be able to share that part of her life with and she had no one but herself to blame.

CHAPTER 3

WHERE THE FUCK ARE YOU?

Shane glanced at the text on his phone and then tossed it back on the coffee table. It was Gabe's third text in the past hour and Logan had already left two messages berating him for being MIA the past three weeks. He leaned back against the couch and looked around the room. It was almost entirely done in white except for the occasional black accent. It made him feel like he was in a hospital or institution of some sort, but Paige insisted it was all the rage. Everything in Paige's life had to be that way – clean, expensive and flawless. At least on the outside where people could see. Inside everything was the color of blood and shit. Dark, swirling and violent. And he had managed to somehow fit perfectly into her fucked up little world. It made sense, he supposed, since he was just as fucked up, if not more so.

The click clack of her stilettos told him she was near, the kitchen probably. Even when they were in her apartment, safe from prying eyes and the ever more important flash of cameras, she was in full garb.

"Babe, don't forget we're having dinner with my parents tonight. Wear the blue Armani," she said as she clicked her way out of the kitchen and towards the front door. She paused at the couch and leaned over the back of it to peck him on the cheek. It took everything in him not to pull away from the sticky, heavily painted red lips. "I left you a little something in the bathroom," she said brightly as she flung her designer bag over her shoulder and left, her perfect body showcased in a tight, white mini-dress. God, sometimes he really hated her.

Paige Moran was a daddy's girl, even at 24 years old. Her rich, banker father had bought her the condo that overlooked Puget Sound and had written her a blank check to stuff it full of whatever useless, trendy crap she could. She "worked" as a part-time interior designer, but as far as Shane knew, her only clients were friends of her father's. Their families had known each other for a few years and he and Paige had had some fun when they were in high school, but it had only been physical. She had had a great body – and knew it – and her dad had given her a BMW Roadster for her 16th birthday which Shane got a kick out of driving, but that was the extent of it. By the time he had made it to college, the majority of his memories of Paige were relegated to the back seat of that car and twisted fuck that he was, he got more of a thrill out of the car than the girl. But two years ago she had wormed her way back into his life and now he was practically living with her in this godforsaken, white mausoleum.

He heard his phone ding again, but ignored it and stood and walked to the floor to ceiling windows that overlooked the Sound. Ironically, he'd never fucked Paige up against these windows, hadn't even considered it. She wouldn't go for it anyway – might scuff up the glass. He studied the street below and then raised his eyes to examine the mountains just beyond the water. It occurred to him that at some point they had stopped amazing him and he tried to pinpoint when that had happened but couldn't. Dropping his eyes to the blue water, he couldn't help but think it was too dark...it should be lighter, paler. Like her eyes. Somehow that was the only shade of blue he liked anymore – crystal clear and swirling with passion. He hadn't actually gotten to see the passion, but his brain had no trouble imagining what her eyes had looked like before he grabbed her. And now it was all he could think about. That and the pure fear when he had twisted her under him and drove into her.

It had been twenty-three days since Savannah had shattered his world with her pleasure and her pain. He'd been a coward to walk out on her in that hotel room when she was hurting, but the helplessness had been too great. His entire life was about becoming what other people needed him to be, but when she had asked for that he had balked. And it wasn't because she was Logan's sister or that she was too young or fresh or innocent. No, he'd been afraid, plain and simple. Afraid she would see right through him, through the person he gave to the outside world. And she'd be horrified by what she found and he couldn't take that – couldn't see that contempt, that disgust in her eyes.

Scrubbing his hand over his face, he felt the sticky residue of Paige's lipstick on his cheek and went towards Paige's bedroom. He refused to think of it as his room, his bed. He passed by the monstrous king-sized bed with the perfectly made white sheets and comforter and went into the bathroom. More white but with a black marble vanity and black and white tiles on the floor. He stuttered to a halt when he saw the "gift" Paige had left him. She was such a bitch.

The small, round mirror lying on top of the middle of the counter stood in sharp contrast to the dark, smooth texture of the marble beneath it. But it was what was on top of the mirror that had his insides churning. Three perfectly straight lines of powder lined up side by side on the mirror, a half-rolled hundred-dollar bill sitting next to them. He swallowed hard as that familiar, metallic taste filled his mouth and his body automatically tightened in anticipation. It would only take a couple of steps, a few good inhales and he could be free.

He moved until he was standing over the mirror. Paige only ever bought the best so he knew what he was looking at would be even better than the shit he'd tried in the past. Curling his hands around the edge of the countertop, he leaned over the mirror and studied himself in the reflection, his image broken up by the lines. This was the guy he recognized, the fuck-up who was always just on the edge of losing it all.

Ten seconds passed, then twenty, then a full minute. And he knew he would do what he had done all the other times Paige had tried to "help him out." He picked up the mirror and dumped the contents in the sink and turned the water on. He didn't even care that the hundred-dollar bill got wet. It was her daddy's money and there was plenty more of it where that had come from.

Shane was lucky that Paige had yet to figure out that cocaine was just a cheap substitute for him – that the drug his body craved and tormented him endlessly for was heroin. One taste eight years ago was all it had taken for the monster to latch onto something inside and never let go. If she'd left him a needle full of the beautifully ugly brown liquid, his former life would already be a distant memory, his friends and family gone. It would only take one hit and he could let everyone and everything around him go. For eight years he had fought it and won, but it was inevitable that there would be a day when he couldn't stop himself from sticking that thin piece of metal in his arm and feeling the pain and pleasure as he pushed the plunger down and watched as the drug burned through his body.

He dropped the mirror on the counter and left the room and went to answer his now ringing phone because he knew that if he didn't, Gabe or Logan would show up on his – no, Paige's – doorstep, and he didn't want the few good pieces of his life anywhere near this piece of shit monstrosity that was his future.

"THOUGHT I MIGHT FIND YOU HERE."

Shane looked up from the bench he was sitting on to see Gabe striding toward him. Shane considered himself to be a fit guy but Gabe had him beat hands down – he was tall, built like a heavyweight champ and Shane had seen his skills in action – the bulging muscles weren't just for show. "How'd you find me?" he asked as his friend stopped beside the bench and looked around before dropping down next to him.

"Riley," was all Gabe said.

"Shit. Your woman has a good memory," Shane muttered as he leaned forward and dropped his elbows on his knees. He'd mentioned once in passing to Gabe's girlfriend Riley, that he stopped by to visit his brother every Saturday morning.

"I didn't know you did this," Gabe said as he motioned around them.

"Yeah, well, Saturday mornings were our thing right?" Gabe smiled and nodded and then fell silent. Shane turned his attention back to his brother's headstone. It was big and garish just like his parents had wanted. All around them were subtle grave markers with simply engraved names and dates with the occasional epitaph or colorful bouquet of flowers, but Michael's grave might as well have had a neon sign flashing over it that said, "Rich, beloved dead kid here." It wasn't true of course, at least not the beloved part. There were pictures engraved into the marble on each sides of Michael's name and fancy calligraphy underneath that said *Gone too soon, forever in our hearts.* He suspected his mother had come up with the phrase – it sounded appropriately dramatic.

"I guess 'disowned gay kid who would rather OD then live in this fucked up world alone,' was too big to fit," Shane said coldly as he motioned to the headstone. Gabe didn't answer and he hadn't expected him to. Michael had been fucked from the get go and they both knew it. His brother had been only nineteen when he'd taken his own life by shoving a needle full of heroin into his arm. It had happened just hours after Michael had come out to their parents about his sexuality and he'd been quickly disowned and abandoned in response. Shane hadn't even been able to say goodbye and by the time he got the suicide note the next morning, it was already over and Michael lay on a metal slab in the coroner's office. Official cause of death – accidental overdose. And it was all because Shane had been too much of a coward to stand up for his big brother. He'd let his parents push his brother away and then cover up the truth about why he was gone.

"It wasn't your fault," Gabe said softly. It wasn't the first time his friend had said it, probably wouldn't be the last either. And it did nothing to ease the guilt that ate away at his insides.

"What are you doing here?" Shane asked.

"Haven't seen you in a while. You missed the last three family dinners."

"Right, family dinner," Shane drawled, emphasizing the word "family." None of them were actually family, but they had started the tradition of meeting on Sunday nights a couple of months ago at Riley's insistence. It usually rotated between Logan and Savannah's house and Gabe and Riley's new apartment. He'd never offered to host it at Paige's place since she and his friends didn't mix well and he was barely living in his own apartment, which he was still hanging onto for some reason he was hesitant to identify.

"It's not the same without you there."

Shane wanted to tell Gabe that it wouldn't be the same if he was there – how could it ever be the same now that he'd fucked his best friend's sister? How could he explain that just looking at her tied him up in knots and knowing everything she'd been through, suffered through alone, would make it impossible to ingest anything, let alone keep it down? "Gotta say man, you're starting to sound like a bit of a girl," Shane joked but there was no laughter behind it.

Gabe wasn't taking the bait. "We're all worried about you."

"Don't be – it's all-"

"Good, I know," Gabe finished for him. "It's all good."

Shane could hear the disappointment in his friend's voice. "You heard from your mom?" He felt Gabe tense next to him and he glanced over at his friend who had gone pale. Gabe's mom was a mess, she'd been a junkie for more than half of Gabe's life and he had spent most of his time bailing her out of jail and getting her into rehab. She'd even resorted to stealing from him, but instead of turning her in, he'd stuck by her.

Gabe had even taken up escorting just so he could get enough money so he could keep paying for the rehab she would always end up leaving early. His friend had hated every second of being paid for sex. He'd even confided to Shane and Logan that he found no physical pleasure in the act. Riley's appearance in his life had changed all that and he was out for good. Shane had never seen his friend more relaxed and happy. "Sorry, I shouldn't have brought it up," Shane said, feeling guilty for putting that darkness back in his friend's eyes.

"She raped me."

Shane froze, sure he had heard the whispered words wrong. "What?"

"Wow, that's the first time I've said that." Amazingly, Gabe relaxed and sat up a little straighter.

"What are you talking about?" Shane stuttered, unable to grasp what his friend was saying.

"My mother raped me," he repeated carefully, as if still testing the words.

"Oh my God. Oh my God!" Shane jumped off the bench and took several clumsy steps away and willed the bile to stay in his gut which was now churning. "When?" he managed to ask in a strangled tone.

"I'm not a hundred percent sure when it started, but I think I was around thirteen."

Shane couldn't support his weight anymore so he dropped down to the grass next to his brother's tombstone. "I'm sorry Gabe, I didn't know...we didn't suspect..." Shane said, motioning to Michael's headstone.

"You couldn't have known Shane. We were kids. It's not something that most people can even conceive of."

Things started clicking into place for Shane. "The escorting..." he breathed in horror. No wonder his friend had hated it. "Oh God!"

Gabe rose from the bench and then sat down next to Shane. "Shane, do you know why I'm telling you this?"

Shane shook his head. He really didn't – part of him wished he hadn't.

"All of this came out because of my feelings for Riley," Gabe started.

"And I encouraged you to go after her," Shane responded, horrified.

Gabe's arm dropped around his shoulder and squeezed hard. "Look at me." When Shane shook his head Gabe nearly shouted, "Look at me!"

Shane forced his eyes up and felt the sting of bitter tears.

"You saved my life Shane. You fucking saved my life!" Gabe dropped his arm and looked around the cemetery. "If I'd lost Riley, I would have ended up here. If you hadn't opened my eyes..." Gabe took a deep breath and then turned his eyes back to Shane.

"I'm worried about you. I see it in your eyes – it haunts you the way it haunted me."

Shane knew what Gabe was talking about, but how could he explain to his best friend something he didn't completely understand himself? He shook his head and heard Gabe sigh in frustration.

"Have you seen your mom since...?" Shane asked carefully.

"No. It's part of the reason Riley and I moved into a new apartment. I've been seeing someone – a therapist – to help me figure out some of the shit going on in my head. I'm still trying to decide out how to deal with her if she shows up or calls looking for bail money." Gabe started picking at the grass. "Can you promise me something Shane?" When Shane didn't answer, Gabe said, "Can you promise me you'll call me if things go bad or when you're ready to talk?"

"Yeah," was all Shane said. It was the first time he'd ever lied directly to his friend's face.

CHAPTER 4

SAVANNAH SAT NERVOUSLY AT THE DESK IN HER NEW CLASSROOM AND waited. She had been more than an hour early to prep for her first class – it was the first day of school for both the kids and for her. As part of her education, she'd assisted other teachers in their classrooms, but it was entirely different when she was the one in charge. She would have volunteer parent helpers throughout the day to help her keep up with the twelve Kindergartners that had been assigned to her, but ultimately she would be the one making the decisions.

She jumped up and made her way around the room to make sure everything was in its place. As she made one final check of all the arts and crafts stuff she'd organized earlier, her phone rang and she had to dig pretty deep into her purse to find it. She tried not to be overly disappointed when she saw that the caller ID showed her brother. It was ridiculous to have expected *him* to call – it had been nearly a month since their disastrous meeting in the hotel room and she hadn't seen or spoken to him since.

"Hi Logan," she said, forcing a brightness into her voice that she wasn't feeling.

"Hi, I just wanted to wish you luck," came the deep voice on the other end.

"You did that already this morning," she laughed.

"I know but I also know how nervous you've been about this – I heard you get up a couple of times last night."

Savannah didn't mention that her restlessness had nothing to do with the new job. "I'm good, I swear."

"Okay. Hey, you want to come by the bar tonight and have a celebratory dinner? I make a mean bowl of peanuts."

Savannah tensed. "Um, no, I'll probably have a lot of prep work to do for tomorrow's class."

Logan was silent for a long time before saying, "They're five year olds Savannah. How much prep work do you need for a group of five year olds?"

"Maybe this weekend," she said. God, she hated lying to him.

"Yeah, okay," he responded. Their conversation had turned awkward quickly and she knew he was confused.

"Um, I gotta go. See you later."

"Bye. Good luck today."

"Thanks," she muttered and disconnected the call. She went back to the desk and sat down, her mood turning sour. She just kept messing things up. She'd been back from school less than three months and she'd alienated Shane and disappointed her brother. And worse, no one understood Shane's defection. He no longer attended dinners or get-togethers and Logan had reached out to him several times to no avail. It was like he had dropped off the map and it was all because of her.

The guilt was eating away at her and she struggled more every day to avoid the darkness that had consumed her these past few years. She had tried to call Shane a dozen times to tell him how sorry she was and to beg him to rejoin their group, but every time she dialed the phone she chickened out. She had used him for her own selfish reasons – she was no better than any of the other women in his life. That familiar itch began under her skin and she stood up to try and distract herself, but luckily her first student came barreling in the door, a haggard looking parent in tow and she was able to push everything else from her mind.

❧

SHANE SNAPPED HIS NOTEBOOK SHUT AND GRABBED HIS STUFF AS THE class dispersed. Most of the other students in his class took their notes on laptops, but he found that he absorbed more the old school way with pen and paper. He was also able to get out of the room faster since everyone else was still trying to shut down and unplug.

It had been another rough class, but not because the material was difficult for him. No, he'd been struggling to keep his attention from drifting like it had been all week. Between his conflicted feelings for Savannah and Gabe's stunning revelation about his mother, Shane could barely keep it together. He had known his friend's mother was messed up – he'd seen it firsthand when they were kids – but he had no idea the extent of Gabe's demons. It was a wonder the man was still upright. He knew Gabe didn't want him to feel any guilt about his part in the whole thing with Riley, but he couldn't help it. He knew in his heart that Riley was the best thing for Gabe, but knowing his actions had brought back so much trauma for his best friend had torn something open inside of him. When he'd gotten back to Paige's that night, he had almost wished she had left him another "gift," but she was off at yet another social gathering so he'd ended up numbing the dull ache in his chest with some really expensive scotch.

He felt his phone vibrate as he walked out of the building, the cool breeze hitting him as darkness started to fall. It was a reminder that time was steamrolling ahead, whether he wanted it to or not. He pulled his phone out of his pocket and checked the caller ID – a text from his father. Which business card did he like better? He didn't bother to look at the images his father attached, the same way he had ignored having to pick out the furniture collection for the corner office waiting for him in some fancy building in the middle of downtown Chicago. He turned the silent switch off and shoved the phone back in his pocket, but the second he did, it started ringing.

He expected it to be his father but didn't recognize the number. "Hello?"

"Is this Shane?" came a man's voice.

"Yeah, who's this?"

"Do you know a young woman named Savannah?"

Shane ground to a halt and felt his heart drop out of his chest. "Yes. Is she okay?"

"She is, but you need to come and get her." The voice on the other end was cool and calm, but laced with concern.

"Where?" Shane asked as he started running towards his car.

"Barretti's-"

"Yes, I know the place. What happened? Is she hurt?"

"She's okay, but she needs you."

"I'm coming!" he shouted and stuffed the phone in his pocket as he raced to his car.

❧

SHANE FIGURED HE BROKE ABOUT TEN TRAFFIC LAWS IN AN EFFORT to get to the small, but well-known Italian restaurant near the waterfront. It actually wasn't far from Logan's bar and he could only wonder why the stranger on the phone hadn't reached out to Logan since he was so much closer. It didn't matter – Savannah needed him. If she was at the restaurant, it couldn't be that bad, right?

He double-parked his car in front of the restaurant and flew through the front door. He took in a dark, cozy atmosphere with small, dimly lit lanterns on each table, elegant tablecloths and plate ware and dark paneled wood walls. He'd actually been here on numerous occasions with clients, but the only thing that registered now was that the place was completely empty – not one single customer. All he saw was a bartender behind the empty bar cleaning glasses. The bearded man in a crisp white shirt and black pants pointed towards the back of the restaurant where the restrooms were located. He rushed around the corner and stopped when he saw another man standing outside the ladies' room door. He was tall, well-built with a buzz cut and a little bit of a five-o clock shadow on his face. Shane guessed he was in his mid-thirties and he was wearing an expensive suit with gold cuffs and what looked like a very expensive watch on his wrist.

"Where is she?"

The man motioned to the door but shot his arm out in front of Shane when he tried to enter.

"Take a breath," the man said calmly and that was when Shane noticed the knife in his other hand. It was a steak knife.

"If you touched her-" he began.

"You need to calm down before you see her."

The man's quiet demeanor was the complete opposite of what was happening inside of Shane, but he forced himself to take a deep breath.

"What happened?"

"She was here with a gentleman – a date I'm guessing."

Shane's breath hitched at the image of her with another man, but he kept his mouth shut.

"They put in their orders with the waiter and then the guy pulled her onto the dance floor. She seemed reluctant, but she went. They were only dancing for a minute or so when she started screaming at him to stop."

Shane started to talk, but the man put up his hand to stop him. "The guy barely touched her. From what I could tell, he was being a gentleman."

"What happened next?"

"She kept saying 'no' over and over. One of the waiters approached her to see if he could help and she ran to the bathroom." He held up the knife. "She grabbed this off a table as she ran by."

Shane took the knife and sucked in a breath when he saw blood on the tip of it.

"Did she..."

"She wasn't trying to kill herself." The man's voice had dropped down a level as if he was trying to prepare Shane for bad news.

"Why is there blood on it?" Shane felt like he was in another dimension because he had no idea what the fuck was going on.

"I saw her take the knife off the table, but she locked the door so it took me a minute to get in." Shane glanced at the door and saw that it had indeed been forced open. "I was able to stop her before she did too much damage."

Shane closed his eyes and shook his head. The man seemed to realize he couldn't get out the words to ask what Savannah had done.

"She cut her arm."

"I don't understand," Shane said quietly even though he did, but he needed someone else to voice it because it couldn't be true.

"It's a coping mechanism – I've seen it before. The cuts aren't too deep so that's why we didn't call the paramedics. We left the cops out of it too because they aren't what she needs right now. My wife is in there with her but she hasn't said much. I couldn't find a cell phone on her – just her license and some credit cards in her wallet. I told her she needed to give me the number of someone to call or I'd have to call the police, so she gave me your name and number. Hasn't said a word since." Shane was numb and he felt the man remove the knife from his limp hand. "Take all the time you need – we cleared out the restaurant and shut it down for the night."

"How?" Shane asked dumbly.

"Let's just say I know the owner." He pushed open the door for Shane.

Shane collected himself and went into the bathroom, steeling himself for whatever he was going to see.

CHAPTER 5

SHOCK WENT THROUGH SHANE WHEN HE FINALLY SAW HER. SHE WAS sitting on the floor, her back against the wall, her knees pulled up to her chest. One hand was resting on top of her knees. A beautiful, slightly older woman with bright blonde hair and wearing a red silk dress was sitting on Savannah's left side, her hand holding a towel over the inside of Savannah's lower arm. He could see that a little bit of blood had dripped down her arm and onto the floor between the two women. Savannah was quiet and deathly pale. But worse, her eyes were empty, like she wasn't even there. Her hand was limp in the other woman's gentle hold.

He dropped down in front of her. "Savannah, sweetheart, it's me. It's Shane." No response. He gently placed his hand over the hand she had on her raised knees. When she still didn't respond, he bit back his frustration and growing concern that maybe he wouldn't be able to reach her. "Savannah, I need you to look at me now, okay?" His voice was firm and he stroked his thumb over her cheek. He saw her flinch and then her pale eyes seemed to focus on him. Her body drew up tight as she looked around in confusion.

"Shane?" she said. She looked at him and then at the woman next to her, then finally at her arm and she let out a whimper as she covered her mouth with her free hand.

"Hi Savannah, my name's Sylvie. I'm going to let you and Shane talk, but I'll be right outside if you need me."

Savannah nodded, but she seemed so confused that Shane wasn't sure if she actually understood what the woman had said. Shane rose to help Sylvie stand and immediately noticed how frail she seemed, especially for a woman her age. When she was upright, she seemed to take a moment to steady herself and he saw pain flash through her eyes. He was about to ask her if she was okay, but then she patted him on the arm.

"I'm okay, take care of your girl here," she said softly. "Dom and I will be outside if you need anything."

The woman left and he took her place on the floor next to Savannah. He took her arm and carefully lifted the towel. There were three, almost perfectly matched cuts on the inside of her forearm. Each one was about an inch long and blood continued to well up on the ends of each wound. The first two were deeper than the others – he guessed that she'd been distracted on the third by the bathroom door being kicked in and hadn't used the same level of force as on the first two. The man – Dom, his wife called him – had been right. They didn't appear deep enough to need stitches but if he put some butterfly bandages on them, they'd be less likely to scar. Not that it mattered because he could see dozens of scars covering her lower arm, some with raised welts meaning they'd been deeper, others just fine lines that could have passed for skin imperfections if someone weren't looking close.

She was silent as he examined her arm, but tears of humiliation flowed down her cheeks. The long sleeve shirts she always wore, even in the summer, made sense now. He couldn't even remember a time when he'd seen her in short sleeves. He carefully replaced the towel and dropped his head back against the tile. God, he wasn't equipped to handle something like this. He needed to tell someone, her brother, a doctor – someone who was strong enough to help her fix whatever was destroying her on the inside. She had screamed for help every time she dragged a sharp blade over her delicate skin and no one had heard, no one had listened. He heard himself choke back a guttural sob and he covered his eyes with the hand that wasn't holding her damaged arm.

"I'm sorr-" she started but he shook his head violently and squeezed her hand.

"No. No, you don't ever say that to me again." She flinched at his tone, but he straightened and gently used his hand to force her chin to move so that she was looking at him. "You have absolutely nothing to be sorry for – nothing!" She didn't look like she believed him, but she didn't say anything. "Can you tell me what happened tonight?" She was quiet for so long that he thought she wasn't going to answer, but then she finally shifted, relaxing the arm he was still holding.

"His name is Robert. His son is in my class."

Shane remembered now that she had started her first teaching job this week.

"His wife died last year...He was really nice and I thought I could handle dinner. I even drove myself here so I wouldn't have to deal with any of the end of the date stuff," she said awkwardly. She used the sleeve of her other arm to wipe at the lines of tears on her face that had blessedly stopped.

"I didn't know this restaurant had dancing. When he asked if I wanted to dance, I didn't really know what to say so he just grabbed my hand and led me to the dance floor. It was okay at first, but when he pulled me a little closer I just kind of froze."

"Did he hurt you?"

She shook her head violently. "That's what's so messed up about this – he was barely touching me, but when I felt his hand tighten on my hip just a little bit everything just went dark and I was back there. No warning or anything – I was just back *there*," she repeated, her head shaking in confusion.

"What happened then?"

"Robert just looked at me – he was so confused and then everyone was looking at me. And my skin, it felt like there were a thousand ants crawling under it and the noise in my head...I could see people talking to me – a waiter, another guy in a suit – but I couldn't hear what they were saying because of the noise. I just had to get away."

"Do you remember picking up the knife?" he asked quietly.

She nodded. "I don't lose time until after the first couple..." her voice dropped off.

"Cuts?" he finished for her. She nodded again. "What do you mean by lose time?"

"I always remember the first couple, but at some point I lose track and I just start to float away and everything gets quiet and warm. I don't ever remember stopping – I just kind of wake up and I just feel..."

"Relieved?" he supplied.

Another nod. She dropped her head back against the tile and pulled her arm free of his hold, the towel dropping to the floor unnoticed. She wrapped both arms around herself protectively and turned her head away from him.

"He's going to put me in a hospital. He won't want to, but he won't know what else to do."

"Who?" Shane asked even though he suspected he knew who she was talking about.

"Logan. He's going to be so hurt that I did this and he's not going to understand and I won't be able to explain it because I don't get it either." She sounded done, broken.

Shane knew he should have already called Logan; he should have done that after that day in the hotel and told him everything, but something had held him back. He knew what Savannah was going through, knew the darkness she fought. He'd done it himself for years, continued to do it. And there were times where he'd lost the battle and given in to the relief like she had. He hadn't used a blade but was snorting shit up your nose any different? Was fucking a woman senseless just for the rush of walking away with a pocket full of cash any different?

"I get it Savannah." When she turned to look at him, he gave her a slow nod. "I get it," he said again softly. "I'm gonna take you home now, okay?"

She nodded shakily and he helped her to her feet. He picked up the towel off the floor and went to get a clean one from the bathroom counter top – he was glad it was a classy place that offered actual hand towels instead of paper ones. He dampened the towel and then used it to clean off some of the blood that had dripped down her arm. He snagged a third towel, folded it up, and then placed it over the cuts. "Hold that there," he ordered gently as he took hold of her elbow on the non-injured arm and pulled her out of the bathroom.

Dom and Sylvie were standing just outside the door, the big man's arm curled protectively around his wife's thin frame. They straightened when they saw him and Savannah. Shane was glad to see Dom had gotten rid of the knife.

"You okay darling?" Dom asked, his eyes searching out Savannah's.

She nodded, but Shane knew she was too overwhelmed and raw to respond.

"Thank you. Thank you both," Shane said, nodding to Dom and then his wife.

"You take care sweetie," Sylvie said as she placed a gentle pat on Savannah's shoulder. She handed Savannah what Shane assumed was Savannah's purse, which she had probably forgotten about in the melee.

"Call me if you need anything," Dom said as he handed Shane a business card. Shane glanced at it long enough to see the name *Dominic Barretti* in bold print. When he looked up at Dom, the man smiled and said, "Told you I knew the owner."

Shane chuckled and starting easing Savannah towards the front door. "I'll be back later to pick up her car." Dom nodded and walked them out the door. He was glad to see his car still sitting parked where he'd left it.

The ride home was silent. Savannah seemed completely drained of energy and Shane was on edge. He had to be careful how he handled the rest of this evening – he had a plan, but if he fucked it up, he would end up hurting her even more. As he pulled into the driveway of the small house she and Logan had grown up in, Shane asked, "Is Logan home?"

"He's working."

Shane glanced at his watch and saw that it would be hours before Logan got home. He got out of the car, helped Savannah out and then led her to the side door. She was still in a daze so he took her purse and dug out her keys. The door led into the small, but clean kitchen that he, Logan and Gabe had spent many nights in just hanging out or playing cards. He'd never met Logan and Savannah's parents, but from the outdated look and feel of the house, he figured they hadn't changed much since their parents were taken from them in a car wreck. He suspected it had more to do with lack of money than sentiment, but he couldn't be sure. He paused to search the fridge for a can of soda. "Do you have any first aid stuff?" he asked. She flinched but nodded.

"In my bathroom." Of course, he realized stupidly. His chest constricted as he realized this wasn't the first time for her and she would have had to take care of the damage she had inflicted upon herself. She followed him silently through the dark living room and then up the stairs to where her bedroom was. Her door was open and he pulled her in and had her sit on the bed. A long, white haired cat jumped on the bed and immediately crawled into her lap. Savannah automatically started stroking the animal.

"How are you Pickles?" Shane said as he gave the cat a quick pet and then reached past Savannah to turn on the light next to the bed.

"Mr.," she corrected.

"Savannah, I'm having a hard enough time calling the cat 'Pickles' – don't ask me to stick a 'Mr.' in front of it." She smiled briefly and for the first time that night, he felt a shard of hope that maybe he could fix this.

"It's not his fault. Logan was the one who said he was a girl when he gave him to me. By the time the vet told us he was a he, it was too late to change his name." Shane chuckled and opened the can of soda and put it in her hands.

"Drink that," he ordered and then went into the bathroom. He rummaged around in the vanity drawers and then went to the cabinet next to the sink. He pulled it open and froze when he saw an assortment of bandages, ointments, gauze pads and band aids. Right next to the medical supplies was a fresh pack of razors. Nausea swept through him and he held on to the cabinet door so hard he feared he might actually rip it from the hinges. He took a deep breath and then grabbed the razors and put them in his pocket – he knew she could easily get more with one trip to the drug store or just do what she'd done tonight and grab a knife from the butcher block downstairs, but it still gave him some comfort to get them out of her reach.

He grabbed some of the band aids and ointment and then found a fresh washcloth which he got wet. When he got back into her room, she was still sitting in the same spot, the cat softly purring in her lap, her fingers idly running down the length of its back. He remembered how those fingers felt on his skin and envied the animal. Shaking the inappropriate thought away, he grabbed the rolling chair that was in front of her small writing table and sat in front of her. He dropped the supplies on the bed next to her and then removed the towel on her arm so he could clean the wounds again.

"When did this start?" he asked, hoping she hadn't drifted too far off into her safe place. She started at the sound of his voice and then snapped her eyes to where he was cleaning her arm. She *had* been somewhere else.

"Does it matter?" she asked.

"It matters to me."

She was quiet for a moment and then said, "Just before I left for college."

"Have you done it a lot?" He tried to keep his tone casual so she would keep talking, but his insides were churning.

"The first year of school was bad." Shane took that to mean that yes, she had done it a lot. "Focusing on my school work helped take my mind off things."

"You mentioned seeing a counselor at school – did you tell them about this?"

She shook her head and whispered, "I was afraid they'd tell Logan and that they'd put me into an institution or something. I knew they'd tell me I was crazy."

He stopped cleaning the cuts and looked up at her, his eyes penetrating hers. "You are not crazy – you've got some stuff you need to work through, but you are not crazy, do you hear me?" She dragged her gaze from his and focused on the cat in her lap. She obviously didn't believe a thing he was saying. He finished cleaning the wounds and then carefully dressed them. His hands drifted down her arm and over her palm and he couldn't help but notice how cold it felt. He placed it between his hands to try and warm it up and marveled at how big he was compared to her.

"You're so strong Savannah," he said, his gaze fixated on where their bodies were temporarily linked. It felt so good to touch her, to feel his warmth seep into hers.

She laughed harshly at his statement and tried to pull her hand away, but he wouldn't release her. She quickly settled and stopped fighting his hold and he couldn't help but be glad she hadn't seemed afraid that he was restraining her – maybe that meant she trusted him just a little.

"I'm not. Strong people don't do this," she said, jutting her chin towards her injured arm. "Strong people don't freak out when someone tries to dance with them. Strong people don't use the people..." she choked back a sob. "They don't use the people they care most about."

A combination of joy and dread shot through him when she said those words. "You didn't use me," he said firmly but she shook her head and ripped her hand from his. The cat, sensing her agitation, jumped off her lap and ran out of the room. She stood up and began pacing and he saw her hands ball up into fists.

"I did! I lied to you, I lied to Logan – I lie to him every day! Weak people lie! Weak people are cruel and selfish."

Anger filtered through him at the rage she was directing at herself. He got up and stalked towards her. She automatically stopped at his approach and then backed up until she hit the wall behind her. She looked scared, but at least he had her attention now. He caged her in with his arms but didn't touch her. "You are none of those things and I don't ever want to hear you use those words to describe yourself again." She was trembling and he knew he was being too rough, but he couldn't listen to her disparage herself like that – if those words were true then it put her in the same category as him and he knew for a fact that she was nothing like him. He'd had choices and made them – nothing that had happened to her had been her choice.

"Someone hurt you Savannah – someone took something from you that they had no right to take and that makes *them* cruel and selfish and weak – not you! The only thing you are guilty of is not asking your brother or me or Gabe for help sooner and my guess is you have your reasons for that, even though I'll be damned if I can figure out what they are."

She swallowed hard but he saw something in her eyes shift briefly – a spark of hope maybe? Was she hearing him? Could he plant a seed in her head that she could draw on later when that darkness came back for her? Maybe that was what he needed to give her – she'd asked him to help her get control back, but maybe she needed more than just control of her body. She needed those pieces inside that that bastard had taken – the ones that reminded her that she was strong and kind and beautiful. Could he give her all of it and still let her go when it was time?

"I'm going to give you what you asked me for Savannah." She sucked in a breath and he knew she understood what he was talking about. "But I have conditions." When she remained silent, he continued. "I'm going to show you that your body is yours – that your choices are yours. But I need three things back from you." He dropped his gaze to her lips which had parted and he was momentarily distracted. He forced his eyes back to hers and said, "One – you have to go talk to someone. A professional. I'll help you find someone and if you don't like them, we keep looking until we find one you do like."

He saw her nod slightly and he felt a shiver of victory go through him. He also felt the stirrings of desire and struggled not to close the distance between their bodies. "Two – you need to understand this isn't about love or emotion. When it's over I need you to be able to walk away."

"You don't want me to fall in love with you," she finally said, her voice barely audible even though she was only a few inches away.

"It wouldn't be love Savannah – at best it would be some kind of knight in shining armor thing."

"Does it happen a lot?" she asked. "Do the women you're with fall in love with you?"

Her change of topic unnerved him because talking about his work was definitely not something he wanted to do with her. "Sometimes," he finally answered truthfully. "But most figure out it's not real."

"And that's how it would be between us."

"You're not a fucking client Savannah. It's not the same thing."

"What's the third thing?" she asked.

He dropped his right hand so it closed around the wrist of her injured arm. "If you feel the need to do this, you have to call me first – no matter where you are, no matter what time it is, no matter what the circumstances."

She wavered for a long moment, but he was patient because he knew what he was asking her to do – she'd have to go without the security that cutting gave her and rely on him to keep her grounded. When she finally nodded, something inside of him let go and he couldn't stop himself from leaning down to kiss her. It was soft, tender and she relaxed instantly under his mouth. He lingered for a moment and then drew his mouth back.

"Meet me at my place tomorrow after work. You know where it is?"

She balked and said, "What about your girlfriend?"

He stiffened at the mention of Paige. He supposed it was just another mark against his character that he had no problem being unfaithful to the woman everyone viewed as his girlfriend, but who was really nothing more than set dressing in the fucked up little play that had become his life.

"She's not part of this. She never comes to my apartment." That was all he was willing to give and she seemed to accept it because she just nodded. The air was awkward between them now, so he drew back. He cast her one last glance as he left her room. Mr. Pickles darted past him and back into the room as he walked out and he was glad that at least she wouldn't be alone the rest of the night.

CHAPTER 6

LOGAN BRADSHAW WATCHED HIS YOUNGER SISTER JUMP UP FROM THE table for a third time to go rummaging in the fridge, this time for some more orange juice. She topped off her nearly full glass and put the carton in the middle of the table. She'd been like this for the last twenty minutes as they worked together to get their breakfast on the table. He'd been up for almost twenty-four hours now and was planning to hit the sack as soon as she headed off to work. He would have gone to bed as soon as he got home from the bar after finishing inventory this morning around five, but his concern for Savannah had kept him sitting at the kitchen table for the last hour while he waited for her to get up. She'd been surprised to see him sitting there, but had managed to squeak out a polite greeting and ask him if he wanted her to make him some breakfast. He hadn't really been hungry, but he was worried that if he said no, she'd grab a protein bar and rush out the door just so she could avoid being around him.

It hadn't always been like this. They'd been very close as children and at five years old, he had taken on the role of protector the moment he met her in the hospital room a few minutes after she'd been born. They'd been a happy family. Busy, but happy. His parents both worked hard, his dad as an engineer, his mom as a teacher. But they both made it to the dinner table each night and he and Savannah had been carted to all the different after-school activities like most kids. His sister had been happy and carefree, always smiling. But one drunk driver on a cold, wet March night had changed all that. He had tried to give that back to her by taking the place of his parents as best as any nineteen-year-old kid could, but she wasn't the same. They hadn't had any other family to rely on, just each other.

The insurance his parents had left behind had helped get them through at the beginning, but between his tuition and everyday bills, the money disappeared quickly. Becoming a professional escort had sounded like the stupidest idea he had ever heard when an Upper-classman at school approached him and Gabe near the end of their freshman year. But when the guy had told them how much money they could make in one night, it became a lot more attractive than the lousy pay he was making bussing tables at a local seafood restaurant. So he'd done it and the money he walked away with made him feel just a little bit less dirty. He could swallow the shame of selling his body for sex if it meant he could keep his sister safe and give her the life she deserved.

But things had changed shortly before she left for school. She'd become withdrawn and anxious and most of her energy had been focused on getting her grades up high enough that she could get enough scholarship money to fund her dream of becoming a teacher like their mother had been. He'd balked when she told him she was going out of state, but she'd worn him down and he knew that he had to let her go. She came home for the occasional holiday, but had decided to stay on campus each summer so she could pick up some extra classes.

His own life had become harried as he and his business partner and one-time former boss, Sam Reynolds, had bought a small bar in the touristy part of downtown Seattle a few years ago and finally started fixing it up earlier this year. Logan had actually started leasing the space while Savannah was still in high school and he'd been working part-time for Sam as a bartender at Sam's trendy sports bar in the heart of downtown. But when the owner of the spot had decided to sell it, Logan had used all the money he'd managed to save from his escorting work – along with a generous cash infusion from Sam for 20 percent of the business – to buy it. It had taken another three years of hard work and countless escort jobs to get enough money together to refurbish the place enough to get the doors open.

He'd learned quickly that being a bartender and being a bar owner were two very different things and he'd been glad to have both Sam's money and his expertise. The work was endless and the hours long, but the escorting had made it possible for him to sink more money into the place to get it to where it needed to be and it wouldn't be too much longer before it was finally operating in the black. His friends often wondered at his simple dream, but it was his and he was okay with that.

Savannah started gathering her dishes up, her food barely touched.

"How was your date last night?" he asked, taking a sip of his coffee. He watched her carefully and didn't miss her hesitate as she started scraping her plate off over the garbage can. The long curtain of her hair was hiding her face from his view.

"He was nice." The brightness in her voice seemed forced.

"You gonna see him again?"

"Maybe." She picked up her pace with cleaning off her dishes as well as the pan they'd used to make the eggs. She stuffed them in the dishwasher hurriedly and then rinsed her hands.

Logan wanted to shout at her and demand she tell him why she was different. He wanted to know where along the way he had fucked up because he didn't recognize this shell of a person in front of him. But he did nothing. He said nothing.

"Bye, sleep good," she said breezily as she grabbed her things and hurried out the door. He waited several seconds and then flung his half full coffee cup against the wall, brown liquid splattering all over the fading yellow paint that his mother had loved so much.

SAVANNAH PAUSED WHEN SHE THOUGHT SHE HEARD SOMETHING shatter inside the house and every instinct told her to go back inside and fix the damage she had done to her brother. But she kept walking to her car which Shane had somehow managed to get back to her in the middle of the night. The keys had been on the usual hook inside the kitchen door. And since her brother hadn't jumped all over her the second she had walked into the room, she figured Shane had kept her secret from Logan.

Bitter tears stung as she thought about her brother's confused look this morning. She had felt his eyes on her all through breakfast, and the few times she had looked up she could see the hurt in them. It would be worse to see what would be in his eyes if he knew how messed up she really was.

She climbed into her car and got on the road. As she got closer to school, she started to hope and pray that Robert wouldn't escort his son into class today; maybe he'd just see him to the door and not come in like he had every other morning. The shame of how she had reacted to him last night burned through her. He'd even admitted to her that it was his first date since his wife had passed and she had gone off on him like a raving maniac. She only remembered flashes of his shocked expression and she had no idea what had happened after she'd taken off for the bathroom...after she grabbed that knife.

She realized suddenly that she didn't even know if Robert had seen that part. If he had and he told the school's principal, she'd be out of a job. It was a sobering thought, but maybe it was the way things should be – what if something one of her kids did set her off and she had a meltdown in front of a group of five year olds? No, she would never hurt them physically, but she could still cause them trauma.

By the time she reached the parking lot, her hands were trembling. How had her life spun so far out of control? All through school she had kept things together. But she'd also hidden herself away from the world too. Lying to her brother had been a little easier when she didn't have to look him in the eye. Envy could be ignored when she didn't have to see people like Gabe and Riley - who were clearly meant to be together – every week at family dinner. Hope was nearly non-existent until she had felt Shane's touch on her skin, his lips on hers, his body buried deep within her.

Maybe if she'd just stayed away...A knock on her window startled her out of her reverie and she looked up to see one of the other teachers smiling and waving at her. Savannah sucked in a breath and forced herself out of the car. If she just kept moving, kept busy, she could do this.

❧

"I NEED A FAVOR. SEVERAL, ACTUALLY," SHANE SAID AS HE DROPPED down into the booth across from Gabe in the diner. Before Gabe could even respond, a menu dropped down in front of Shane and he looked up to see Nell, one of the diner's owners, looking at him with accusing eyes. She was a larger woman with grey hair and a round face. Her arms were crossed in front of her and she was actually tapping one foot. Glancing at Gabe, he saw his friend smile and then pretend to read the menu – bastard ordered the same thing every time and didn't need a fucking menu to do it. He turned his attention back to Nell.

"So, big high class lawyer - Pete's Eats not fancy enough for you anymore?" Shane almost smiled at the name of the diner – it never failed to amuse him that the place was named after Nell's husband, a huge tattoo wearing, ex-military guy who did all the cooking in a little white chef hat that was too small for his big, bald head. Nell was clearly in charge of everything when it came to the diner and the way she was looking at him now, he figured he had some fancy footwork to do before she got her big ass husband to throw him out the front door.

"I'm not a lawyer yet and it hasn't been that long since I was in last-"

"Three months," she cut in.

God love this woman, he thought, as he stood and wrapped his arms around her thick frame. She stood stiffly, testament to the fact that she was actually a little angry with him, and then he felt her let out a little huff and hug him back.

"Sorry Nell, things have been busy," he said.

She nodded against and then released him. "Okay, what are you going to have today? Besides the cherry pie," she said as she pulled out her order pad.

"Just the pie – I've got a class in a bit." She jotted it down.

"I'll have the-" Gabe started, but she snatched the menu from him.

"Oh shut it Gabe. I know what you're having and why you think you can fake read this menu while I'm standing right in front of you, I'll never know. Thank God you're pretty," she laughed as she shook her head at him and then took Shane's menu and moved on to the next table. Gabe covered his smile until she was gone.

"Name it," Gabe said to him.

"What?"

"The favors, they're yours." Typical Gabe; unquestioning and loyal to a fault.

Shane felt a longing come over him and he realized he actually missed his best friend which was incredibly stupid since Shane was the one pulling away. He shook off the morose feeling.

"I need the name of your therapist."

Gabe whipped out his phone and a few seconds later Shane heard his own phone ding.

"Done," Gabe said.

"I also need you to teach someone some basic self-defense stuff." Gabe leaned back against his seat and Shane knew his mind was turning. His friend had probably thought Shane was asking for the therapist for himself, but he also knew that Shane was fully capable of taking care of himself and didn't need self-defense training.

"Who?" Gabe asked.

"Well, that's the third favor. I need you to keep this from Logan. It's Savannah."

Gabe instantly tensed and sat forward. He was in full protective mode now and Shane could see his uber alpha male coming out.

"Tell me," Gabe ordered.

"Gabe, my last favor is that you not ask a lot of questions." Gabe wasn't liking that one bit, but before he could respond, Shane said, "It's not my story to tell." Gabe snapped his mouth shut and then finally nodded.

Shane knew he wasn't getting away scot-free when Gabe asked, "What's your relationship with her?"

"There's no relationship. I'm just helping her work through a few things. I'll get her to a place where she can talk to Logan, but I need a little time." Gabe looked like he wanted to argue the point but he didn't.

"Have her meet me at the gym tomorrow night at seven." Shane was saved from having to say anything else because their food arrived. It was the first time he actually had to force Nell's famous cherry pie down.

❧

SAVANNAH WRUNG HER HANDS AS SHE WAITED FOR THE DOOR TO open. She knew this was a mistake – there was no way she would be able to go through with this. She would tell him what a bad idea this was and go. But when the door swung open and he smiled in greeting, she knew she was a big fat liar. He was wearing jeans and a gray T-shirt and his hair was damp, probably from showering.

"Hey," he said, swinging the door open to let her in.

Walk away Savannah. Walk away. She told the voice in her head to shove it and entered the apartment. From the outside, his apartment actually looked more like a warehouse, but it had clearly been renovated into modern, spacious living units. It was an open floor plan with very contemporary fixtures and his décor was masculine but welcoming. The hardwood floor gleamed where the fading sunlight hit it through the floor to ceiling windows. There were actually windows on all three sides of his corner unit so he had a nearly 360-degree view of the city and the water. To her right was a narrow set of spiral stairs leading up to what looked like a bedroom loft. Beyond the stairs was a huge kitchen with cherry cabinets and stainless steel appliances. Directly in front of her was a spacious seating area with plush, oversized brown furniture and a flat screen TV in the corner.

It was very warm and inviting, but what surprised her more than anything were the pictures. Dozens of them all over the bookshelves and side tables and hanging in various sized frames on the walls. They weren't fancy pieces of art or professionally taken photos – they were pictures of his friends. Shane and Gabe at what looked like the finish line of a race, Gabe and Riley with huge smiles as they mugged for the camera, even a picture of her and Logan from when they were younger. Distracted, she moved closer to the table along the back of the sofa and picked up a picture of a young man she didn't recognize. He was handsome with an effervescent smile – the mirror image of Shane's smile on the few occasions she'd seem him truly let loose and be himself.

"My brother, Michael," he said from behind her. She remembered her brother telling her about Michael's death when she was younger and her heart had broken for Shane.

"How old was he in this?" she asked.

"Eighteen – that's his senior picture. Can I get you something to drink?"

"Water please," she said absent-mindedly as her nerves started to pick up again. He returned a moment later with the water and a beer for himself.

She turned to face him and saw that he was holding the water out to her. He looked so young and so old at the same time. She wondered what had done that to him. As a girl, she hadn't been attuned enough to recognize how life could beat you down so she couldn't be sure if he had always been like this, alive but not living; in the present but not in the moment. He looked how she felt – broken and lost.

Before she could second guess herself, she moved past his outstretched arm, ignored the water and pulled his head down so she could seal her mouth over his. He was caught off guard for a second and stiffened against her, but then he was kissing her back, his lips opening against hers and drawing her tongue into his mouth. Both his hands were full, so he ended up resting the two different bottles against her sides as he leaned into her and took over the kiss.

His mouth was hard, ruthless as it plundered hers and she felt her body responding instantly. Everything this man did to her set her on fire. When she drew back just a little to try and draw in some much needed oxygen, he was following her, refusing to let her go. She felt his arms close around her back, the bottles thumping together and then coming to rest against her lower back as he claimed her mouth again. Fear lanced through her at the feel of his arms tightening like steel bands, but she forced it away and focused on him instead. His lips were both hard and soft at the same time and his tongue worshipped every part of her mouth. She could hear his harsh breathing and felt the muscles in his neck tighten and she realized that he was just as affected as she was. He finally released her mouth and then dropped his arms, seemingly confused by how they'd ended up around her in the first place.

"Sorry, I just had to do that in case..." she mumbled as her body howled at the loss of his warmth.

"In case what?"

She shrugged and took a few steps back so she wouldn't be tempted to reach for him again.

"In case I backed out? Or is that what you were thinking of doing?" he asked, suddenly angry.

"I don't want to be like the others. I don't want to use-" she stopped quickly when he jerked away from her.

"Goddamn it Savannah!" he yelled as he spun around and went back to the kitchen. He slammed the two bottles down on the counter and then gripped the edges of the black granite hard. She'd never seen him this angry before and fear skittered up her spine. She didn't even realize she was edging towards the door until he softly said, "Please don't go." If he'd yelled it, she would have been out of there in a heartbeat, but he'd said it so quietly, so desperately that she swore she could actually feel the words on her skin the same as a caress. She remained perfectly still and watched while he took several deep breaths to get himself under control.

"Did you ever think I might need this?" he asked, his eyes still on the bottles sitting on the counter in front of him. "Did you ever think that maybe I was using you?"

"But you're not," she responded, completely confused. "I was the one that lied..."

"I don't care about how you got me to that hotel room. I'm glad you chose me." That shut her up. He stood up and walked towards her, no longer angry, just quiet...eerily so. "Why does it have to be that word? Using? Why can't it be needing? You needed me. That's it. You. Needed. Me." He stopped in front of her, but didn't touch her.

"You needed me to hear you a long time ago and I didn't and I'm going to regret that forever." She started shaking her head, but he stopped her by framing her cheek with his hand and holding her still. Her breath hitched when he ran his thumb over her lips. "Those women – they don't need me – they'd take whatever guy walked through their door. That's why they pay for it – so that it *isn't* about needing. That's not what this is; that's not who you are."

He dropped his hand and suddenly moved past her and opened his apartment door. "I can't do this if you only see me the way those women do. I don't want to be just any guy to you. I can't give you love or be your happily ever after, but I'm not going to play the whore for you like I do all the other women in my life, so if that's what you want then yeah, you should go."

Tears burned in her eyes as she walked up to him and then carefully pushed the door closed.

"Shane," she began but he cut her off.

"And Savannah, I swear to God, if I hear you tell me you're sorry one more time, I'm going to fucking lose it."

"You will never just be 'any guy' to me. I want you – the you that no one else gets to see. The you that's kind and loyal and strong-" She couldn't finish her thought because his mouth was on hers again. This kiss was softer, searching. And when his arms closed around her this time, the only fear she felt was knowing that she wouldn't be able to keep her promise to not to fall in love with him because she was already more than halfway there.

CHAPTER 7

SHANE HAD KISSED HER TO PREVENT HER FROM SAYING ANYTHING else to describe him because all the words she used were built on a lie. Like everyone else in his life, she'd believed in the façade he had created. She couldn't know that for every time she thought he was strong, he'd been weak a dozen times more. Yes, he was loyal to his friends, but his dead brother was proof that he was capable of failing even those he was closest to.

He didn't want her to know any of that because then she wouldn't look at him the way she did – she wouldn't soften and melt under him every time he kissed her; she wouldn't get that bright color in her cheeks whenever he looked at her. Her eyes wouldn't flare up with desire around him - they'd burn him with condemnation.

He took another sip of her lips and then drew back and noticed his arms were around her once again. Damn, how did she manage to sap whatever control he had? He was glad she hadn't freaked out at his hold, but he was going to have to come up with a game plan for how to keep his desire under wraps if and when they ever got past the kissing stage.

"Are you hungry? I was thinking we could order some Chinese and watch a movie." She was flushed from his kiss and a little dazed, but she nodded so he took her hand and led her to the couch. He retrieved their drinks from the kitchen and then dropped down next to her. He made sure their thighs were lined up and she was pressed against him. She shifted a little bit so she could draw her legs up under her, but didn't try to move away from him. He pulled up the menu for the Chinese place on his phone so she could pick what she wanted and then got a movie started.

"TELL ME ABOUT YOUR BROTHER."

Shane heard and felt her voice at the same time. At some point after they'd eaten and well into the movie, she had fallen asleep and had ended up curled against him, her head on his shoulder. Her lips were just inches from his neck and he felt her soft breath caress him. Her hand had come to rest on his chest. The movie had ended a good twenty minutes earlier, but he'd been reluctant to wake her so he had just sat there and enjoyed how her warm body fit perfectly against his. He told himself that the position they were in was too comfortable and would send out all the wrong signals, but he couldn't force himself to change it, so at some point he had let his arm curl around her, the tips of his fingers playing with her sleek hair.

"What do you want to know?" he responded.

"Were you guys close as kids?"

"Very. Gabe too – he lived down the street from us and he and Michael were in the same class. They let me hang out with them even though they were three years older."

"What kinds of things did you guys do?"

Shane felt her fingers start to drum against his chest softly and he was suddenly glad he was wearing jeans because his dick started to harden.

"Typical boy stuff – sports, video games; our dad took us out on his boat fishing. Our big thing was basketball though. We met every Saturday morning like clockwork to play – even after Gabe moved to a different neighborhood, he figured out how to use the bus to get back to our house to play. We kept doing it up until Michael died. Logan joined in too after he met Michael and Gabe in school." Her fingers stopped their movement for a second at her brother's name, but then she seemed to relax further into him and her fingers started repeating a small, circular motion in the middle of his chest.

"How did your brother die?" she asked carefully.

It was an emotional line that he knew he shouldn't cross, but he couldn't stop himself from answering.

"He killed himself."

She let out a gasp and then lifted her eyes from where they'd been watching her fingers draw on him.

"Shane," she began but he gently covered her lips with one of his fingers from his free hand. He didn't want to hear her apology because everyone did that as soon as he told them his brother was dead. As if their apology could somehow make up for the agony and guilt he felt every time he thought of his big brother, his hero. He should have glossed over the truth with her like he usually did with everyone else and just say he overdosed, but for some reason the lies wouldn't fall out of his mouth as seamlessly when he was around her. She seemed to get his message about the unspoken apology because she nodded slightly and then dropped her head back down on his chest.

"He was a drug addict – heroin mostly, but he'd do whatever he could get his hands on." He felt her stiffen against him but she didn't look at him or try to speak. "It started when he was sixteen – pot mostly, then some cocaine here and there. By the time he graduated from high school, he was a full blown addict."

"Did your parents know?"

He started to shake his head and then realized she wouldn't be able to see it so he said, "No – he was able to keep his grades up and was good about keeping up with appearances and that was all they cared about."

"But you knew," she observed.

"Not at first, but then I started to figure it out because he started acting different – more agitated and paranoid."

"Did Gabe or Logan know?"

"I think Logan may have suspected something towards the end, but Gabe had no idea – Michael had pulled back from Gabe a lot and Gabe was so busy with dealing with his mom's bullshit that he didn't see what was happening."

"She's an addict too, right?" Savannah asked.

"Yeah." He realized the word probably came out more sharply than he had intended, but his body was starting to burn from Savannah's innocent caresses. The pressure of her fingers had increased somewhat and his body was demanding more.

"Why did he do it?" she asked quietly, clearly unaware of the effect she was having on him.

"The drugs or the suicide?" he asked.

"Both I guess."

"It started off the same way it does for most; he fell into the wrong crowd and got caught up in all of it. But he kept doing it because of the pressure he was under from our parents. They had his life all planned out – school, career, marriage."

"And he didn't want the same things," she stated.

"He wasn't sure what he wanted in terms of career and school. But he knew that the one thing he did want, they would never be okay with."

She was silent for a long time before saying, "He was gay, wasn't he?"

"Yeah, he was. He tried to tell our parents when he was seventeen or so. He was trying to feel them out I guess. Anyway, it didn't go well and that's when his drug use blew up. I told him I didn't care if he was gay – he was still my big brother – but I guess it wasn't enough. I'd find him sometimes, when he was high. He even blurted out to me once that he was in love with Gabe."

She inhaled sharply, but kept quiet. He felt her hand drift to his side as if she was trying to draw him closer to her. He needed to finish this because it was getting way too intense.

"He knew Gabe was straight so he never told him. He finally told my parents just after he started his second semester, but they flipped out and disowned him on the spot. Told him they would take everything away. He wouldn't even be allowed to see me anymore." He felt her fingers bite into his sides but he pushed on.

"My father took away my phone and laptop so I couldn't even reach out to Michael to tell him it wasn't true – that I'd always be there. He went back to his dorm and shot himself full of enough shit to take down a horse. Didn't even get it all in before it killed him."

Shane took a deep breath and then realized that in his growing distress, he had actually fisted his hand against Savannah's back, some of her hair still in his hand. He instantly relaxed his hand and breathed a sigh of relief when he realized she hadn't noticed.

"Everyone thought it was just an accidental overdose, but he emailed me a suicide note. I showed it to my parents, but they convinced me it would be better for Michael's memory if I didn't tell anyone so I didn't."

She didn't say anything right away but kept holding on to him. He felt her gaze come up to meet his. "Thank you for telling me about him. I wish I could have met him." He nodded but didn't trust himself to respond. She lay there for a few more moments, her hand back to petting his chest, but this time there was no pattern to her stroking and her hand start drifting down to his abdomen. He heard her breathing increase and felt lust tear through him as he realized she had just started to recognize her own desire.

"Shane?" she said slowly and he both dreaded and needed her next words. "Can I kiss you?"

"Yes," he managed to croak. Instead of just lifting her head so he could take her lips, he watched her shift so she was kneeling next to him. Her hand had stopped exploring his chest and moved up next to his head so it could rest on the back of the couch. He didn't realize what she was doing until she actually did it – she moved her left leg over him and in one swift, graceful motion she was straddling him. He forced his hands to remain on the couch but when he felt the first touch of her lips against his, he clenched his fists into the cushions.

There was no hesitation on her part as she sought entry into his mouth. He opened on a groan and then felt her delicate hands come to rest on each side of his face as if to keep him steady for her assault on his mouth. Her tongue swept in and explored every surface of his mouth and then she was caressing his tongue, urging it to join hers. His cock became painful as he felt her settle further into his lap, heat radiating from her core. She slanted her mouth further over his so she could get at more of him and then her hips started rocking back and forth.

"Will you kiss me back?" she whispered as she separated their mouths, her breathing harsh. He didn't answer, just closed the distance between their lips and crushed his mouth down on hers. Her fingers still gripped his jaw, but then her arms drifted around his neck to support herself as he thrust into her mouth, his tongue doing what his cock so badly wanted to do. Her mouth was hot and lush, her tongue strong as it met his plunging strokes. When she finally pulled her mouth back to try and catch her breath, he dropped his lips to the smooth column of her throat and made his way to the sensitive shell of her ear. He forced his hands to stay at his sides as he traced the rim of her ear, and then let his tongue dip inside for a moment. She shuddered and let out a whimper as the pace of her rocking grew more frantic.

The pressure in his pants was too much, so he leaned back against the couch and sucked in several deep breaths. "I need you to take me out," he said harshly as he raised his arms up and held them crosswise over his face. He knew if he actually saw her hand anywhere near his dick, he'd completely lose it. Luckily, she seemed to understand his predicament and she lifted up enough so that she could reach the button and zipper of his pants. She fumbled awkwardly for several torturous moments, but then finally had his pants and underwear loose enough that his cock could spring free. His relief was short-lived because he felt her hand close over his hot length. Her thumb traced the head and swirled the pre-come that had already started to collect at the tip.

Dropping his arms along the top of the couch, he watched as her body instinctively began to take over. Her hand carefully pulled his hardness against her pelvis as her hips slid back and forth over his lap. She brought one of her hands down on his shoulders so she could support herself as she angled her body so that her clit bumped against the hardness of his cock on every up stroke. She was still fully clothed, but the slacks she wore were thin enough that she could clearly feel it every time she rubbed against him and as her movements became jerkier, he realized she was close. Her fingers gripped him hard on the shoulder but the hand around his cock was careful as it began stroking up and down to match the motion of her body. Her eyes were closed as she concentrated on the rhythm and he forced himself to remain perfectly still as he watched her.

He was completely devastated by how beautiful she was like this, her head thrown back, her small, perfect breasts jutting out, her hair cascading down around her like a dark waterfall. Even through the dual layers of her shirt and bra, he could see that her nipples were hard and he imagined sucking on them.

"Shane, I need you to touch me," she managed to whisper as she released his cock long enough to reach for his arm. She pulled his hand down to where their bodies met and pressed him against, her but then returned her hand to his cock so she could continue stroking him. He felt the moisture through her slacks and underwear, but knew he needed to be closer, so he slipped his hand into her pants, grateful that they were loose enough that he wouldn't need to work with the button or zipper. He found her clit easily and began stroking it hard to match what she was doing to him. She cried out and then opened her eyes so that she could look at him. He could tell that whatever she was feeling was overwhelming in its newness to her. She began to ride him harder and faster, her grip on his cock tighter as she used more of the pre-come now dripping steadily out of the head to make the glide easier.

"Shane," she cried out in confusion along with a little bit of fear.

"It's okay, sweetheart, you can let go. I'm here," he whispered and then she was coming apart. He shifted his hand so that he could continue to stroke her clit with his thumb, but also allow his fingers to cup her opening. As he felt the moisture bathe his hand, he felt his own release come out of nowhere and he gripped her reflexively in his palm as semen shot out of his dick and spurted all over his shirt and her hand. His guttural shout of pleasure in the quiet apartment sounded harsh, even to his own ears.

As their bodies eased and started to relax, he watched her carefully release him and then she raised her hand up to study the white fluid coating some of her fingers. His body instantly hardened when she looked at him as if asking permission. With his nod, he watched her little pink tongue dart out and lick her hand so she could taste him.

"Jesus," he muttered as he automatically stroked her clit. Only at her soft shudder did he remember that he still had his hands in her pants. Realizing that his body already wanted hers again, he carefully disengaged his hand and then gently lowered her so she was sitting on the couch.

"I'll be right back," he said softly and straightened his clothes. She watched him in silence, still dazed. He returned within moments, a damp washcloth in his hand, a fresh T-shirt replacing the cum-stained one. She blushed as he cleaned her hand off with the washcloth.

"Is it always like that?" she finally asked him.

He desperately wanted to lie to her but couldn't, so he shook his head. When she mistook his response as saying it hadn't been good and her face fell, he gripped her chin in his hand and forced her eyes up to his. "It's never been like that for me. Never." His firm tone made it clear that he meant what he said.

She smiled shyly and then dropped her eyes to her lap. "Thank you Shane. Even if this is all it ever is...thank you." She suddenly gave him a quick hug and then stood. "I should probably get going. I have to work tomorrow."

"Right," he said and then reached for his phone. "I have something for you. It's the number for someone you can talk to – a professional." She stiffened at his words and he hated having to remind her of the fact that they had an agreement that included his conditions. But she nodded as they both heard her phone announcing the arrival of his text. She started making her way to his door and then stopped and spun around so suddenly that he nearly ran into her.

"Will I get to see you again?" she blurted out, heat suffusing her already bright cheeks.

Instead of answering her, he leaned down and kissed her hard, his tongue not asking for permission as it swept into her mouth. She instantly wrapped her arms around his waist and he used his hands on each side of her neck to control her movement so he could dominate the kiss. When he finally pulled back, they were both breathless.

"We can do dinner after your session at the gym." He felt her fingers tighten and she looked at him in confusion. "I signed you up for a self-defense course."

She started to protest but then snapped her mouth shut and he could see she was mulling the idea over. He was worried that his high-handedness would piss her off, but when he felt her fingers relax against his sides, he knew he had bypassed the storm.

"Okay," she said.

He rewarded her with another kiss, but when he felt her warmth press against him and his cock sprang to life again, he forced himself to release her and took a step back. "I'll walk you to your car."

She smiled serenely at him and he couldn't help but be arrogantly pleased with himself, knowing he had put that happy, sated look on her face.

"Okay," she said again. When he felt his body tighten at her submissive tone, he quickly grabbed her jacket and purse off the side table, grabbed her hand, and nearly dragged her out of the apartment.

"ANOTHER HOT DATE?"

Savannah practically jumped out of her skin at her brother's voice and she slammed her back against the kitchen door so hard she was sure the doorknob would leave marks on her spine.

"Jesus, Logan, you scared the crap out of me!" she shrieked.

"Sorry," he said sheepishly. He was sitting at the kitchen table with a ledger open flat in front of him, a cup of coffee near his hand. The kitchen wasn't completely dark, but he appeared to only be using the light they routinely left on above the sink to do his work by.

"What are you doing here? I thought you were working."

"Sam offered to cover for me so I could get some paperwork done," he said, motioning to the ledger in front of him.

"Where's your car?" She knew her voice sounded high-pitched and almost accusing, but she was still on edge from being caught completely off guard.

"It's out front. I left the driveway for you to use," he said, suspicion creeping into his voice at her odd behavior. Thoughts of Shane had taken over as soon as he helped her into her car, but not before he'd turned her into mush with another one of his devastating kisses. Her lips still tingled and she barely stopped herself from reaching up to touch them.

"Savannah!" She jumped as she heard her name. Logan was watching her with obvious frustration.

"What?" she asked, realizing that he had asked her a question but she had no idea what it was.

"I asked if you went out with that guy from your class again."

Crap. She hated lying to him, but she certainly couldn't tell him who she'd been with, much less what they'd been doing. "Um, no, I just had dinner and caught a movie with a friend." That was close enough to the truth, right? Before he could question her further, she hung up her jacket and then hurried past him. "Goodnight Logan." She heard him mutter the same back to her as she darted out of the room and up the stairs to her bedroom. Mr. Pickles was on the bed and greeted her with a soft meow when she hurried into the room and shut the door. She dropped down on her bed and the cat immediately started climbing all over her. She automatically ran her hands over the animal's soft fur, but her thoughts were once again on Shane.

She hadn't meant to fall asleep and definitely not on him. She hadn't even managed to make it through the movie; not that she had really watched any of it because she'd been too nervous at Shane's proximity to pay attention to what was going on on the television. She'd felt like she was on fire in all the places his body had been pressed up against hers and she'd had to stifle a cry of protest when he'd gotten up to answer the door for their Chinese food.

They'd eaten in silence as the movie played and when she was done, the combination of good food and a hard, warm male body did her in and she'd fallen asleep. When she'd come to, she'd found herself sprawled over him and felt his fingers playing with the strands of her hair. It would have been smart to pull back and move away, but she hadn't been able to force herself to do it – it had just felt too good to feel his strong heartbeat under her fingers as she'd caressed him.

Her desire to know more about him had led to her questions about his brother and hearing the truth had been upsetting. She'd regretted almost instantly that she'd dampened their night with such a dark topic. She couldn't remember actually meeting his brother when she was younger since Logan had lived in the dorms at that time and she'd lived at home with their parents. Michael's death had come a couple months before her parents' own deaths. Knowing that he'd taken his own life and that Shane had to deal with the guilt of that had broken her heart, but she was grateful that he'd been willing to share so much of himself with her.

Kissing him hadn't been part of her plan at all and she definitely hadn't intended to crawl all over him like a monkey before she even got her lips on his. It was like something inside had just taken over her body and knew what it needed. There'd been no fear this time and she wasn't sure if that was because he hadn't reached for her or if it was because her body instinctively knew he wouldn't hurt her. A thrill had run through her when he finally kissed her back and her insides had melted when he told her to pull him free of the confinement of his jeans. It was thrilling to know she'd put him into that state and the rush of removing his cock from his pants while he forced himself to keep his hands off her had given her the strength she needed to follow through with the task.

Seeing his hard, nearly purple cock leaking that clear fluid against her fingers had turned her on in a way that she didn't know was possible and she'd only managed to give him a few strokes before she felt the need to rub up against him. Sensation had shot through her body as her clit came into contact with his hardness and the pure want had taken over as she gyrated against him, searching for more. Grabbing his hand had been bold, but she'd known he could give her what she desperately craved and within seconds of his hand touching her, she felt everything inside tighten up into an almost unbearable coil of raw need.

She'd had no idea what she was reaching for but as it sucked her in, she'd felt a moment of panic and had tried to draw back. But his deep, gentle voice – strangled with his own desire – had given her the lifeline she needed as she flung herself over the edge. Everything had gone dark for a split second and then it was like lights and sparks lashed through every cell in her body. She'd had absolutely no control as her body twisted and thrashed against his and it had been unbelievably freeing.

As the liquid fire had raced through her veins, she had felt his hips push up and his cock thickened in her hand and then suddenly there was hot liquid splashing down over her fingers and all over his chest and abdomen. She'd wished she had thought to push up his shirt so she could see the milky white fluid covering his rippling muscles. It would have been more fun to learn his taste that way. Heat washed through her cheeks as she remembered the look he had given her when she licked the salty, bitter substance from her finger.

When he had pulled free of her and gone to get the washcloth, a rush of doubt had swept through her. The silence had been awkward and she should have kept her mouth shut because a sexually self-confident woman wouldn't desperately need her partner's reassurance. And then the words had just tumbled from her mouth and then a rush of humiliation when he shook his head. But his next words had had her flying high. If he was telling her the truth that it had never been like that for him with another woman, then maybe it meant there was something more than the obvious physical attraction between them. She knew it was a risky line of thought, but her heart refused to crush that little shard of hope that had flared to life.

The talk about seeing a therapist as well as his decision to sign her up for a self-defense course had been a stark reminder of why he was doing this, but she couldn't find it in herself to be angry. She wasn't as sure about the therapist, but she wanted desperately to be free of the darkness that still had a grip on her. And the idea of learning how to defend herself was quickly growing on her. It surprised her that it had never even crossed her mind to look into something like that – she supposed she had just gotten used to being a victim and her perspective was skewed. If nothing else happened between her and Shane, she'd at least be grateful that he had shown her what her body was capable of and that maybe, just maybe, she was strong enough to defend it from anyone or anything ever hurting it again, even if that person was herself.

CHAPTER 8

SHANE KNEW HE WASN'T GOING TO BE ABLE TO GO THROUGH WITH what he'd agreed to. He'd thought he could keep Savannah separate from his professional life, but still maintain the emotional distance he would need. But last night had fucked with his head big time.

"More coffee honey?" Nell asked as she went ahead and filled up his nearly empty mug. He'd barely touched the food in front of him, but was on his third cup of coffee and it was barely noon.

"Thanks Nell."

"Sure thing." She looked at him fondly and then wandered off to see to her other customers. It had been a spur of the moment decision to have lunch at the diner, but one look at Nell's pleased expression as he walked through the door and he'd known it was the right choice. He took another long draw on the bitter coffee and then forced a French fry into his mouth. The delicious combination of salt and grease flooded his taste buds, but there was no pleasure in it. He chewed automatically and finally gave up and pushed the plate away from him.

"Nell's gonna skin you alive if you don't eat that," Riley said as she suddenly dropped into the seat across from him. Gabe's girlfriend wasn't beautiful in the typical sense, but something about her always made him feel a little lighter inside. Her long blonde hair was neatly braided and she wore a set of scrubs with puppies and kittens on them.

He pushed the plate across the table to her and she snagged a fry. Her gray eyes bore into him as she leaned back against the cushion and studied him.

"This is our table you know," she remarked casually.

He looked around and realized that they were in fact sitting in the same booth they'd sat in all those months ago when he had told her about Gabe's childhood in hopes that she would understand the circumstances that had shaped the broody man's dark life. That was also the day Shane had told her what he did for a living.

"Let me guess. Nell," he stated as he cast a look over to the counter where Nell was serving customers. The woman gave him a big, unabashed smile and then winked at him.

"Gabe said he met you here yesterday and Nell gave you the third degree. Since you can't take it upon yourself to show up for family dinner or answer any of my calls, I asked Nell to keep an eye out for you in case you showed up here again today." She grabbed another fry and then pushed the plate back towards him. "You should eat – you look like you're losing weight."

He hadn't, but he secretly enjoyed her nagging so he reached for the burger and took a bite.

"He misses you. We all do," she said quietly.

"I've been busy," he began.

"Bullshit," she cut him off. The fact that she was swearing was a bad sign.

He put the burger down and leaned back. "What do you want Riley?"

"How about the truth? Why do you look like shit? Why does your smile never reach your eyes? Why are you lying to us? To me? Why do you keep pulling further and further away from us?"

Hurt accompanied every one of her words and he actually felt pain in his chest.

"What difference does it make? I'm out of here in less than a year. I've got a whole new life waiting for me." He tried to inject excitement into his voice, but his words felt flat, even to his own ears.

"So you're breaking up with us before we can break up with you?" she said snidely.

If she hadn't been so upset, he would have found her analogy amusing. "I just have different priorities." Might as well turn the knife a little deeper he thought.

She was silent for a long time, her eyes sharp and calculating as they studied him. He actually started to squirm under her intense gaze. The woman was definitely in the wrong profession – she belonged in a prison somewhere, intimidating criminals into confessions. She finally leaned forward, her arms folded on the table.

"Well, guess what Shane? You don't get to walk away from this. We aren't some girl you're trying to ditch after a one night stand or some client who's gotten a little bit too clingy for your liking. And we're not "The Bitch" who doesn't give a shit whether you're coming or going. We're your family."

Her use of the nickname his friends had given Paige would have made him laugh, but pinpricks of fear were skittering up and down his spine because he believed every word she was saying. His friends were loyal, unbending. It had been idiotic to think he could just brush them off and they'd disappear. Frustration and anger boiled up. Why didn't she get that he was trying to protect them from the truth? He wanted them to keep the image of good old, fun loving, happy go lucky Shane. He'd worked hard to keep them from knowing who he was inside, the demons that haunted him.

Shane stood up and pulled some money from his wallet. "You know what Riley? You're not my family and unlike the rest of you, I already have a family, a real one." She flinched when he said "real" but he forced himself to ignore it. "At best, you guys have been a placeholder."

Sharp heat flooded through him at his own cruelty and his throat closed up as he tossed the money down on the table and walked away from her. The image of tears pooling in her eyes caused his own eyes to burn, but he forced himself to walk out of the diner, ignoring Nell's confused and hurt look as he slammed out the door.

SAVANNAH WAS NERVOUS AS SHE ENTERED THE GYM. SHE'D CHANGED into sweats before she left school so she wouldn't have to deal with changing in the gym's locker room. Shane had given her directions to the gym which was north of the city, but she'd been surprised to find that it wasn't some big fancy fitness place. In fact, if she hadn't confirmed the address twice, she wouldn't have known it was the gym at all. As she entered, she expected to see walls and walls of various workout machines but there was none. No weight machines either. She came to a stop when she realized she wasn't actually in a gym but a boxing center. In the middle of the room was a boxing ring where two bulky men in headgear and gloves were pounding on each other. Along the sides stood several men shouting instructions and encouragement and lining the back wall were various types of weights and boxing bags.

Terror went through her as she realized there weren't any women around and when several men looked up from what they were doing, she nearly choked on her fear. That terrible itch began and she swung around to hurry back out the door.

"Savannah!"

She knew that voice. Turning around, she saw Gabe striding confidently towards her, his face etched with concern. He was wearing a pair of sweats and a tank top that showed off his huge muscles and from the layer of sweat on his skin, she figured he'd already been working out before her arrival. She knew Gabe, trusted Gabe, she reminded herself, but couldn't stop her body from automatically taking a few steps back as he closed the distance between them. He seemed to sense her tension because he stopped a good couple feet from her.

"How you doin, darling?" His voice was light, casual.

She managed a stiff nod, but nothing else.

"He didn't tell you I would be the one teaching you today, did he?" When she shook her head, he chuckled and said, "He's such an asshole." She could tell he was kidding, but couldn't force herself to relax enough to enjoy his teasing.

Hurt went through her at Shane's betrayal. He'd told Gabe about what had happened to her. Her skin was crawling now and she started scratching at her left arm, her nails scraping over the scabs that had just started forming on the cuts that were there. Gabe seemed to sense her agitation and sharply called her name. His tone was firm, his voice authoritative when he said, "Savannah, look at me."

Temporarily distracted by his commanding nature, she stopped her scratching and looked up.

"Shane didn't betray you – he didn't tell me anything other than you wanted to learn a few self-defense moves. That's all I need to know."

If she knew anything about Gabe, it was that he didn't lie. The man was honest to a fault, sometimes too much so, and if he said Shane hadn't told her secrets then she believed him. The itching eased, but she could still feel it there and she debated whether or not she should just go.

GABE WATCHED SAVANNAH CONSIDER HER OPTIONS AND FELT HIS heart sink when he realized that whatever she'd been through was bad. It had been hard to not probe Shane for details, but one look at her stiff posture and her ready to flee stance gave him everything he needed to know. She kept rubbing her left arm and he guessed it was some type of subconscious, coping thing that she wasn't even aware she was doing. He knew that teaching her self-defense was going to be a challenge because there was no way she'd be able to tolerate his hands on her, at least not until he'd reestablished some of the trust that he had just assumed would always be there between them. He hadn't seen much of Savannah in recent years since she'd been gone at school, but early on when he and Michael had become friends with Logan, he remembered a gangly, always smiling Savannah trying to horn in on her big brother's get togethers. She'd become like a little sister to all of them and guilt poured through him as he realized someone had hurt her at some point and none of them had known.

"How about we warm up with a couple of laps?" he said as he pointed to the small jogging track that the gym's owner had been smart enough to install. It ran along the top of the wall and had been a significant expense, but allowed the gym goers access to a cardio workout when they didn't have the time to run outside or the desire to be caught in a Seattle downpour.

She looked up at the track and then back at him. He sighed in relief at her nod, then led her to the stairs. They started off with a brisk walk and then a light jog. After a few laps he could see her starting to feel more comfortable in her stride so he took them back down to a walk and then led her down to the mats. She immediately tensed up when she realized what was next.

"Savannah, we're just going to cover the basic movements today – no one is going to touch you or grab you in any way. If and when we get to that point, it will be when you're ready and not a second sooner. Okay?"

She relaxed and he spent the next forty-five minutes breaking down various moves and showing them to her so she could mimic him.

"Nice," he said when she completed the final move. She'd worked up a nice sweat and he was pleased to see that she seemed more at ease around him now. "You ever try using a speed bag?"

"A what?" she asked in confusion.

He took that as a no and led her to one of the small punching bags nearby. "These are great for hand-eye coordination." He didn't mention that they were an excellent outlet for one's frustrations too, but based on her earlier agitation, he guessed that she could use something to vent her anxiety on. He gave her a brief demo of how to hit the bag and then stepped back to let her try. Her hits were awkward at first and she laughed a couple times when she completely missed the bag all together. It was a good sound and he suddenly realized why Shane had sent her to him. He was an asshole but a smart one, Gabe mused.

SAVANNAH'S ARMS FELT LIKE NOODLES, BUT SATISFACTION ROARED through her at her accomplishment. She'd kicked that little bag's ass and it had felt great. Sure, hitting the bag in the beginning had felt weird and awkward, but after she got the rhythm going, it had felt smooth and natural. And when Gabe had patted her on the back afterwards, all she'd felt was pride. No, she wasn't ready to go out walking the streets at night by herself, but maybe it was a start. She could have run when she realized Gabe would be her instructor, but she hadn't.

And even if Shane hadn't revealed all her secrets, the fact that Gabe hadn't touched her during their training indicated that he suspected what had happened to her. But she'd stuck it out and absorbed as much information as she could about the different techniques she could use to defend herself.

Electricity hummed through her all the way home. She took just a few minutes to get showered and blew her hair just dry enough so that it wouldn't leave wet marks along her back. She threw on her favorite yellow spring dress that fell in soft waves around her knees and grabbed a pale blue, long sleeved cardigan from her closet. She texted Logan a brief message saying she was out meeting with a friend and then rushed back out the door. She'd seen Shane less than twenty-four hours ago, but it had felt like a lifetime. They'd agreed to meet at his apartment so they could drive to dinner together. He was waiting for her on the curb near his car. As she parked her car next to his, he opened her door. Before he could even speak, she was kissing him, her arms up and around his neck, her body pressed against the full length of his. If he was surprised, he didn't show it because he kissed her back and then used his arm to brace them both so she wouldn't get pushed back against the body of the car as he leaned into her.

When they finally separated he said, "I'm really starting to like when you do that." She blushed when she realized that she had initiated their kisses on more than one occasion.

"I guess you had a good day?" he asked, somewhat cautious.

"I did. I'll tell you all about it over dinner."

He nodded and then went to close her door. She noticed the wariness almost instantly and then the sadness in his eyes.

"What's wrong?" she asked. He looked up at her, seemingly surprised at her observation. He instantly pasted a smile to his mouth and shook his head as if in confusion.

"Nothing," he said easily. She didn't believe him, but didn't say anything when he pulled her to his car and deposited her in the passenger seat. He made casual conversation throughout the drive but it was hollow and her previous excitement drained away. She wanted to beg him to tell her what was going on, but that didn't fall under the purview of their relationship, did it?

"Maybe I can help," she said finally.

He looked at her and then back at the road.

"With what?"

"With whatever is bothering you."

She saw him tighten his jaw, but then he relaxed again and smiled brightly. "I'm good, swear."

Cold swamped her at the obvious lie and she couldn't help but wonder how many times she and the other people in his life had fallen for that easy, charming smile and upbeat voice. This wasn't the Shane she knew, but she had met him before in the past. She'd been too caught up in her naïve, schoolgirl crush to recognize that he was pulling away even then, but she saw it now.

The rest of the ride was made in silence. Dinner was awkward and impersonal and was only interspersed with the occasional comment about how good the food was or what the weather had done today. When he asked for details about her training with Gabe she gave him quick, simple answers because she didn't want to share her excitement with this Shane. He was absolutely perfect to the outside eye. Impeccable manners, expensive clothes, polite and charming to the hostess and waiter, complimentary to her – any woman watching would have envied her. She just felt sick because she had no idea how to reach him.

When they arrived back at his place, she debated whether or not she should just go home. He invited her up for a drink and she agreed. After showing her into the apartment, he took her coat and hung it up, then asked her what she wanted. She watched him get the soda she asked for and then he prepared himself a drink. It was all completely wrong and her skin crawled as she realized what he was doing.

"Is this the part where you fuck me now?"

SHANE FROZE AT HER WORDS, THE SWEAR WORD SOUNDING unnatural from her lips. When she'd arrived at his place, he had an excuse loaded and ready to go as to why he couldn't have dinner with her tonight, but then she'd gone and kissed him and the excuse was wiped away. Her entire day had been in that kiss – whatever had happened with Gabe had obviously gone as well as he'd hoped, because she'd put every ounce of her joy and confidence in that kiss. But then her sharp gaze had picked up on the sadness that still lurked in his head after his confrontation with Riley in the diner. And when Savannah had offered him help, something inside of him shifted and changed. He'd entered his safe mode – the place he could go and be whoever he needed to be in that moment. Savannah needed the strong, confident, fun-loving Shane who she could share her day with, not the broody, angry Shane that wanted desperately to find the relief that a few straight, clean lines of coke could bring him.

He'd struggled all day with not calling his old contacts. He'd deleted them from his phone, but he had memorized the numbers long ago. He'd entered them more than once into the keypad on his phone, but hadn't hit the dial button. The things he'd said to Riley today were cold and cruel and completely untrue, but he couldn't sit there and let her strip any more layers from him. How could he explain to her that he was always balanced just on the edge of the cliff, his foothold precarious? The slightest thing could send him over into the darkness that he wouldn't be able to escape this time and he feared he would take those closest with him. After all, his own brother had done it to him. But as bad as he hurt Riley, it paled compared to the agony that knifed through him when he realized Savannah knew exactly what he was doing.

"I mean, that's what happens next, right Shane?"

He put the soda he'd been getting for her back in the fridge and closed the door. She was still by the door, her body tense, her angry eyes glittering.

"But *I* paid to fuck *you* so I guess that means I get to say what happens next."

If he didn't know how much she hurt underneath, he would have found this Savannah intriguing. He loved when she was soft and compliant and curious, but seeing her try to take control called out to his baser needs.

"Take off your shirt," she ordered coldly.

He knew this game far better than she did and maybe this was the best way to end things between them. He'd been a fool to think he could help her. She was so much stronger then he was. After whatever they were doing here was over, he'd betray her one last time and tell her brother the truth about her and then he'd walk away from all of them.

He reached for the buttons on his shirt and undid them slowly. Women always liked it that way. But her eyes never even left his as he stripped the shirt off and dropped it to the floor. He was standing just over the threshold of the kitchen. She closed the distance between them, her eyes still on his.

"This is what you want, right Shane? You want to give me what I need? I can take whatever I want from you. Like in the hotel room."

He nodded curtly. She still hadn't looked at anything but his eyes and had made no effort to touch him.

"I want one kiss," she said. "Kiss me once like you do all the other women." She took a step back from him. "If you can keep yourself from me during the kiss like you did at dinner tonight, then I'll go right now and tell Logan everything. About the rape, about the cutting. You won't have to stick around out of some sense of guilt or worry that I'll hurt myself again."

He knew he was going to fail even as he closed the distance between them and slashed his mouth over hers. He guessed she knew it too. She held herself back at first, probably testing him or judging his kiss. But he wasn't going to even bother trying to deny what was between them. It didn't change how things would end, but at least he could have this moment. He bent down and grabbed her around the backs of the thighs and lifted her against him. She squeaked in surprise as he carried her the few steps to the kitchen and deposited her on the counter, stepping between her legs. He took advantage of her open mouth to steal back into it, his hand wrapping around her head and fisting in her hair to keep her from trying to escape him. He knew he was being too aggressive, but when she kissed him back and then wrapped her arms around him, he knew she was still with him.

Tipping her head back, he kissed his way down her throat and then sucked on the spot where her neck met her collar bone. He used his other hand to push the cardigan she was wearing off her shoulder and was glad to see the dress she had on had only a thin strap holding it up – he slid that out of his way too and trailed his lips along her shoulder and then down her breastbone. As he neared the upper slope of her breast, he felt her thighs tighten around his hips. But before he could go any further there was pounding on his front door. Savannah tried to scramble away from him, but he grabbed her hips gently and then waited for her to settle. When she did, he straightened her clothing and then lifted her off the counter. The banging on his door grew heavier and a sinking feeling hit him when he guessed who it might be.

"Stay here," he said to Savannah as he went to the door and pulled it open. Gabe strode in and instantly grabbed him and slammed him back against the wall next to the door.

"You made her cry you son of a bitch! Are you happy with yourself now?" His friend was beyond enraged, but Shane didn't struggle or try to break free of his hold. He didn't try to come up with some flimsy excuse or smartass comeback either because he'd given up that right when he went after Gabe's girl.

"She even defended you tonight! She's crying her eyes out and then telling me it wasn't your fault!" Gabe slammed his head back against the wall hard and Shane shut his eyes. The pain inside was so much worse.

"Gabe!" Savannah's trembling voice was like a gunshot to both men.

Gabe released him and then took in Savannah's appearance including the mussed hair and swollen lips. Stunned, he pushed back from Shane, his hands fisting.

"Are you fucking kidding me with this?" he hissed as he motioned to Savannah. "Your best friend's kid sister?" He shook his head. "Is this why you didn't want me telling Logan? So you could fuck around with his sister?"

"Stop it!" Savannah shouted at Gabe and then she was standing in front of him, her small frame dwarfed by the big man. If the situation hadn't been so fucked up, Shane would have enjoyed watching his friend confront an enraged female who didn't even make it to his shoulder.

"You have no right to judge what's between Shane and me, Gabe!" She actually gave him a shove even though it had no effect on Gabe's stance. "Now I'm sorry for whatever happened between Shane and Riley, but you don't get to come in his home and attack him!"

"Savannah-" Shane started.

"No!" she said to him over her shoulder, but she calmed a bit. "Gabe, please," she said softly. He must have picked up on something Savannah hadn't said, because he relaxed and took a couple of steps back, his hand running through his hair in agitation.

"Shane, whatever shit you're going through – she didn't deserve that, man." Gabe's voice was heavy with pain, whether for him or for Riley, he wasn't sure.

"I'm sorry Gabe. Tell her I'm sorry." He felt his voice crack. He pushed away from the wall and headed towards the stairs. "Can you make sure Savannah gets to her car okay?" he said as he passed them and went up the spiral staircase and into his room. He felt both of them watching him, but he was too tired to care.

❧

SAVANNAH WATCHED GABE GET HIS ANGER UNDER CONTROL. Whatever had happened between Shane and Riley must have been bad because she couldn't imagine anything else that would make Gabe turn on Shane.

"What happened?" she finally asked.

Gabe repeated what Shane had told Riley and Savannah stifled a gasp. It was cruel and unfeeling and not at all like the Shane she knew.

"I don't know him anymore," Gabe muttered sadly, his thoughts clearly mirroring hers. "Come on, get your stuff. I'll walk you to your car."

"I'm staying."

"Savannah..."

"Gabe, I'm not a kid anymore. I haven't been in a really long time." Pain lanced through his features as he realized she was referring to her stolen innocence. "He may not want me here, but he needs me."

"He could end up destroying you, Savannah."

She took in a deep breath because she was well aware that was the likely outcome, but it didn't change things. "At least it will be my choice."

Gabe studied her for a long time and then nodded. He glanced up towards the loft once more, shook his head and then left, closing the door softly behind him.

CHAPTER 9

"YOU SHOULDN'T BE HERE SAVANNAH," HE SAID QUIETLY FROM where he sat on the bed. The room was almost completely dark except for a dim lamp on his nightstand. She could see his hunched back, his head in his hands. Pain radiated off him in waves.

"I know," she said as she moved to stand in front of him. She pressed forward a little bit and he instantly opened his legs so she could stand between them. He lowered his arms and she leaned down to kiss the top of his head.

"Things will be the same tomorrow," he said weakly.

"I know," she said as she lowered herself so that she straddled his lap.

"I'll still have clients."

"I know." She tipped his head back and brushed her lips briefly over his.

"I'll still have a girlfriend."

"I know," she whispered as she settled more fully against him. She felt his arms come up to wrap around her waist.

"I may not be able to stop if you need me to," he said unevenly even as he slid one of his hands up towards her breast.

"You will."

He groaned and kissed her as his hand skimmed her breast. Sensation shot through her at the contact and when he tweaked her nipple through the fabric of her clothes, she hissed at the unexpected pleasure. His hands worked to pull her cardigan off and then he was kissing a path down her neck. His nimble fingers pulled both of the shoulder straps of her dress down and since her small size meant she could forgo a bra if she wanted to, his lips found skin right away. He gave her no warning, just sucked one of her nipples into his mouth and bit down lightly. She cried out and then fisted her hands in his hair to hold him closer as he laved her taut skin with his tongue.

His fingers pressed against her back to pull her even closer and then his attention was on her other breast. She bit her lip to stifle a scream and then his tongue was back in her mouth, searching, loving. Any fear she had flew out the window when she pulled back and saw his dark, hooded gaze watching her. She knew things were going to change between them – and probably not for the better – but walking away was no longer an option.

SHANE WILLED HIS HANDS TO STOP AS THEY SLID DOWN HER SIDES TO her hips and then along her thighs. They were both vulnerable right now and doing this would just make everything worse, but his mind and body seemed disconnected. He felt the muscles in her thighs tighten as he pushed the thin material of her skirt up and felt her smooth skin. He realized then that in the few times he'd been with her, he hadn't actually seen her without her clothes. His body was screaming at him to take her, to relieve the ache inside of him, but he didn't want it to be over too quickly because this was the only time he would have with her. He let his fingers curl around the backs of her thighs and then up to cup her ass, the thin fabric of her panties blocking him from feeling everything he wanted to feel.

"I need to see you this time," he muttered as he tugged at the dress and started pulling it up. She lifted her arms willingly as he pulled it up and over her head. Her trust humbled him. Throwing the dress aside, he pulled her back down for another scorching kiss. He loosened her hair which she had fashioned into a simple ponytail at the nape of her neck. The black waves flowed over his hands as he stroked up and down her back and she began to fervently kiss him back.

Her hot little tongue dueled with his and then she was in his mouth, her lips slanting over his as she tried to get as deep as she could. Her fingers actually grabbed his ears in a bid to keep him still so she could do what she wanted to his mouth. He complied, but let his fingers drift along the edge of her panties where the silky fabric met the soft skin of her lower back. When he dipped one of his hands under the material to skim the perfect globes of her ass, she shuddered and dropped her head back.

Her position gave him perfect access to her breasts so he licked and sucked on each one in turn. He ran his tongue down between them and then explored the supple skin of each mound of flesh. He stopped when he reached a patch of skin that was slightly raised just to the right of her nipple. A scar, he realized. He explored the other breast and found another scar, this one seemed to actually circle the nipple. She didn't give him time to ponder the origin of the marks because her hips pushed hard against him as her hands curled around his shoulders.

Suddenly she was tugging at his shirt, trying to pull it over his head. He reluctantly released his hold on her breast to get rid of the offending fabric, not even bothering to unbutton it first – he just jerked it up and over his head. Her hands were all over him then, touching, stroking and the flexible fabric of the dress slacks he was wearing became increasingly uncomfortable as his cock sought her warmth. He grabbed the backs of her legs and then stood so he could lay her down on the bed underneath him. When his weight settled on her, he felt her stiffen and he froze. A flash of panic went through her eyes.

"Savannah," he said softly. His voice seemed to be what she needed to ground her back in the present and he felt her relax and open her legs so that his hips could fit more freely against hers. He kissed her again until he felt her start to squirm with need and then he worked his way down her body. They were near the edge of the bed so when he reached her thighs, he actually dropped his knees down to the floor and pulled her so that her legs dangled off the mattress. There was just enough light from the tiny lamp on his nightstand to show her splayed before him, her plump, wet lips slightly parted, her eyes bright with lust. Her arms rested at her sides, her fingers pressed into the bedding. Her breasts rose and fell with each rapid breath. He watched for fear as he caressed her stomach and when he saw none, he put his fingers under the waistband of her panties and stripped them off her.

He kept eye contact with her as his fingers searched out her clit. She had only a thin strip of smooth hair just above it and when he ran the rough pads of his fingertips over the swollen bud, she shuddered and closed her eyes at the contact. He lowered his mouth and stroked the little nub with his tongue. She cried out and pushed her hips up against his hands, but he held her down. When he sucked her into his mouth, he heard her say his name in a harsh whisper and then she was dropping her legs open further for him.

He used one hand under her ass to lift her higher as he alternated between stroking and sucking her while his other hand sought out her opening. He tensed when he felt how wet she already was. He pressed one finger in just a little and felt her instantly tighten. He glanced up to check that she was okay and was caught off guard to see her watching him, her mouth parted as little pants escaped her lips. Seeing her watch what he was doing turned him on even more and he began to furiously stroke her clit with his tongue as he pressed his finger further inside of her. Her body was tight around his digit and she was desperately lifting her hips to match the rhythm his probing tongue had set.

When he added another finger and began thrusting them in and out of her, he felt her body start to ripple and he knew it wouldn't take much more to send her over. She was clawing at the bed frantically and then one of her hands was in his hair, her grip stinging his scalp as she tried to speed him up. He gave her what she wanted and sucked hard on her clit as he curled his fingers inside of her. Her body tightened further and with one more thrust and stroke combination she was coming and he felt her insides clamp down on his fingers to keep him there. She screamed his name and forced herself down on his fingers as far as she could and then her body was beyond her control as she helplessly rode out the spasms of her release. She went limp around him but even then her body twitched with aftershocks.

He pulled free of her and she watched as he licked his fingers clean. He lifted up and over her and kissed her, letting her taste herself. Even in her sated state, she kissed him back with the same passion she did every time their mouths met. "I need you," he whispered against her lips.

"Yes," she responded as she ran her hands down his back, her legs lifting so that her hips could hold his. "I need you. All of you," she muttered before he claimed her mouth again. Her breasts rubbed against his chest and he could feel her arousal building all over again. He lifted himself off her and removed his pants. She watched him with open curiosity and hunger as he fumbled around in his nightstand drawer for the foil packet he knew was there. It felt like hours before he managed to get the condom on. He leaned back over her, but held his weight off of her.

"Scoot back a little," he said. When she had moved closer to the middle of the mattress, he settled a knee between hers and leaned down to kiss her.

"Is this position okay?" he asked.

She seemed too overwhelmed to speak so she just nodded. He reached down to her entrance to make sure she was still ready for him and when his fingers came away slick, he carefully lowered his hips until he was resting against her. He used his hands to angle her hips higher and felt his tip press against her. He pressed in a little and when he heard only a gasp of awareness from her, he used more pressure to breach her. Her hands were wrapped around his upper arms and he felt the tips of her fingers bite into his skin.

"It's so good Shane," she cried as he gained another inch. She was hot and tight around him and he felt like his head was going to explode from the sheer pleasure. Sweat dripped down his brow as he slowly thrust in and out, his dick sinking in a little further each time. He lost his control after a few strokes and pushed into her as far as he could go. She cried out, but when he felt her legs wrap around him he knew she was okay and he pulled almost all the way out before sliding back in.

"You're so tight...so perfect," he mumbled as his lips sought out hers, his tongue mimicking what his lower body was doing. He felt his balls start to tighten and knew he wasn't going to last much longer. The way she met his strokes with her hips told him she was close too and he increased his pace. His heavy lunges were pushing her farther up the bed so he curled his body around hers to use his weight to keep her upper body still while his lower body hammered in and out of her.

He felt her lips against his neck, her gasps matching his thrusts. He shifted his hips so that his pelvis stroked her clit on each upward stroke and she began crying in earnest. Within moments, her inner muscles were tightening on him and she began to pulse around him as a scream ripped from her lips. He pumped into her a few more times and then followed her with his own release. He shouted into the bedding next to her head at the pleasure that raced through him and the last thing he remembered was her whispering his name in his ear as she clung to him.

SAVANNAH KNEW SHANE WAS GONE BEFORE SHE WAS EVEN FULLY awake the next morning. She was surprised that he'd stayed in bed with her as long as he had because as soon as their passion had cooled, she felt him start to pull away from her. Physically he had stayed and held her in his arms, but the emotional distance had been obvious and not a word had been spoken between them once he got her settled under the covers. She'd known this would be the likely outcome, but it didn't hurt any less, especially after the way he had made her feel the night before.

From the second his lips had brushed hers and his hands caressed her, she was a goner. Even in his heightened state of arousal, everything he'd done had been for her. He'd even felt her momentary surge of fear when he had placed her beneath him, but instead of backing off or ignoring it, he'd simply said her name to bring her back, to remind her who she was with and then he had rekindled the flame of passion that had initially fled at the change in position. When he'd made her come with just his mouth, it was unlike anything she'd ever felt until he had joined his body with hers. At that point she knew that he would be the only one for her because what she felt went so much deeper than the physical. He had filled the parts inside her that always seemed to be empty and hollow. She just hadn't been able to do the same for him and it was a harsh truth to accept.

Forcing herself to sit up, she looked around the dark room, secretly hoping there would be a note, but there wasn't one. She got out of the bed, her body still deliciously sore, and searched out her clothes. At some point he had neatly folded them and placed them on a chair in the corner of the room. Seeing them that way actually hurt because it made her feel like he'd done it to further distance himself from what they'd done – cleaning up after an unruly guest, not leaving behind an impassioned lover. Pulling on her clothes, she went downstairs and gathered her jacket and purse. She didn't bother to look for a note down there because there wouldn't be one – she was getting the message loud and clear. She forced herself not to take one more desperate glance around her before she left the apartment.

Savannah entered the coffee shop and instantly found Riley sitting at a table in the corner by the window. She waved and then went to the counter to place her order. She'd gotten off of work a half an hour ago and had every intention of going home and confiding her sorrows to Mr. Pickles, but when the text from Riley came through on her phone, she was both interested and wary at the timing of Gabe's girlfriend's invitation.

Riley had only recently moved to Seattle and had hooked up with Gabe less than six months ago. Savannah had finished school and moved back home within weeks of the drama that had brought Gabe and Riley together. While they had hung out and politely chatted every week at family dinner, which Riley had instituted right after she and Gabe moved in together, they hadn't really grown close. Savannah knew that was mostly her fault since Riley had actually reached out to her numerous times. But college had been a harsh lesson in what friendship really was and Savannah found building connections with anyone, man or woman, was nearly impossible when she kept hearing the cruel taunts of her classmates in her head. She'd had many friends in middle school but after her parents had died, most of her friends didn't know how to be around her and had distanced themselves. After she'd been assaulted, the idea of trying to make friends was the last thing on her mind.

She actually liked Riley and had learned that the young woman was just a few years older than her. They'd even had lunch a few times but Riley was usually the instigator and typically carried any stilted conversation they had. Savannah just found it hard to take that last step and trust her, even if she was a part of the family now. As the Barista handed her her order, she weaved her way in and out of the busy crowd and reached the table. Riley's eyes were puffy, proof she was still hurting from Shane's verbal attack.

"Hi," Riley said as Savannah sat across from her. She was a pretty young woman with long blonde hair and kind gray eyes. She worked as a vet tech, which didn't surprise Savannah when she saw the way Riley interacted with Mr. Pickles when she and Gabe came over.

"Hi. Thanks for inviting me," she said somewhat awkwardly.

"Gabe told me he was teaching you some self-defense stuff," Riley ventured. Savannah wondered what else Gabe had told her, but simply nodded her head in response. "It's smart," Riley continued. "I can't believe I never even thought to learn something like that, especially after some of the stuff that happened."

Savannah knew she was referring to an attack against Riley by her ex-fiancé. The lunatic had actually followed her from Texas, trashed her apartment and then held her at gunpoint when he tried to abduct her in broad daylight in front of her apartment. Luckily, Gabe and his dog Bella had been there or things would have ended in tragedy.

Riley smiled and took a sip of her drink. "I asked Gabe to teach me some moves last night but I guess it's different when it's your boyfriend that has his hands all over you instead of an actual instructor." Riley blushed and Savannah couldn't help but laugh.

"I'm sorry for what Shane said to you yesterday. Gabe told me," Savannah said quietly and watched Riley's face fall.

"I begged Gabe not to go over there."

"Shane shouldn't have said it. I don't know why he did, but in my heart I don't think it's what he really believes," Savannah offered.

"He's been like a brother to me. He's a big part of why Gabe and I are together." Riley shook her head. "But it's like we're losing him."

Savannah didn't respond, but found herself reaching across the table to pat Riley's hand. Riley responded by grabbing her hand and holding it for a moment, seemingly grateful for the show of support.

"How long have you been in love with him?" Riley suddenly asked, her voice gentle.

Savannah gasped at the question and then straightened in her chair. She should deny it because to do anything else would be foolish and expose how sad and pathetic she was to be in love with someone so far out of her league. But instead she said, "How did you know?"

"You look at him the way I used to look at Gabe when I thought he wasn't watching. It's like a hunger you can't feed or a thirst you can't quench."

Savannah nodded at the description because the young woman across from her was spot on. "It started off as a childish crush I guess."

"But things have changed?" Riley prompted and Savannah nodded.

"I have a confession to make," Savannah blurted. "That day we had lunch and I asked to borrow some tissues from your purse, I found his card." Riley looked surprised but stayed quiet. "I knew what he did – what they all did."

"Logan told you?" Riley asked, clearly surprised.

"No, definitely not. I overheard the three of them talking about it one night while they were at our house. They were still in college and they were hanging out in our kitchen playing poker and drinking. I came down to get something to drink and overheard them. I never told Logan that I knew."

"So when you saw his card, you guessed what it was for?" At Savannah's nod, Riley blanched and said, "Savannah, you know nothing happened between me and Shane, right? The card was a message-" she stuttered.

Savannah laughed and shook her head. "I know. I saw what was on the back of the card and figured that was why he gave it to you." Riley was visibly relieved so Savannah continued. "I memorized the email address and contacted him."

Riley shook her head in confusion. "I don't understand. Why would you need the email from his card to do that? You saw him all the time."

Savannah bit her lip. She was risking a lot by telling Riley this, but truth be told, she really needed someone to talk to. And since she'd been taking a lot of risks lately anyway, why stop now? Hopefully this one wouldn't end in disastrous results like the others. It was likely that Riley already knew she'd been at Shane's apartment last night and that she had stayed after Gabe had left.

"I have some hang-ups...sexually," she began. "I emailed Shane pretending to be a potential client and paid him to meet me at a hotel. I insisted he wear a blindfold so he wouldn't know it was me."

Riley was clearly shocked. "Holy crap," she muttered. Savannah almost smiled because as much as her brother and his friends used various and colorful swear words, Riley rarely ever did so it always amused Savannah to hear Riley's version of it. "What happened?"

Savannah decided to forgo the details and just said, "He figured out it was me anyway."

"So, is that why you were there last night?"

"He agreed to help me figure out some of the stuff I was trying to work through, but I thought maybe it was turning into something else." Her voice faltered and she felt tears sting her eyes.

"What happened?" Riley asked gently.

"It was amazing. I thought it meant the same to him but after... after, he pulled back from me. He was there, but he wasn't. He was gone this morning – no note, no goodbye."

This time it was Riley who reached for her hand to offer comfort. "I'm sorry, Savannah."

She nodded and then took the napkin Riley offered her so she could dab at her watery eyes. "It's ridiculous that I could feel this much, this fast, isn't it?"

"Part of me wishes I could tell you it is, but that's how it happened for me. I knew pretty much right away that Gabe was my future. It hurt like hell when he pushed me away. I was all set to leave - my bags were literally packed."

"What happened?"

"Shane happened."

Savannah sucked in a breath. "What do you mean?"

"He kept sticking his nose in – wouldn't let Gabe let me go, wouldn't let me give up on Gabe."

Riley's answer actually hurt Savannah physically. Shane would bend over backwards to help his friends find each other, but he wouldn't even consider pursuing something with her. Hurt lanced through her and she dropped her eyes to her hands, more bitter tears threatening to fall. Something hit the tips of her fingers and she looked up to see Riley pressing Shane's business card against her splayed hand. She lifted the tips of her fingers and Riley pushed the card under them. The side that said *'Don't give up on him'* was facing up and she ran her fingers over the ink. Riley's hand closed over hers and Savannah let out a deep breath, then squeezed Riley's hand back.

CHAPTER 10

SHANE HEARD THE DING ON HIS PHONE INDICATING HE HAD AN email but ignored it. He reached down and grabbed the straw that Paige had so considerately left him this time instead of a rolled hundred-dollar bill. He'd seen the drugs sitting on the coffee table the second he walked into the apartment and his control had snapped. He'd spent the entire day struggling to get through his classes and had ended up skipping the last two because he was too on edge to focus. His night with Savannah had destroyed him and he had walked out on her like the coward he was. He hadn't even left a note because there was absolutely nothing he could say that would justify what he'd done. As soon as she had dropped down on his lap, he had known he was going to take her and didn't care that she would be the one to suffer. He'd been too raw from his fight with Gabe and his cruelty to Riley to even consider trying to do what was best for Savannah and force her to go.

His plan had always been to let Savannah experiment on him, test her boundaries. He hadn't even really been sure she'd want to do more than some heavy petting. Keeping an emotional distance from her during any sexual act should have been the easiest thing in the world – he did it for a fucking living for Christ's sake. But even he couldn't deny the connection between them as he made love to her. And that's what they'd done – made love, not fucked. He'd asked her not to let her emotions play into what they were doing, but then he'd gone and done exactly that.

His skin crawled as he imagined Savannah waking up alone in his big bed. She was better off, he reminded himself as he leaned over the mirror that Paige had left in invitation. She'd done all the work and prepared the lines. She hadn't even been home when he got there, but she'd made sure to leave her "greeting" where he would find it right away. He guessed she also knew it would be harder to get rid of if it couldn't be quickly disposed of in a sink or toilet. It had been twenty minutes since he'd walked in and seen his salvation, but he had hesitated. His mind knew that if he did this there would be no going back, but his churning gut and burning tongue didn't care. He was a fool to think he could ever escape this part of his life.

As he leaned over and positioned the straw, he heard his email ding again. A second later there was another, and then another. He could tell by the tone that it was the email he used for escorting. It wasn't unusual to get the occasional email, but several in a row was something new. Putting the straw back down on the table, he reached for his phone and opened his email. When he saw who the new emails were from, his fingers actually trembled as he opened the first.

I need you.

-S

Shane took a deep breath and scrolled through the rest.

I can't stop thinking about how hard you were inside me last night.

-S

I want to taste you again like that first time but I don't want to stop this time.

-S

Each one was dirtier than the next and Shane leaned back to give his hardening cock a little more breathing room. He never would have guessed how naughty his little Savannah could actually be.

I'm in our room.

-S

God, he wanted her again. All the arguments for why he needed to stay away from her fled and he was up and moving. His car seemed to drive itself to the hotel and every time he had a moment of weakness and went to turn the car around, he heard that email tone again. Each little ding had his blood racing and he was afraid he wouldn't be able to make it up to the room before his cock betrayed him.

By the time he found a parking spot and got the room key from the front desk, he felt like he was on fire. The anticipation of having her sweet mouth wrapped around him was nearly too much and he fumbled to open the door. He stopped at the sight of her lying naked on the bed, her luminous eyes watching him. He saw relief etch her features, but he tried not to give that too much thought as he banged the door closed behind him, reached the bed in two long strides and then slammed his mouth down on hers as he covered her with his body. She immediately began working the buttons on his shirt, even as her tongue stroked his.

Rearing back, he discarded his shirt and then sat back to study her. Her hair was spread out beneath her like a dark pool and her lips were parted slightly. His knees were on each side of her hips which prevented her from moving her lower body, but that didn't stop her arms from coming up. He thought she would reach for him, but he watched in stunned silence as she caressed her own breasts. His breath stopped as she tentatively tweaked the nipples and then palmed them. She took her right hand and sucked one of her fingers into her mouth, soaking it with saliva. When she dipped the wet finger around one of her nipples, he actually moaned and dropped down so he could replace her finger with his lips. She arched up against him as he sucked her nipple into his mouth and his teeth bit down on the tip. She cried out against the sting of pain and then groaned when he licked her. As her hips thrust up against him, he reached for the zipper on his pants.

Before he could comprehend what she was doing, she sat up against him and then used his momentary fumbling with his pants to her advantage. She reached into his pants and closed her hand around him. It felt so good that he gave in to the pressure of her hand on his chest and dropped down on the bed so that he was on his back. Her hand stayed on him and stroked as her other hand worked his pants down. He was already leaking fluid from his cock so she used the makeshift lubricant to ease her stroking. On each glide, she twisted her hand and tightened her grip and he couldn't bite back the sound of pleasure that escaped from his lips. He dropped his head back on the bed to just relish in the sensation of it all, but nearly came when he felt her hair skim his thighs. Moments later, her hot mouth was scorching a path up and down his length and then she was sucking him deep. He shouted at the contact and then leaned up on his elbows so he could watch.

She was bent over him, her long hair hiding his view so he quickly pushed it back so he could see as her mouth drew him in as far as she could and then pulled back up. Zaps of electricity fired through him as she kept repeating the motion and when she cupped his balls with her hand, he actually knotted her hair around his fist so he could keep her there. But from the way she was working him, he knew she wasn't going anywhere until she sucked him dry.

"Take me deeper," he whispered harshly and she complied. He heard her gag a couple of times but then she seemed to figure out how to relax her throat because she was taking him all the way to the base. She came up for air every couple strokes, but in between she sucked him as hard as she could. When she swallowed around him, he started fucking her mouth.

"I'm gonna come," he said hoarsely. She tightened her hold on his cock with her mouth and then he felt her fingers playing with the skin behind his balls. Shockwaves went through him as his balls drew up and he started shooting into her mouth. She kept sucking him even as the proof of his release leaked out of her mouth and down his dick. He cried out her name and then fell back on the bed as his orgasm slowly started to wane. She licked him clean and then crawled up his body and kissed him. He tasted himself on her as she thrust her tongue into his mouth and explored every inch of him. He knew he should get her off too, but he couldn't quite make his body respond yet. He kissed her back and then let his eyes drift shut as she gently ran her lips all over his sated body. He just needed a minute, he told himself, then he would reciprocate. That was the last thing he remembered before he drifted off to sleep.

SAVANNAH WATCHED SHANE SLEEP AND COULDN'T HELP BUT MARVEL how young and relaxed he looked. It was so different from the constant darkness she saw in his eyes. She was glad she'd given him that, even if it was just temporary. It had been a huge risk to bait him the way she had, but drastic times called for drastic measures. As she had lain there naked and waiting for him, she couldn't help but wonder at the change that had come over her after being with him. He made her feel powerful and beautiful without even having to say the words. The way he'd worshipped her last night had inspired her to want to do the same for him. She knew it was still just sex to him, but if that was the only way she could even reach him, she was willing to try it.

She'd enjoyed watching his reaction to her, especially when she touched herself. It was thrilling to have so much power over a man, but she'd enjoyed the orders he had given her too. It made her feel like they were equal when they came together – they could each gain pleasure from both giving and taking. She doubted it would be like that with all men and at this point it didn't matter because she couldn't see herself feeling that free to follow her baser instincts with anyone but Shane. He shifted beneath her and she felt an arm curl around her as he drew her closer. He was still asleep so she pressed her advantage and wrapped one of her legs over his. She'd managed to get the rest of his clothes off after he'd fallen asleep, but they were still on top of the covers so the heat of his body where it rested against hers was very welcome. She placed her hand over his chest, felt his strong heartbeat and then nuzzled her lips against his neck and breathed him in. He reflexively tightened his arm around her and she finally closed her eyes.

"SHANE."

He heard his name being whispered but it sounded far away.

"Shane, please."

When he heard the fear in her voice, he awoke with a start. Savannah was no longer lying next to him and he looked around the dark room for her. The clock showed it was just after midnight. There was only a little bit of light coming from the bathroom, but the door was partially ajar. He got out of the bed and yanked on his underwear as he hurried across the room.

She was sitting on the edge of the tub, her left arm laying exposed in her lap, her right hand resting on her thigh, a shiny silver letter opener clutched in her fist. She was wearing his shirt and staring blankly straight ahead. He dropped to his knees in front of her and pulled the letter opener from her hand. He examined her left arm but saw no new wounds.

"Savannah," he said softly as he quickly checked the rest of her body for any injuries. There were none. She still didn't seem to register his presence so he gave her a hard shake and said her name again, this time more firmly. Her eyes seemed to focus and he heard her pull in a deep breath as she looked at him and then around the bathroom as if trying to figure out how they'd gotten there. When she saw the letter opener in his hand, she recoiled and then looked down at her arm.

"It's okay, sweetheart. "You're okay," he said gently as he stroked her bare thigh.

"I didn't..." she said as her fingers skimmed over the scars on her arm.

"No, you called for me just like I asked you to."

She looked up at him in confusion and then finally seemed to remember where they were. "I had a nightmare. I didn't want to wake you, so I got out of bed to get some water."

He was amazed that he hadn't felt any of it.

"Do you remember what your dream was about?"

She nodded but said nothing more and he realized that she'd been dreaming about her assault.

"I thought I was getting better," she cried hoarsely.

"You are, sweetheart. Look," he said, pointing at her arm. "You called out for me even when you weren't really aware of it – your mind knew to ask for help."

She considered his words and then nodded. "Thank you Shane."

He leaned in and kissed her. He pulled her up and led her out of the bathroom. He dropped the letter opener back on the writing desk where it had come from and then steered Savannah back to bed. Stripping the shirt off her, he pulled back the covers so she could crawl under. He got rid of his briefs and got in next to her. He leaned over her so that his chest covered hers and he kissed her over and over again, soft, gentle kisses that were meant to comfort. She relaxed under him and as he began to explore the rest of her body with his lips, he felt her fingers comb through his hair.

He skimmed her collar bone and then made his way down her chest. His exploration came to a halt when he felt the scar on her breast. He licked it gently and then used his fingers to trace the outline of the other scar on the opposite breast. He was trying to make sense of the unusual patterns.

She must have sensed his thoughts because she stilled and then carefully said, "He bit me."

It didn't register what she said at first, but when the words did finally sink in, he felt rage surge through him. The amount of pain that bastard had to have inflicted to leave that much damage on such sensitive skin was mind blowing. He heard her choke back a sob and then she covered her eyes with her hand.

"If I just hadn't opened the door..." she began but then became overwhelmed with sobs.

He gathered her in his arms and whispered, "It's not your fault" over and over again. As he held her, he thought about the last thing she said about opening the door. Logan often had to leave her alone when they were younger because he was working so much, but he would have taught her not to open the door to strangers. Nausea rolled through him as he realized what that meant – she'd been raped by someone she had known, someone she had trusted. He'd already figured out from their conversation on that first day in the hotel room that it had happened before she left for college so in all likelihood, the assault had happened in her own home.

She quieted beneath him and as her breathing evened out, he realized she had fallen asleep. He held her that way for a long time. Before he closed his own eyes, he heard her whisper, "Please don't leave in the morning without saying goodbye."

❧

IT WAS STILL DARK WHEN SHANE AWOKE, BUT HE COULD TELL BY THE light filtering through the split in the curtains that it was morning. A glance at the clock confirmed it was still early and since it was a Saturday, neither he nor Savannah had to get to school. She was still wrapped in his arms, her legs entangled with his. It was probably her way of trying to make sure he didn't sneak out on her again. He carefully disengaged himself and slipped out of bed. He made his way to the bathroom and took care of business and started the shower. He made sure to leave the door open so he'd be able to hear if she called out to him. He was only in there a few minutes when he felt the shower curtain behind him move and he watched in silence as she stepped inside. He didn't bother with words and neither did she as she leaned into his embrace.

Pressing her back against the wall, he took his time exploring her body with his hands and mouth. She reached between their bodies and stroked his erection as he thumbed her pebbled nipples and then bent to suck the drops of water off them. He closed his mouth over hers and reached to lift one of her legs as his cock searched out her warmth. It took only a few thrusts to be sheathed completely inside of her and the hot grip of her body had him rutting against her like an animal. When it finally registered why she felt like a furnace around him, he stuttered to a halt and buried his mouth against her neck in an effort to try and catch his breath.

"Shit, I forgot the condom," he muttered in shock. He had never been bare inside a woman and he couldn't believe his lust had overridden his common sense when it came to protecting her.

Savannah was breathing heavy against his ear, her breasts brushing his chest. The contact was making him crazy and he actually thrust against her again before he could stop himself.

"It's okay, I'm on the pill," she whispered.

"No, it's not safe," he responded, shaking his head even as he felt her flex her internal muscles. His shaft swelled and he forced himself to pull back, but she reached down and dug her hands into the globes of his ass and wrapped her leg tighter around him.

"I trust you," she said and then she lifted her other leg and he instinctively grabbed it to give her the support she needed to wrap it around his other side. Gravity helped her to slide down his length and he couldn't help but match the motion with a shift of his hips.

It was stupid and crazy to do this, but he knew he was physically safe – he'd been tested regularly and had never gone without a condom, so the risk was minimal. If he were a better man he would have pulled out of her and done this right, but as her body rippled around his, he knew it was just another notch in the failure column that was his life. He kissed her hard as he began plunging in and out of her. She met his every thrust as her hands wrapped around his upper arms for support.

The hot water caressed them both as he worked their bodies closer and closer to the edge. He felt her start to pulse around him and knew she was close. He reached between their slick bodies and found her clit. He showed her no mercy as he stroked it hard and then felt her nails rake his back as she suddenly wrapped her arms around him and screamed his name. His own orgasm tore through him as he felt the heat of her release all around his throbbing dick and then he was emptying himself inside her.

As her body's aftershocks milked him dry, he called on his reserve energy to keep them upright because everything in him relaxed as the pleasure snaked through his veins. When their bodies had finally stilled, he pulled free of her and then tugged her under the shower spray and washed her body. She did the same to him and after running towels briefly over each of them, he lifted her in his arms and carried her back to the bed. Within minutes she fell asleep, but Shane lay there for a long time, wide awake and lost in turbulent thought.

Savannah woke slowly, her hand automatically searching for Shane in the dim room. Disappointment flooded her when she realized the other side of the bed was empty. She flopped onto her back and dropped her arm over her face as hurt lanced through her – she'd really believed something had shifted between them. She lay there like that for a moment and then pulled herself up. She nearly screamed when she saw Shane sitting by the desk in the wooden chair, his tall frame relaxed.

"You're still here," she said stupidly. When he didn't answer, she pulled the sheet up tighter around her chest. He dropped his eyes at the movement and then looked back up. She was pleased to see desire there.

"I don't know what to do with you," he finally admitted.

She had an answer for him but doubted he would like it so she kept her mouth shut.

"I told you things couldn't be different for us – not like you want – but you still keep coming back to me." He seemed both sad and confused.

"I just want you Shane. I'll take what I can get." She hesitated for a moment and then said, "But it has to be you, the real you. I don't want the Shane that you want everyone else to see."

He stiffened and she guessed he was unnerved by her honest observation. He had been fooling people so long with his persona that she supposed it was odd for him to be seen as anything else.

"You're only going to get hurt when whatever this is ends. And Savannah, it will end."

She was silent for a moment and then drew her knees up to her chest. "Do you need me Shane?" She pinned him with her gaze. "Do you need me the way I need you? Do you need me to make things hurt just a little bit less? To ease that knot in your stomach that never quite goes away? Because that's what you do for me. And if that's all I can ever be for you, I can learn to live with that."

He was silent for a long time and she held her breath when he stood. In seconds he was over her and pushing her back on the bed so that the sheet loosened and fell to her waist. She wasn't sure but she swore she heard him mutter, "Yes" an instant before his mouth covered hers and after that there was no longer the need for words.

CHAPTER 11

DR. HENDERSON WAS AN EVIL GENIUS, SAVANAH MUSED AS SHE LEFT the therapist's downtown office. She had walked into the doctor's office with every intention of clamming up and brushing off all the inevitable talk about tools and resources she had access to in her mind to fix herself, but then the guy had gone and used his magic on her by simply sitting there. The silence had become awkward and then unnerving, but the man just sat across from her and smiled. He didn't even have a notepad in his lap so that he could write down what a crazy nut job she was.

Gary Henderson had to be in his late fifties, tall and skinny with a head of thick, white hair. He had sat comfortably in a well-worn, leather desk chair that he placed across from her where she had sat in the center of the plush, cream colored couch. Her legs crossed, arms wrapped protectively around her middle and stiff back had sent her message loud and clear, but he'd just leaned back against that squeaky chair, braced one leg on the other and rested his hands in his lap and smiled at her. No talk of weather, no asking why she was there.

A good ten minutes had passed before she had blurted out that he couldn't help her, that she had tried therapy before. He'd shrugged. That was it. Savannah had fallen silent again and then her anxiety had started to creep in. That familiar itching had returned and she had begun scratching at her arm. The doctor had watched her for a moment and then stood up and retrieved something from his desk. He had returned to his chair and then scooched it right up to the edge of the couch. If he had sensed her tension at how close he was, he had ignored it and held up what was in his hand.

"Put out your hand," he had said, motioning to the arm that she was still scratching. She had hesitated when she saw the band he was holding, but then stuck out her left hand. He had quickly placed the band onto her wrist – it was snug, but not uncomfortable. Upon closer inspection, she had realized it was some type of hair tie. The doctor had pushed his chair back to its original position and then had said, "Snap it."

She'd been confused but had done what he said. The resulting sting was sharp, but the pain had dissipated quickly. She'd done it once more for good measure and then sat back further against the couch to look at the man in front of her in confusion.

In response he'd said, "I'm not here to take away the one thing that brings you comfort, Savannah. And I'm not here to lecture you on how you should stop or get over it. I don't have some magic words that will fix you. I'm here to listen, to be a sounding board. And if I have a couple of insights along the way, like that," he said, pointing to the band on her wrist, "Then I'll give them to you and you decide for yourself if it's something you want to try."

She'd relaxed after that - marginally at least, because a part of her was still waiting for the guys in white coats to come in and drag her to a padded cell – and they'd talked about the basics. Her childhood, what she did for a living, the easy stuff. And then it was over and she was walking to her car and somehow had felt a tiny bit lighter – not because she was fixed or cured or even close to any of that, but because the clever bastard had made everything she said or didn't say her choice to do so. He'd even offered to give her the names of other therapists so she could see which one was the best fit for her and when she'd inquired about another appointment, he'd simply told her to call if and when she was ready to see him again. He'd handed her a business card which included his direct emergency phone number and that was it.

As she crossed the parking lot to her car, her thoughts drifted to Shane. They'd spent most of Saturday in bed at the hotel. When they'd gone past the checkout time, Shane had called down and arranged for them to stay another day and had even had the previous night's charge moved to his credit card, something she'd fought him on but when he kissed her long and deep, that thought had disappeared pretty quick. He'd returned to using condoms which disappointed her because having him completely naked inside of her had made her feel like maybe there was a connection between them that he would never have with someone else. But she figured it was his way of getting them back on common ground where what was happening to them was about physical need and nothing more.

When their bodies were completely drained, they'd ordered room service which they had shared on the bed, naked. It was only Logan's phone call to check in with her that had dampened their evening. She'd told her brother she was spending the weekend at a girlfriend's house for an extended "girls' night" and that she would be home on Sunday. Since he didn't know she had no girlfriends, he easily bought the lie and when she had crawled back into bed, the awkwardness between her and Shane was like a lead ball. Before she could tell Shane that she would tell Logan soon, he'd pulled her against him and set them back against the headboard and ordered a movie on the hotel TV for them to watch – another romantic comedy. They'd made it less than halfway through it before they were on each other again and by the time Sunday morning rolled around she could barely walk. He'd walked her to her car, kissed her hard, told her no more hotel rooms and then he'd watch her drive away. There'd been no discussion of their next rendezvous or if there would even be one.

As she reached her car, she thought about calling Shane to let him know about her session but then decided against it. She wasn't sure what the rules were for who called who the day after a weekend of marathon sex, but since their relationship was anything but normal, she guessed those rules wouldn't apply anyway. The fact that Shane had stayed with her in the hotel room made her want to declare victory, but maybe he'd just been trying to get what was between them out of his system. And as he had reminded her, everything else was staying the same – he had a girlfriend, a new life in Chicago next year and a passel of beautiful, rich women who were more than willing to pay big bucks to spend time with him.

Self-preservation should have her running for the hills, but she'd meant what she'd said – she would take whatever she could get because he made her feel things that she hadn't known were possible, and not just sexually. When he gave her one of his secret smiles because she said something silly or said her name in that smooth, silky voice of his, she felt everything inside of her light up. It was foolish because there was only one likely outcome – she would walk away with a broken heart. But at least she'd have the memories to hang on to and that was a lot more than she had before.

LOGAN CHECKED THE FIGURES ON HIS LAPTOP FOR A SECOND TIME and sighed. The money just wasn't there. He'd stretched and strained wherever he could, but there was just no way he'd be in the black this year. The renovations would drain everything he had and then some, but it was the only way to make the place profitable. That meant the escort work would have to continue for the foreseeable future. It wasn't necessarily that he hated the work, it was just something he could live without – it had been and still was a means to an end and nothing more.

Escorting had never been for him what it was for Shane who had seemed to thrive on the endless women and mounds of money. He'd never seen someone who could so easily turn themselves into whatever the customer wanted. The man was a chameleon. But he had started to sense something shift in Shane over the past few years. He'd noticed the physical signs first – he'd become curter and irritable and instead of two drinks he'd have four or five. Not enough to get stone drunk, but as a bartender, Logan could read when people were reaching the point where they were nearing the line from buzzed to blitzed.

It was the darkness in Shane's eyes and his withdrawal from their group that had Logan most concerned. He had tried attributing it to stress from trying to keep up with the demands of law school and an overbearing father who had decided Shane's future the moment Michael's body had been placed in the cold, damp earth. But Shane remained at the top of his class and his mind was one of the sharpest Logan had ever known. And his friend seemed perfectly content to allow his father to decide his fate. He and Gabe had both tried approaching Shane on multiple occasions to try and feel him out about how he really felt about moving to Chicago to take his place in his father's law firm, but Shane would just wave a hand and say it was what it was.

Logan heard the front door open and light poured into the dark interior as his sister entered. He was sitting behind the bar and immediately stood. "What is it? What's wrong?" he said tensely as she hurried toward him. She paused at his tone, but then continued her quick pace.

"Nothing. Why?" she asked. She looked nervously around the room but seemed to relax when she saw the place was empty. She'd only been in his bar once when he first began leasing the space and that was when she was much younger. He had tried coaxing her back in on more than one occasion so she could see what he spent so much of his time trying to build, but she had always balked and found some reason not to come. So to see her now made him extremely nervous.

"You never come in here," he said bluntly.

She looked pained for a moment and then she reached into her purse and put his phone on the counter. "I found this on the table when I got home today. I thought you might need it so I decided to bring it by."

He relaxed when he saw the phone and then chuckled at his overreaction. Things had been off for so long between him and Savannah that he realized he was always walking on eggshells around her and had no idea what was going on in her life and in her head. Their contact had become so mechanical and non-committal that he had instantly jumped to the conclusion that something terrible had happened.

"How did we get here Savannah?" he wondered aloud.

He saw her stiffen. "What do you mean?" she asked carefully.

"How did we become strangers?" He pulled the phone across the bar and then set it aside. "Did I do something to make you pull away from me?"

She dropped her eyes, but he swore he saw moisture in them. She was silent for so long he was afraid she wouldn't answer. "I'm just working through some stuff Logan. I just need a little more time."

He nodded slowly, ignoring the constriction in his chest. He wanted to know more. No, he *needed* to know more – more about whatever had taken the light from her eyes so many years ago and caused her to turn away from him rather than towards him.

"Okay," he said. "I can wait."

She nodded and then suddenly reached out to grab his hand and gave it a hard squeeze. She let go before he could respond and then she turned to leave.

"Are you going out again tonight?" he called to her as she neared the door.

"Um, not sure – maybe. I'll text you if I do." She disappeared back into the bright light and then he was plunged into darkness once more as the door closed behind her.

"Was that your sister?" came a voice behind him. Sam was walking towards the bar, a box in his burly arms.

"Yeah, I left my phone at home so she was dropping it off."

"I didn't know she was back," Sam commented as he began emptying the box. Sam Reynolds was older than Logan by more than twenty years but his business knowledge and support had saved Logan time and money on more than one occasion. He was a boisterous individual with a thick, deep voice that matched his portly figure – he looked like someone that spent a lot of time watching football on the big screen while downing a bucket of fried chicken. But it was an illusion. His friend was actually quite strong from years of lifting heavy bottles and kegs around, but he also had no problem partying with the patrons of the popular sports bar he ran on the other side of town. Logan had always wondered why his former boss was so willing to help him with the business since Logan's goal was to have a bar that would ultimately be in direct competition with Sam's. He supposed that was why the man had bought in as an investor – Logan had actually had to say no when Sam asked for fifty percent so they'd be equal partners.

Remembering Sam's comment about Savannah, Logan said, "Yeah, she's been back a few months now. Just started teaching over at the elementary school in Queen Anne. I think she's dating the father of one of the kids in her class."

"Good for her," Sam responded as he placed the last bottle behind the bar and then grabbed the box and headed towards the storage area. "I'll bring the rest of these up," he said as he waved the box around.

"Thanks Sam," Logan said as he went back to work on his laptop to try and find money that just wasn't there.

❧

"BABE, YOU HERE?"

Shane flinched at her high-pitched tone, but didn't respond to Paige's inquiry. He heard the snick of her shoes as she made her way to the bedroom where he waited on her perfectly made bed.

"There you are," she muttered with irritation as she strode past him and disappeared into the bathroom. "Jerry's gallery opening is tonight." She reappeared in the bedroom looking exactly the same so Shane guessed she must have gone in there for one of her many daily make-up checks. She was dressed in a white pantsuit with sparkling diamonds and bright gold accessories. If it hadn't been for the ugly red silk scarf she had draped around her thin neck, she could have easily blended into the wall, the nauseatingly white wall in yet another white room. "You should wear the Valentino tonight – the black one but not that god awful teal tie you like so much...it won't go with my dress."

She hurried past him and into her walk in closet. He could see her searching the endless racks of clothes until she found the dress she wanted.

"Do you remember my brother?" he asked quietly.

"Um, yeah, sure," she mumbled as she started scanning her shoe collection. "The fag, right?"

He fisted his hands at her slur. When she glanced at him and saw his reaction she tried to backpedal. "Well, that's what everyone was saying about him at school."

Shane stood and went to the closet door, his icy expression causing her to take a step back. He'd never struck a woman and he wasn't going to now, but he'd never been more tempted.

"You know how he died?"

She nodded, but wisely kept her mouth shut.

"You know how he died, yet you keep leaving me your little gifts. Why?"

"Come on Shane," she laughed. "I just thought you might want to loosen up a bit. Your brother was..." she stuttered to a halt at his dark look. "Look," she began again. "You're under a lot of pressure and I thought you might need a little help to unwind – be yourself again."

"Be myself?" he repeated coldly.

She huffed in frustration and then grabbed a pair of shoes. "Can we do this later? I promised Jerry I'd be there for his speech."

"There's no later Paige."

When she looked at him, he motioned with his head to his side of the massive closet. There were a few suits hanging there – the ridiculously expensive, designer ones that she had bought him – and several empty clothes hangers but nothing else. She studied the nearly bare rack for a moment and then laughed shrilly. "God, you're such a loser Shane." She began stripping off her clothes and he found it amusing that she did so while watching herself in the mirror. Her perfectly tanned and toned body did nothing for him.

"You think your folks will be okay with this?" she muttered as she worked the dress over her body. "Face it Shane, for whatever reason, we make sense together. You know any other woman who's going to let you stick your dick into strangers for money because I sure don't."

"And what if I do it when there's no money involved? Would that even bother you?"

She shrugged. "As long as you show up where and when I need you, I don't care if you fuck every woman in the city." She smoothed her hands over the dress and checked herself at different angles. "Hell, I actually like watching some of those hags you service turn all red when we walk into a place together – Cecilia Harrington actually asked me to co-chair a couple of her stuffy fundraising committees after she saw me with you – bitch has been snubbing me for years."

Cecilia Harrington was a quiet, older woman whose wealthy husband had recently been diagnosed with dementia and often forgot who his wife even was. She'd caved under the stress of caring for a man in declining health and trying to run his many philanthropic organizations and had hired Shane for companionship more than a year ago. They'd been together only a few times, but he'd always thought she was nice. But it had never even occurred to him that Paige would stoop to blackmailing his customers. If he ever ran into any of them while with Paige, he made sure to treat them like he'd never met them before but some, like Cecilia, weren't good at hiding their surprise at seeing him within their own social circles.

"You're a piece of work Paige."

"Spare me, Shane. You've got a good thing going here – you want to try walking away from it, go ahead. But we both know you'll be back. You haven't come this far just to throw it all away."

He heard her nasally voice drag on as he turned and left the closet and by the time he had grabbed his bag and left the bedroom, he knew she hadn't even noticed his departure because she was still railing at him about how he was going to be sorry.

"Savannah?"

Savannah froze at the sound of Robert's voice behind her. In the melee of the kids being dismissed for the day, she hadn't heard him come into the room. Most of the kids had already torn out of the room to meet their parents but, Robert's son, Nicholas, was busily packing up his belongings from the bin each child in the class had been assigned to keep their stuff in.

"Robert," she managed to say pleasantly but her stomach churned. This man had seen her at her worst. It hadn't appeared that he'd shared her bout of craziness with anyone at the school because she still had her job, but he had stopped bringing his son to class himself, instead tasking the child's nanny with that chore.

"How are you?" he asked carefully.

She nodded almost violently and then tried to smile brightly. "I'm good, really good."

"Good," he said awkwardly and then paused. "I...I didn't know after what happened," he slowed and then stopped mid thought. "I'm sorry if I did something to frighten you," he blurted out.

She was sure her mouth was opening and closing like some demented fish struggling for air, but she couldn't believe *he* was apologizing to *her*. "No, Robert, you did nothing wrong."

He seemed visibly relieved and she realized what a truly nice man he was.

"Daddy, daddy!" Nicholas shouted as he ran up to his father and thrust a big, colorful piece of paper into the man's hands. "I painted today!"

Robert and Savannah both laughed when the still wet finger-paint smeared all over Robert's hands and sleeve. "Wow, good job buddy. I love it!" he declared as he admired his son's effort. "Why don't you go find your jacket while I talk to Miss Bradshaw some more, okay?"

The little boy nodded heartily and then took off to do his father's bidding.

"He's an amazing boy, Robert. Your wife would be so proud of how you're raising him."

Robert's eyes darkened with pain for a moment at the mention of his dead wife, but then he looked at his son and smiled. "Thank you. He can't stop talking about you – you're his favorite teacher."

Savannah smiled and then went around to her desk to grab some hand wipes that she kept stashed there. "He's really sweet – and such a talker," she commented as she absently wiped at one of Robert's paint covered hands.

"Savannah, I was wondering if you might want to try things again. We could go someplace quieter," he offered.

She stilled at his words. The last thing she expected was him to ask her out on another date. He was so sweet and thoughtful and a few weeks ago she would have said yes – had in fact said yes. What she had with Shane wasn't really a relationship, so saying yes to this man was what she should do – it would be the healthy thing to do.

"Robert," she began as she wiped his other hand and then handed him a fresh wipe so he could get the rest.

"It's okay," he said, cutting her off. "You have someone else in your life...someone important," he mused. When she just looked at him in surprise, he said, "Just a guess. You seem lighter than last time," he finished and then carefully adjusted his son's artwork so that he wouldn't get any more paint on himself. "Nicholas, come on, time to go. Bye Savannah."

"Bye Robert." She watched him leave through the door on the far end of the room.

"You should have said yes." Shane watched Savannah jump back in surprise at the sight of him in the doorway. He should have felt guilty for scaring her, but he was seething with too much jealousy to do much else besides stare at her. He'd heard her entire conversation with the sharply dressed young father from his spot at the second of two doorways that led into the classroom. He had figured out pretty quickly who the man was and it had taken everything in him not to stride into the room and stake his claim on Savannah. Robert was exactly what Savannah needed - handsome, responsible, clearly successful from the cut of his expensive suit and smart enough not to want to let a woman like Savannah get away, even after their disastrous first date. He hated the guy.

Savannah watched him silently, but her stony gaze was sending a clear message that she was pissed, not scared. He knew why. It had been nearly a week since their rendezvous in the hotel room and he hadn't called or texted her. She didn't need to know that he picked up the phone a dozen times, but always chickened out before completing the call. He'd written her some racy texts too and had imagined what she'd look like as she blushed while reading them. But he'd wimped out there too and canceled them all instead of sending them. But his body hadn't stopped craving her and he'd finally given up the battle today during class when he'd actually found himself writing her name in his notebook like a teenage girl. And now he was here, watching her get asked out by another man and being both overjoyed and troubled when she declined.

"Why didn't you say yes?" he finally asked as he stepped into the classroom. It was a large room, but surprisingly clean. He saw more than a dozen openings in the cubby shelf on the opposite side of the room and marveled that someone as young and quiet as Savannah could control and nurture that many kids at once. He'd seen her as the kids had run out of the room and nearly all had stopped to hug her. She had given each one a squeeze and some personal, endearing comment that left them hurrying out of the room with big, goofy grins on their little faces. He'd never really been around children, but even he knew she was a natural. And then she'd gone and touched Robert and any warm, fuzzy feelings left behind by watching her with the kids had dissolved into a jealous, simmering rage.

"You know why," she responded. She crossed her arms over her chest and he knew she wasn't going to make it easy for him to get back in her good graces. The twisted side of him was excited to have to convince her though.

"He's perfect for you."

"He's not you." The response nearly knocked him to his knees. He actually stopped and stared at her. Warning bells blared in his head. He'd held onto a shred of hope that she wasn't becoming too emotionally attached to him, but her response made it clear that she was already in deeper than she should be.

"Savannah-" he began, but she put up a hand to cut him off.

"Don't Shane. I don't want to hear it." She started moving around the room and snatching up discarded toys and art supplies. "You've made yourself clear about what our relationship is and isn't. But I'm not going to lie about how I feel...I'm already lying too much as it is."

He felt a pang of guilt at her reference. Since Logan hadn't shown up to kick his ass, he had already figured she was still keeping her brother in the dark, but he could see now how hard that was for her.

"You could tell him," he said quietly as he leaned down to pick up some kind of building block toy at his feet.

"I have to be able to tell him everything and I'm just not there yet."

"He'll understand why you kept it from him Savannah," he offered.

She didn't respond, just kept cleaning up.

"Do you remember what you asked me in the hotel room last weekend?" She looked up at him, clearly not sure what he was referring to. He took a few steps closer to her. "You asked me if I needed you to ease the knot in my stomach – the one that never goes away. Do you remember?"

She nodded, but remained silent.

"Did you hear my answer?"

"I've been trying to convince myself that you didn't say yes," she whispered as he reached her.

"I did say it. And that pain does ease when we're together, but it comes back worse every time because I know that no matter what I say or do, you are going to get hurt. Nothing you say will convince me that you can walk away from this unscathed." He palmed her cheek, rubbing the rough pad of his thumb against her silky skin. "But I'm such a bastard that I'm going to take what you're giving and try to figure out how to live with the regret and guilt after you're gone."

When he brushed his lips over hers, he heard her sigh and then she was wrapping around him, instantly welcoming him against her body. Her mouth opened beneath his and he kissed her every way he could think of, soft and hard, fast and slow, shallow and deep.

"How about we get some coffee?" he said against her lips as he forced himself to pull back. "Otherwise I'm going to try out my newest fantasy of spreading you out on your desk and-" he began, but she laughed and slapped her hand over his mouth.

"There could still be parents around." As she pulled her hand back, she brushed her thumb tantalizingly over his lips and then pulled back. "I'll get my stuff."

CHAPTER 12

"WHY DID YOUR PARENTS MOVE TO CHICAGO?" SAVANNAH ASKED AS she watched him take a sip of his coffee. She'd followed him in her car to a small deli near his apartment that also served espresso. They'd been lucky enough to grab one of the back tables away from the counter so it was relatively quiet.

"I'd like to say it was because they needed a fresh start after Michael, but their motives were more financial and social than anything else."

"What do you mean?"

"My father got an offer from a former colleague to start a practice together. The firm does mostly criminal defense law, but throws in some Pro Bono stuff on the side. In exchange, my mom gets to sit on several boards of the different charities my father's company 'gives back to' so it's a win-win for both of them." She didn't miss the condemnation in his tone.

"So you're going to be a defense lawyer too?"

"Yep, you're looking at the reason future pedophiles, mobsters and murderers are going to walk away scot free so they can hurt more people."

She reared back in shock at both his words and the venom behind them. He seemed to have realized he had revealed too much and began drumming his fingers on the table. She could tell he didn't want her to ask, but she had to know. "Why?" was all she said.

"It's expected," was his curt answer.

"Do you even want to be a lawyer?" she asked softly.

"Why'd you choose to be a teacher?" he asked suddenly.

"Because my mother was a teacher," she began, but at his "there you go" look she finished with, "And because I love it."

Her answer seemed to irritate him, but she guessed it had more to do with him not getting off so easy on explaining away his career choices. He looked around the deli and then said, "Let's just say I inherited my future."

"From Michael?" she ventured.

He was quiet for a moment and then suddenly let out a sigh of resignation. "It was supposed to be him. He was the oldest, the prodigal son. I was sloppy seconds." He started drumming his fingers louder and she stifled the urge to cover his hand with hers. "I think he was open to the whole idea of being a lawyer – he was always good at arguing. Our parents had drilled the idea into his head from the time he was old enough to understand what our dad did for a living and the idea of having his name next to Dad's on the letterhead gave him a connection to our father that he couldn't have gotten any other way."

"What about you?"

"As long as I got good grades and stayed out of trouble, they didn't seem to really care what direction I was headed in. I was only sixteen when Michael died and hadn't really made any plans at that point. After he was gone, everything just shifted onto me. I was so overwhelmed by the attention that I didn't even think to argue."

"And now?"

"And now it doesn't matter anymore. My parents lost a son. They may not have agreed with Michael's decision to be who he was, but they loved him. I know they love me too. I won't fail them like I did him."

"You didn't fail your brother," she said automatically and this time she did close her hand over his. He stopped drumming his fingers, but didn't pull away from her.

"I didn't like seeing you touch him," he said quietly, his dark eyes on hers.

"Who?" she asked, confused by the abrupt change in topic. Instead of answering, he studied her. "Robert?" she finally asked.

"When I saw you touch his hand, I wanted to beat the shit out of him."

"I was just cleaning-" she began.

"I didn't say it was reasonable, Savannah. I said I didn't like it." He shifted his hand beneath her so that his palm faced up and he could stroke the inside of her wrist with his fingers. Satisfaction went through him when she shuddered at the contact. "It made me realize how you must feel when you think of me with all those women."

He saw her bite her lip and pain flickered across her features. He was surprised when she suddenly reached out to snap a band that was wrapped around the wrist he'd been stroking. Shock ran through him as it registered that the rubber band he thought was just a hair tie was something else entirely. He tightened his hand on hers and then he was standing, pulling her up behind him. She barely had time to grab her purse before he was pulling her towards the back of the deli. He pushed open the bathroom door, flipped on the light and dragged her into the small space. He slammed the door closed and locked it, then leaned back against the door and pulled her tight against his body.

"I'm sorry. I shouldn't have said it that way," he muttered against her hair as she wrapped her arms around him. "I was trying to tell you that I haven't been with anyone since that first night in the hotel."

She lifted her head, her eyes wide. "But your girlfriend-"

"Not my girlfriend anymore. I wasn't with her either. There's been no one else."

"Why?" she asked, clearly surprised.

"I can't answer that. I'm trying really hard not to try and figure it out myself because it won't change anything. It can't."

"I don't want Robert or anyone else," she whispered firmly.

He nodded and then dropped a kiss on the top of her head before saying, "Let's get out of here."

Savannah moaned as Shane slammed his apartment door closed and kissed her. He'd been on her before they even made it to the door and she'd welcomed it. They'd been making out against the locked front door so fervently that it had taken a polite cough from a passing neighbor to drag them apart. Shane had wrestled with the lock and had his lips back on hers before the door even latched closed. Their conversation at the deli and his subsequent confession about the other women had done nothing to cement what their relationship actually was, but she didn't care. The jealousy and pain she'd been feeling about the other women in his life had needled her since their first time together. Being the other woman was something she never wanted to be and knowing the relationship between him and his girlfriend had already been on the rocks made her feel a little less like a home wrecker.

Shane pulled away from her long enough to free her of the silk blouse she'd been wearing and then he went to work on her pants. As he fumbled with the zipper, she put her hand over the bulge in his pants and rubbed him lightly.

"Shit," he growled as he stripped the pants from her. She was glad she had picked slip on shoes today instead of the ones with the laces because Shane seemed to have lost all patience for foreplay. She loved how rough he was, but still gentle at the same time. As he began working the buttons of his own shirt free, she released his cock from his pants. He'd managed to get the buttons undone on his shirt but then gave up and maneuvered her so she was bent over the side of the couch, her arms braced on the plush arm beneath her. Within seconds her panties were gone and his thick fingers were probing her. She knew what he'd find, since her desire was ripping through every nerve in her body.

"Now Shane, please," she cried brokenly and before she could even finish the desperate plea he was pushing his length inside of her. It burned as he stretched her, but also felt so incredible that she had to fight back tears. He kept working himself in and out of her until he could go no further and then he hung there, his front pressed against her back, his lips on the back of her neck as he sucked in deep breaths.

Her inner muscles clung to him and she could tell he was bare inside her again.

As he began long, slow thrusts, he played with her breasts through her bra. She locked her elbows to brace herself against the force of him plunging in and out of her. "It's so good Savannah," he groaned as he stilled inside her once more. She cried out in frustration, but he remained still and then turned her head so their mouths could meet. As he played with her tongue, she felt him withdraw from her.

"No," she whispered at his departure but he stilled her with a hand on her hips. He pulled his lips from hers and she hung her head down as the need in her body crawled through her like a living thing. Within seconds he was back inside her and this time she could feel the latex separating them. Disappointment flared through her, but it was short-lived as he began hammering into her, his own body forcing hers further down over the arm of the couch. He'd never taken her this hard or this fast and she loved every second of it. His fingers bit hard into her hips and she knew she'd have bruises tomorrow.

She could feel her orgasm building and she automatically tightened her inner muscles around him every time he pulled out. He was groaning harshly and one of his hands moved up to close around her lower neck. His hold was gentle, but firm and she knew he needed to control her body's movement. In the past, the move would have brought back all her old fears, but now she reveled in how he mastered her body, owned it. She couldn't wait to return the favor.

Her orgasm hit her harder and faster than she expected. One minute it was building and building, the next minute it had rocketed through her – there was no in between this time. She screamed and dug her fingers into the soft fabric beneath her. As the pleasure rolled through her in waves, she actually felt Shane slow his pace so that he was gently rocking in and out of her. Sweat rolled down her brow and her muscles gave out as she relaxed her weight all the way down on the arm of the couch. Shane returned his hand to her hip and pulled her back hard on his cock. When he began stroking her overly sensitive clit, she cried out and put her hand over his, but he kept rubbing her slowly, his hips matching the pace.

"No more Shane," she muttered, but he leaned down so that his lips were by her ear.

"One more Savannah." And then he was stroking her with more urgency and lunging into her again. Her body began to respond, but her muscles were still too lax to do anything but lay there and take the pounding. He gave her one last final hard pinch on her clit and then another orgasm tore through her. He shouted against her neck as his body jerked inside of hers. He kept stroking in and out of her as his body emptied itself and then he fell against her back, her body still clutched tightly around him. She would have been content to lay there underneath him all night, but he eventually pulled out of her, disposed of the condom and then dragged her sated body up the stairs and into the shower.

"DOES THIS HELP?" SHANE ASKED AS HE FINGERED THE BAND ON Savannah's wrist. She was sprawled over him, her naked, relaxed body warming him wherever their skin touched. The room was dark and quiet except for a ceiling fan that he'd turned on to cool them down after another round of scorching sex. He'd taken her again in the shower, this time remembering to grab a condom from the drawer in the bathroom, and then again after the water had finally turned cold on them and they'd managed to crawl into his bed. This last time had been less frenzied and he'd taken the time to explore every part of her body and then she'd done the same to him. He knew he needed to feed her since it was well past dinner time, but he just couldn't find the energy or desire to move yet.

She nodded against him. "Dr. Henderson suggested it."

Since he'd gotten the doctor's name from Gabe, he knew who the man was, but he hadn't been sure if Savannah would follow through and make the appointment.

"Did you like him?" He felt her smile against his chest.

"I was determined not to, but he was actually really nice."

"Are you going to go see him again?" he prodded.

"I have an appointment on Monday." He felt her soft lips graze his chest and his relaxed body immediately tightened. "I thought he'd be this stuffy old guy who would tell me to stop the cutting or he'd have to send me somewhere. But he didn't – he said he wouldn't try to take it away from me. This," she said, lifting her wrist to look at the band, "brings me back from the place I start to go."

"I'm proud of you, Savannah. I know it's not easy to have to open up about that part of your life."

She snuggled further into him. "I don't know how I can love and hate it at the same time. It gives me so much, but it takes so much too. I'm worried that it will take everything someday."

He tightened his arm around her. "Logan will understand – so will your friends. They won't judge you for it and they won't turn their backs on you. It doesn't make you weak – it shows how badly you want to live despite the pain inside."

"You know what it's like, don't you?" she whispered. "When the pain goes so deep inside that you need to try and find a way to let some of it out?"

She braced her arms on his chest so she could look at him and even despite the darkness in the room, he could feel her eyes on him. "But you don't actually let it out, do you? You become someone else – someone who doesn't hurt, someone who doesn't have to hide."

Her perceptiveness chilled his blood and any desire he was feeling was quickly replaced with fear. She was way too close to the truth. She must have felt his withdrawal because she sighed and dropped her head back on his chest. "I think you need to feed me," she said casually and then suddenly ran her tongue over one of his nipples. He let out a hiss at the pleasure that coursed through him.

"Otherwise I might need to find something else to taste," she said wickedly as her hand traveled down his abdomen. Had his own stomach not been growling, he gladly would have let her follow through on her threat, but instead he grabbed her straying hand and dragged her out of the bed after him.

Ten minutes later they were on his couch, her wearing just his shirt and him wearing a pair of sweats. He'd thrown together a couple of sandwiches and she'd rummaged up some sodas for them. He hadn't missed her sending a text, presumably to Logan to let him know she'd once again be out all night. He felt a pang of guilt, but forced it down.

Once they were settled on the couch, he turned on the TV. He noticed she kept glancing at the arm of the couch where he'd fucked her long and hard just a few hours ago. When she found him watching her, she blushed. He laughed and kissed her, then began searching for a movie.

As he pressed the play button on the remote, she said, "Okay, I gotta know - what's with all the romantic comedies?"

"What?" he said.

"You're like obsessed with chick flicks. What's that all about?" She was completely serious.

"Are you kidding me? They're for you."

"For me?" she asked.

"Yeah, I figured..."

"What? That just because I'm a girl, I only like to watch ridiculous movies about love and happily ever afters?" He heard the teasing in her voice and smiled.

"Okay, what kinds of movies *do* you like?"

She sat back against the couch and took a huge bite of her sandwich. "Violent ones – the more deaths, the better." He was sure he was gaping at her. "I really like the natural disaster ones – you know, meteors destroying the world, tidal waves, earthquakes...as long as the body count is high."

Shane laughed and it felt so good, so foreign that he did it again. At her mock look of outrage, he tried to stifle himself, but failed and laughed some more. "Have at it," he said as he handed her the remote and then swung an arm around her shoulders. It took her only a couple of minutes to find something about the world being threatened by aliens and when the bodies started dropping like flies, she relaxed against him. He chuckled again and then started on his sandwich – she never stopped surprising him and he guessed, and hoped, that she probably never would either.

"Savannah, you need to focus," Gabe said to her and she snapped herself out of her reverie and focused on the big man in front of her. He'd been showing her the basic technique for a move that was supposed to allow someone of her size to drop a man even as big and strong as Gabe. Her thoughts had been where they almost always were now, on Shane. They'd spent the entire weekend together both in bed and out of it.

He'd taken her downtown to see the sights and they'd even gone up in the Space Needle, something she hadn't done since she was a child. She'd lived in Seattle almost her entire life, but had somehow forgotten how beautiful the city was and how much it had to offer. They'd shopped at the busy marketplace and then gone to the small aquarium on the waterfront. After lunch, they had hopped on one of the ferries that crossed over to Bainbridge Island and then they'd explored a couple of beaches. At one point he had even taken her hand as they walked and she'd never felt more complete and at peace in her life.

"Hello? Savannah?"

"What? Sorry," she muttered and then shook her head to clear it. She heard her phone ding with a new text and she wanted very badly to dart around Gabe and run over to the bench where she'd left her stuff to see if it was another dirty message from Shane telling her what he was going to do to her the next time he saw her. She smiled sheepishly at Gabe and then tried to focus on her stance so that she was mimicking his. She watched as he awkwardly tried to explain her position versus that of her imaginary attacker.

"Hold on," he said and then looked around the gym. "Hey Jim, can you come here a second?" he motioned to a guy lifting free weights against the back wall. "I'll show you what I mean on Jim."

"Gabe, it's okay. You can show me on me." Gabe studied her for a moment and then shook his head at Jim as he neared the mat.

"Are you sure?" he asked. She nodded and he said, "Thanks anyway, Jim. We're good," but his eyes never left hers. He was trying to make sure she was really okay with him putting his hands on her. And for the first time, she really was. They'd only had a few sessions, but her trust in him had grown with each one. She'd also found herself less nervous in a crowd and had even managed friendly "hellos" and polite conversations with a few of the male teachers at work. The shift had been so subtle that she hadn't really realized it until now.

Gabe reached around her tentatively at first to position himself as if he were attacking her, then relaxed when she didn't have a meltdown. A shimmer of self-pride went through her and her first thought was that she couldn't wait to tell Shane about it. She forced herself to focus on Gabe's instructions, and then went about learning how to bring a man nearly twice her size to his knees. Another check in the victory column, she thought to herself and then proceeded to ask Gabe if she could knock him down again.

"You knocked Gabe on his ass and I missed it?" Shane said in utter disbelief as he watched Savannah cutting up vegetables on the butcher block island in his kitchen. Apparently his menu of sandwiches and take-out food no longer impressed her, so she'd brought sustenance with her in two overstuffed, cloth grocery bags. He had cringed when he saw her pull vegetable after vegetable out of the bag but then felt relief – and a little bit of drool – when she dropped two huge rib eye steaks on the counter.

"Twice – it was awesome."

"Two words Savannah. Video," he said holding up one finger to count off with. "YouTube," he said as he added a second finger to the first.

She laughed and tossed the vegetables into a skillet. "There was no way I was going to get my phone out with Gabe around – not after all those dirty texts you kept sending me."

"I wanted to send a picture too, but figured it might offend your innocent sensibilities," he said teasingly and ducked when she threw a piece of red pepper at him. It felt right having her in his kitchen, not because he expected her to cook for him – although he was okay with that since his "specialty" dish involved a box of mac-n-cheese, a couple of hot dogs and a microwave – but because he liked how at home she looked. It was like they were two kids playing house and it was wrong on so many levels because it just added another complicated layer to their already unhealthy relationship.

"Shane, can I ask you something?" she said as she stirred the vegetables in the skillet.

"Sure."

"Would you come to family dinner on Sunday? It's at Gabe and Riley's place."

"Savannah," he began but she cut him off.

"Logan won't be there – he has to work. And it's not like we'd go together or anything. I just think Gabe and Riley would really like to see you."

Shane stood and thrust his hands into his pants. He so wanted to make things right with his friends, but that would just fuck everything up even more. It seemed like the more he pulled away, the harder they fought to keep him. It didn't make any sense.

"Think about it," was all she said as she kept her eyes on the food in front of her.

On edge now, Shane paced around. He finally went and got himself a beer from the fridge.

"Can I ask you another question?" she asked, not looking up at all. He hated her timid tone. He didn't want her to feel like she had to walk on eggshells around him.

"Sure," he said quietly.

"Will you let me finish what I started in the hotel room the first time we were together?" He saw a blush creep into her cheeks. "Not because I need it that way anymore," she stammered. "I just really liked it..."

His body had knotted with lust the second she mentioned their first encounter. He knew exactly what she was asking – she had enjoyed being the one in control. A lot of men might find it difficult to give complete control over to a woman, but he had no such qualms. He put down his beer and walked up behind her. She still seemed embarrassed and wouldn't face him so he caged her in with his body and reached past her to turn off the flame on the burner. He pushed her hair aside and brushed his lips over the nape of her neck. "Where do you want me?" he asked before sucking on her sensitive skin and then soothing it with his tongue. He hoped there would be a mark there tomorrow, reminding her of him.

"Upstairs."

IT WAS RIDICULOUS TO BE NERVOUS AFTER ALL THEY'D DONE TO EACH other, but Savannah couldn't help but feel a knot of anxiety building in her stomach as Shane led her up to the bedroom. She'd been fantasizing for a while now about being the one that controlled their pleasure, but she hadn't known if he'd be open to it. He'd seemed to enjoy it that first day, but then everything had gone to hell because of her meltdown. She'd gotten to taste him again when she summoned him back to the hotel room, but she hadn't gotten the opportunity to feel him inside of her as she rode him. As he drew her closer to the bed, she braced herself against him and he instantly stopped.

"What's wrong?" he asked, concerned.

"I don't want you to think it's like it was the first time – I don't want you to think I'm using you," she said cautiously, her voice heavy with worry.

He leaned down and kissed her hard, then again for good measure. He held her face in his hands as he said, "I've dreamed of this – of you riding me. Slow or fast for as long as you want." He stroked her cheeks with his thumbs and then he dropped his hands and went to his closet. He was gone for only a few seconds and when he returned he had two neckties in his hand. He flicked the lamp next to the bed on and then tugged her forward. "You'll need to use these because there's no way I'm going to be able to keep my hands off of you otherwise." He dropped the ties onto the bed and began stripping off his shirt.

She sucked in her breath when he mentioned using the ties as restraints. He'd been adamant about not being bound that first day, so the trust he showed her now was humbling. It was also unnerving because he would truly be at her mercy.

When the shirt was gone, he dropped his hands to his pants, but she stopped him from undoing them by putting her hand over his. "Leave them. Get on the bed."

There was no hesitation as he stretched himself out on the bed. She slipped her shoes off and then climbed onto the bed next to him, grateful she'd had the foresight to wear a dress to work this morning and had changed back into it after her training with Gabe. She grabbed the neckties and then straddled Shane, pulling the skirt of her dress high. The fabric of his pants was rough against her thighs and she could feel his hardness already pressing firmly against her ass. She rubbed back and forth over him a couple times and was pleased to see his breathing grow heavy.

Savannah tugged the dress off over her head. This time she had worn a bra and she had to stifle a laugh when she saw Shane's disappointment that she wasn't bare. But when she leaned over him, her breasts nearly even with his mouth, she felt him brush his lips over the tip of one, the fabric doing little to quell the sensation that shot through her at the contact.

"Hands," she ordered as she ignored the throbbing nipple that wanted more of his attention. He stretched his hands towards each side of the bed and she quickly tied each wrist to the bed posts. She drew back to admire him splayed out before her. His eyes glittered only with lust, not fear or trepidation at being tied down. She rewarded him with a long deep kiss, her tongue greeting his. When she pulled back, he tried to follow.

"I love how you feel beneath me," she murmured as she shifted her hips against him once more. "So powerful and strong." She skimmed her nails down his chest and then began a slow exploration of every muscle with her tongue. "I love how you taste," she whispered before dipping her mouth lower to his abdomen and she felt him shudder when she searched out his navel and laved it with her tongue. She slid further down his body and cupped his length through his pants. Her movements were purposefully slow as she worked the button free and pulled down the zipper. He groaned when her fingers brushed his cock as she pulled his pants and underwear down his hips. It took a bit of maneuvering but she finally got the clothes off of him.

His cock was huge, its engorged tip almost purple in color. It jetted out from a nest of blonde curls and lay flat against his belly. She bent down to lick her way up the length of it and then swirled her tongue briefly around the head. He was groaning now, his body drawn tight and she looked up to check the bindings – his muscles were rippling from the tension he was putting on the fabric. Satisfied that he wasn't getting free anytime soon, she returned her attention back to his eager cock. Pulling it away from his body, she gave him no warning as she sucked him deep inside of her mouth. He shouted and thrust up into her but she was prepared and held his pelvis down with her free hand. It took several attempts, but she was finally able to work him deeper down her throat and concentrated on relaxing her jaw and throat so she wouldn't gag. The smooth skin intrigued her because it was so different from the hardness rippling just underneath.

She gave him a few more hard pulls and then released him. He was panting hard now, his face red and sweat beading on his brow. His eyes were almost black with lust and she was glad he'd turned the light on so she could see everything he was feeling. She pulled herself up to kiss him again so he could taste his own, unique musky flavor. He fervently glided his tongue over hers. Sitting back up, she worked the clasp on her bra free and then pulled the rubber band holding her hair back free so that her hair fell loose around her the way he liked. When she caressed her breasts with her own hands, she heard him curse and saw him yank hard at the bindings.

"You want a taste?" she asked as she pinched her nipples.

When he nodded, she leaned down enough so that he could reach her left breast. He sucked as much as he could in his mouth and then licked the turgid tip. She closed her eyes at the sparks that coursed straight down to her clit and she began rubbing against him. She offered him the other breast and he gave it the same ardent attention as the first. When she pulled back, he released her with a pop and then dropped his head back on the bed, his eyes closed, his frustration becoming more obvious. Climbing off of him, she worked her now soaked panties off and threw them to the floor.

"Shane," she whispered and he opened his eyes. "Can you make sure I'm ready?" she asked. He glanced at her thighs and saw the moisture glistening there.

"Yes, but you'll have to untie one of my hands," he said softly. She looked up at his hands and then crawled up the length of his body. But instead of releasing him, she shifted her body so that her core was directly over his mouth. A startled sound left him at her brazenness, but his tongue instantly searched out her clit and began loving it. Electricity jolted through her and she braced her hands on the headboard so she didn't put all her weight on him. His expert tongue had her moaning in exquisite agony within seconds and she began rubbing against his face shamelessly. She felt his teeth close over her bud and then he sucked hard. She came apart instantly and screamed his name as pulses shot out from deep inside her womb and spread throughout her entire body. The pleasure continued for several long moments as the tension in her body eased and she barely managed to pull off of him before her muscles went lax.

As she tried to recover from the soul stopping orgasm, she saw her moisture still coating his lips. When his tongue flicked out to lick it off, she felt another wave of desire surge through her. She worked her way down his body and then went searching for the condoms she knew she would find in his nightstand drawer. His body was still tight with unspent passion and she was careful as she rolled the condom over his leaking cock. Her own lust was back in full force and she had no more desire to tease him. She positioned him at her opening and then sank down as far as she could. She loved how her body burned as it stretched to accommodate him. Even with her slickness to ease his entry, it was still tight and she had to lift herself up and down his length several times before his dick slipped past the last bit of muscle trying to bar his entry. She gasped as he slid all the way inside and then went still so she could just enjoy being connected to him in this way again.

It took everything in Shane not to thrust up into her. After she had worked him all the way inside of her, a look of contentment had taken over her features and had he not been so tightly strung with his need to find his own release, he would have taken his time to commit the image to his mind.

"Savannah," he finally growled. She opened her eyes and then seemed to realize he was in need of relief because she began to move. Slowly at first, experimenting to find the pace that would work for her. He itched to touch her breasts, to suck them into his mouth as she rode him while his hands knotted in her hair, forcing her head back so that he could control her movements. But she was in charge and as much as he was loving every second of it, it was also torture. He'd been shocked when she had ridden his face and the feeling of her orgasm coating his mouth had been like nothing he'd ever known. He knew he would have bruises on his wrists from all the pressure he was putting on his arms. Maybe if he had invested in cheaper ties, he'd be free by now.

A moan slid out of him as she began to ride him more quickly. He felt her sleek hair brush his thighs every time she dropped down harder on him. When she angled her body back and supported her hands behind her on his legs so that the head of his cock kept hitting the same spot deep inside her, he gave up the battle and began meeting her thrusts. Either she didn't notice or didn't care at his level of participation because she was working his cock in and out of her in a frenzy now. He could feel her inner muscles tightening on him.

One of her hands reached around her body to start stroking her clit and he actually bit his tongue at the sight. He wrapped his hands around the bindings since he had nothing else to hold on to and pounded into her as hard as he could. He felt her orgasm rip through her and then she was crying out in relief. The second he felt her body clamp down on his, he gave it up and shot into the condom. She kept riding him well after his release as little aftershocks quaked through her body and then she relaxed and just hung there, head back, eyes closed, her hand still covering her mound. At some point she pulled free of him and removed the condom from his sated body but he was too worn out to care. And when she released his wrists, he didn't even have the energy to move so he just kissed the top of her head when she snuggled up against him and then went to sleep.

CHAPTER 13

SAVANNAH GLANCED AT HER WATCH AS SHE FINISHED THE FINAL progress report form. It was nearing three o' clock on Sunday afternoon so she still had time to get home and get cleaned up before heading to Gabe and Riley's for dinner. She'd come into work nearly three hours ago to finish up the paperwork that she had left behind when she'd left early on Friday so she could grab some groceries and head to Shane's to cook him dinner. The school was eerily quiet and had been since the custodian popped in to say goodbye an hour earlier. Truth be told, she would have been done much sooner if her thoughts didn't keep drifting back to where they always did.

Shane had assured her that he had liked everything she'd done to him, even when she'd seen the red marks on his wrists the next morning. She'd nearly started crying at the thought that she had caused the damage but when he started telling her in explicit detail what he'd been thinking as she had owned him, her dismay had quickly turned to desire and they didn't even make it to the bedroom – she was glad his dining room table proved to be so sturdy but she knew that eating on it would never be the same again.

She laughed out loud and then signed the document in front of her before adding a personal note about how much she enjoyed having the student in her class. The evaluations weren't really meant to be very formal considering how young the children in her class were, but she liked using the opportunity to share with the parents how well their son or daughter was doing and always tried to add some extra information on personality, creativity or anything else that would let the parents know that she didn't just view their child as another faceless body that she was charged with watching for a handful of hours each day.

As she began cleaning up her desk, she stilled when she heard what sounded like footsteps in the hallway. Silence was all that greeted her. She waited another second but heard nothing, so she finished organizing her things. Her meetings with parents were scheduled over the next couple of weeks and she was looking forward to them since this would be the first time she would be doing them herself versus when she just sat in on them while acting as a teacher's aide during her schooling.

Grabbing her purse and jacket, she closed her classroom door behind her and then headed to the stairwell that would take her down to the first level of the large building. As she reached the bottom step, she heard the distinctive snick of a door closing from somewhere above her. The school had four floors total so there were several flights directly above her. She froze and waited but didn't hear any steps or movement.

A chill went through her as visions of all the horror movies she watched with guilty pleasure flashed through her brain. Served her right for enjoying watching some young group of dumb college kids get tormented and ultimately picked off one by one by a crazed serial killer in some tiny, backwoods town. She hurried through the door and then began the long walk down the corridor that led to the side of the building where employees parked. She kept looking over her shoulder but saw nothing and heard no one. Fear niggled through her, but she forced it back and increased her pace. She had nothing to be worried about, she assured herself. The school was locked and the wealthy, upscale neighborhood of Queen Anne wasn't exactly teaming with criminals. She exited the school and saw that her car was the only one in the parking lot.

As she reached the car, she noticed it was tilted at a strange angle and then realized why. She went around to the passenger side and sure enough, the front tire was flat. She bit back a curse and then reached for her phone. She knew Logan was at work and it would be hard for him to get away. She wasn't sure what Shane was up to – he'd been non-committal about whether or not he would join them for family dinner and had mentioned something about needing to study. If he was even at home, it would take him a good thirty minutes to get to the school. A tow truck was another option, she supposed. She started searching for the nearest garage on her phone, but then stopped when she realized the solution was right in front of her. She had a spare, she had the jack and other tools needed to change the tire, all she needed were the steps to do it and a little elbow grease. It wasn't like she had some big, monster SUV where the tire weighed almost as much as she did.

Feeling empowered, she searched for instructions to change a tire on her phone, then dug out everything she would need from the trunk. Every once in a while as she worked, she'd get this feeling of being watched but when she looked around there was absolutely no one – not even another car. The school was set back from the main road in a way that she couldn't even see the traffic from her position, so it seemed unlikely that someone could be watching her. It still creeped her out though and she tried to work just a little bit faster. But the feeling never quite went away and her constant checking of her surroundings ended up slowing her pace dramatically.

"WHAT HAPPENED TO YOU?" RILEY ASKED AS SHE PULLED OPEN THE door and saw all the black grease that clung to much of Savannah's clothing. She never would have guessed that changing a tire would be such a messy process although she'd been supremely proud of herself when she'd gotten the task done. She now knew why mechanics always seemed to be covered in a perpetual layer of grime. She'd thought her hands had taken the worst of it and had figured a wet wipe would solve the problem, but then she had looked down at her shirt and pants. As she had lifted and handled the two tires, each had left muck on her favorite shirt and the knees of her pants were covered with dirt and debris from kneeling in the parking lot.

"I had a flat," she muttered as she carefully kept her hands from touching any part of the pristine white door of Riley and Gabe's apartment. "It took a lot longer to fix than I thought it would, so I didn't have time to go home and change. I was hoping I could borrow a shirt?" she said.

"Of course," Riley laughed and Savannah frowned at her obvious enjoyment of her predicament.

"Why didn't you call someone?" Riley asked as she led her into the bedroom. Gabe and Riley's dog, a Pit Bull named Bella, jumped off the couch and weaved dangerously in between the two women as they walked.

"Hi sweetie," Savannah said to the dog. She turned her attention back to Riley. "I figured it would be faster just to do it myself."

"And was it?" the other woman asked with a snicker.

"Shut it Riley or say goodbye to your nice clean walls," Savannah threatened as she reached out as if to rub her still grimy hands on the pretty yellow paint that the couple had used on the living room wall.

"Okay, okay," Riley said in mock surrender, her arms raised.

"What the hell happened to you?" Gabe said as he walked out of the bedroom and towards them.

"Don't ask," Riley warned him. She stopped to give him a quick kiss as he passed, but a brief touch of the lips turned into something more and Savannah had to finally cough to remind them she was there and then reached out threateningly towards the wall again.

"Sorry, sorry," Riley said as she pulled free of Gabe and grabbed Savannah by her elbow, one of the few clean areas on her body. Gabe watched them curiously, then headed towards the kitchen, Bella now trailing him. Riley led her into the bathroom which was huge. It had a wide vanity with dual sinks. There was a nice walk in shower, but also a jetted tub that actually sat up against a window. She could only assume that the frosted part of the glass offered enough privacy so that the occupant or occupants could still enjoy the view without putting on a display for anyone strolling in the wooded area below.

"Dinner's not for another twenty minutes – why don't you take a shower? I can lend you some clothes."

"Yes please," Savannah said gratefully. Riley pulled out some towels for her and then left her alone. She showered quickly and found the clothes Riley had left for her on the countertop. Riley was curvier than her, so she didn't quite fill them out in the same places that Riley would have, but they were clean and that made her supremely grateful. No amount of scrubbing had removed all the oil from her hands, but at least she could touch things now. She'd have to remember to ask Riley for some wipes so she could clean her steering wheel.

As she exited the bedroom, Bella came to greet her and this time she dropped down to her knees and gave the happy dog the attention the sweet animal deserved. She could feel the scars that still littered the animal's body. Gabe and Riley had suspected she'd been used as a bait dog for dog fighting and had been cruelly dumped next to a garbage can in an alley, blood oozing from dozens of bite wounds. Luckily, Gabe had found her and Riley's background as a veterinary technician had gotten the dog back on track for a full recovery. Bella had repaid them a dozen times over after attacking Riley's ex when he had tried to abduct her and threatened her with a gun.

Hearing a soft lilt of laughter, Savannah glanced up to see Gabe standing behind Riley as she was trying to stir something in a pot on the stove. The big man's arms were wrapped around her and his mouth was by her ear, whispering naughty things, no doubt, from the way Riley was blushing. When Riley turned in his arms and started kissing him, Savannah felt envious. The twosome just couldn't seem to get enough of each other, and not just physically. Even when they weren't in close proximity to one another, they were still connected. She'd heard Gabe talking to Riley on his cell phone on several occasions during breaks in their training sessions and the deference in his voice always moved her. And when he closed the call each time by telling Riley he loved her, she found herself wanting that same bond with Shane.

Riley finally noticed her and reluctantly pulled back from Gabe. "Better?" she asked Savannah as Gabe allowed her to turn back to the stove. His hands lingered on her waist for another moment before releasing her and grabbing some plates from the cabinet.

"Much," she said. "Thanks."

There was a knock on the door and Savannah's insides locked up. It was wrong to hope it was him – it could be a neighbor stopping by to borrow something or to drop off some mail delivered to the wrong box. But in her heart she knew who was on the other side of that door and she hurried to open it.

"I'll get it," she said quickly and then she was drinking her fill at the sight of him. He seemed surprised to see her opening the door and his nervous stance seemed to relax for a moment as his eyes drifted up and down the length of her body. She wanted to throw herself in his arms and give him a proper welcome, but that wasn't allowed. Even if Gabe and Riley both knew something was up between them, their relationship wasn't something that could be shared. It hurt, but she knew that was the way he wanted it.

"Hi," she said as she opened the door.

"Hi," he returned. He was wearing black slacks and a blue dress shirt and a light whiff of cologne brushed over her senses as he moved past her. She felt his right hand briefly caress her hip in greeting as he entered the apartment, a move she felt in her bones, but knew Gabe and Riley wouldn't have been able to see. The fact that he had even done it made that little spark of hope inside her flare up.

As he moved further into the apartment, she saw his body tighten as he met Gabe's cool stare from where he stood by the dining room table. Riley was silent and stiff as she stood in the kitchen, her cooking temporarily forgotten. They'd both known he might be coming, but it was clear that none of them knew who should make the first move. She was glad when Shane finally moved forward and then reached out his hand to Gabe. Gabe didn't even hesitate to take it. He pulled Shane in for a brief, but hard hug and then patted him lightly on the back.

Savannah closed the door and watched as Shane went to the kitchen and stood in front of Riley who had turned around, her back now to the stove. The air was tense between them and she knew they were both remembering the cruel way he had treated her at the diner. Savannah felt a sigh of relief when Shane reached out and pulled Riley into his arms for a hug. He whispered something into the woman's ear. Riley let out a soft, choking sound and then nodded and closed her arms around the taller man. Gabe, who had been watching the pair carefully, clearly ready to intervene on his girlfriend's behalf if needed, relaxed and then went to work setting the table. Maybe, just maybe this would work out, Savannah thought as she went to help Gabe.

❧

DINNER WAS AWKWARD AND QUIET AT FIRST AS EVERYONE TRIED TO get their bearings. The dining room table actually seated six people and it would have made sense for Riley and Gabe to each sit at the ends. But it seemed like the couple couldn't even bear to be that far apart, so Gabe and Riley had sat on one side, putting her and Shane on the other.

It physically hurt to sit next to Shane and act as if they were nothing more than acquaintances linked through her brother, especially after she remembered the way he'd taken her early this morning. He'd been slow and worshipping, bringing her release twice before he sought his own. His mouth had languished everywhere and he'd whispered things in her ear about how beautiful she was and how much he needed her. She had tried to remind herself that his words were part of being a good and experienced lover, but her heart only wanted to believe he'd ever said those kinds of things to her. And now, to sit next to him, to be so physically close but not be able to acknowledge what he meant to her made her ache.

"So, I heard Savannah knocked you on your ass last week Gabe," Shane said out of nowhere and everyone froze as if he had yelled the words. Not only was he trying to ease the tension in the stilted room, he'd referenced that Savannah and him had had a conversation, a clear sign that they were more than they were pretending to be. She held her breath as Gabe lifted his eyes to meet Shane's smirk. She saw Riley hide a smile and then Gabe chuckled.

"She's got some skills," Gabe acknowledged and then winked at her. After that, it was like time had been turned back because the two men were joking and sniping at each other in the way that only best friends who've been doing it for years know how to do. And when she felt Shane's hand drop down under the table and stroke her thigh through the thin leggings that Riley had lent her, that damn spark of hope turned into a raging wildfire.

◈

"Is this oil?" Shane asked as he studied her fingers. After dinner, she had followed him back to his place and they'd made love on the couch. She was lying on top of him, a thin throw barely covering their still heaving bodies.

"I had a flat tire today. I changed it by myself," she offered, strangely proud of her little victory and needing to share that with him.

"Why didn't you call me?" he asked.

She shrugged. "I figured, how hard could it be? People change tires every day. Even though it probably would have been faster and cleaner to call someone, I like knowing I didn't need someone coming to my rescue."

"You know that I've never thought of you that way, right?"

"What, as someone who could change a tire?" she asked, jokingly.

He laughed but then clarified, "As someone who needed rescuing." He intertwined their fingers. "You're one of the strongest people I know Savannah." She felt tears sting her eyes and then leaned down to kiss him. "Would you go to dinner with me tomorrow night?" he asked.

She nodded and then his tongue was inside her mouth and she knew they were both done talking for a while.

◈

From his peripheral view, Shane watched as Savannah fidgeted in the passenger seat of his car. He was glad to see she wasn't snapping the band on her wrist, but he could tell she was starting to suspect their destination as he turned the final corner. She'd shown up at his place for the scheduled date looking relaxed and even flirting with him about skipping dinner and starting on dessert as she rubbed her body against his. Had their evening not been so important, he would have taken her up on her offer in a heartbeat.

His relationship with Savannah was moving at lightning speed and every day he spent with her, he found it harder and harder to consider letting her go. She'd even managed to pull him back into Gabe and Riley's lives and his friends had been more forgiving than he deserved. Shame still ate at him when he thought of how Logan remained in the dark and he was nearing the point where he was going to come clean with his friend whether Savannah was ready or not. No, he wouldn't divulge her secrets, but he also couldn't keep hiding the truth about his and Savannah's relationship either.

He heard her distressed cry when he pulled to a stop in front of the restaurant.

"No," she muttered in disbelief. "Why?" she asked as she turned to face him in the seat, her eyes unable to hide the betrayal she was feeling.

He grabbed her hand and said, "You can do this." She looked back at the restaurant and then the valet was there opening her door. Shane held her hand until she released him and got out of the car. The second she did, he was out and tossing the keys to the valet and then taking her hand in his. Her eyes were on the door, the word "Barretti's" etched into the glass. She had every reason to not want to go into the restaurant where she'd had her meltdown just a few weeks ago, but he knew she needed to face what had happened. He gave her a tug to get her moving and when he felt her squeeze his hand and her eyes sharpened with resolve, he sighed in relief.

The restaurant was packed for a Monday night. The hostess seated them right away at a table near the back. At the opposite corner from where they sat was the dance floor, a few couples swaying to the music. Her fingers trembled as she reached for the menu, but she still hadn't gone for the band. She'd had another session with her therapist just that day and had told him before they left his place how well it had gone. He suspected that having to expose herself like that to a virtual stranger left her raw, but he guessed that she also felt empowered afterwards because a little bit more of the pain that had festered inside of her for so long was being allowed to seep out.

The waiter appeared and took their drink orders. Savannah

nervously took a sip of water, then started clenching her hands together in front of her.

"I was wondering if you would come with me somewhere on Saturday morning."

That got her attention. "Of course. Where?" she asked.

"I want to introduce you to my brother."

If she was phased by the way he had mentioned meeting his brother as if he were still alive, she didn't show it. She smiled gently and said, "I'd like that."

The waiter brought their drinks and they placed their orders. When they were alone again, Shane asked, "You want to dance?"

She tensed, but then smiled and said, "Shane, we don't have to do that. I think we both know that I won't freak out if you put your hands on me." He loved her sexy, suggestive smile and couldn't help but marvel at how she was so much more comfortable with her sexual side than he ever would have guessed.

"I wasn't thinking it would be us dancing," he said calmly. At her confusion, he motioned over his shoulder and said, "I was thinking you could dance with him."

Her eyes widened as she saw Dominic Barretti heading their way. He stopped at their table and reached out to shake Shane's hand, then his dark eyes gentled as he extended his hand to Savannah.

"Miss Bradshaw, it's good to see you again." It took her several long seconds to finally take his hand. "Will you join me for a dance?" he asked. She looked back at Shane uncertainly and then firmed her shoulders and dipped her head in a brief nod. Both men watched her carefully as she stood and when she forced a tremulous smile to her lips, Shane never felt prouder of her. She was clearly terrified, but she was facing her fear head on. He just hoped that he hadn't overplayed his hand by testing her newfound strength before she was ready.

SAVANNAH FOUGHT BACK THE NAUSEA THAT THREATENED TO overtake her as Dom led her to the dance floor. The man was huge like Gabe, but unlike her friend, she didn't know this man. She'd been too far gone in her meltdown the last time she was here to even recognize him as the man who had not only emptied the restaurant of all the patrons so she wouldn't have to face them when she left, but had also broken a door down so that he could take the knife away from her before she could cause any significant harm to herself. She did remember his pretty, sweet wife who had comforted her on that cold bathroom floor, her gentle touch and soft voice urging her to come back to reality.

Truth be told, she was a little angry at Shane for clearly orchestrating the entire evening, including the unwanted contact with this man, but the bottom line was that she never would have been able to attempt something like this on her own. Shane clearly trusted this man or he never would have put her in this position.

Her hand felt cold and clammy in Dom's huge grip, but he was gentle and if she wanted to pull free, she could. When they reached the dance floor, he kept her on the outskirts of the small group of dancers. She closed her eyes as she waited for him to grab her around the waist and she immediately reached for the band on her wrist.

"Sweetheart," he said gently, his voice incredibly quiet for such a large, imposing person. "Nothing happens here tonight unless you say it does." He was giving her an out and she badly wanted to take it. She looked over her shoulder at Shane to find him watching her intently. She saw his concern and then he was getting up, clearly about to come rescue her. She shook her head at him and he stopped, but didn't sit back down. Sucking in a deep breath, she turned back to Dom and stepped closer to him so she could put her hand on his wide shoulder. As his arm slipped lightly around her waist, he held out his other hand and she took it. As he began to move them to the music, he left a wide gap between their bodies.

Her shoulders started to ache from the stiff way she was holding herself so she took another deep breath and forced her muscles to relax. Dom kept them on the outer edge of the dance floor and never once tried to pull her closer.

"Try not to be too pissed at him."

"What?" she asked in confusion, startled by the intrusion of his voice.

Dom motioned over her shoulder with his head to where Shane had returned to his seat. "I can tell he wants nothing more than to come over here and beat the shit out of me for touching you, even though he's the one that set this up."

Dom turned them so she could connect with Shane visually. He did look pretty angry and part of her was glad that he didn't find handing her off to someone else so easy. The other part of her was grateful for the strides he had taken to try and help her gain some of her confidence back.

"Why are you doing this?" she asked as she watched Shane get up and go over to the bar where Dom's wife sat. He spoke with her briefly and then the woman was taking his hand and following him to the dance floor. A little bit of jealousy surged through her but when she saw how indifferent Shane's hold was, how it was as impersonal as the one Dom had on her, she felt marginally better.

"My wife has taken a fondness to you. I give my wife whatever she wants," he said simply but something in his voice dragged Savannah's eyes to his. There was pain there – a lot of it. She'd also felt the briefest tightening of his grip at her waist, not enough to frighten her, just enough to show that the man wasn't as unaffected by emotion as he appeared to be. Whatever he felt for his wife ran deep, but there was some turmoil there too.

"Thank you for doing this Mr. Barretti. And for what you did that night," she said.

"It's Dom and you're welcome sweetheart. Now let's go get you back to your man." He led her to where Shane and Sylvie were dancing and the exchange was quick and effortless. She instantly pressed up against Shane. It felt like coming home. They didn't speak, he just held her against him as they swayed slowly back and forth. Her body had the same sated feeling she got after a night of lovemaking with this man and she couldn't help but wonder at what that meant.

When the music ended, he led her back to their table and they talked about mundane things. It was comfortable and natural. As they finished off with dessert, she excused herself to go to the restroom.

SHANE WATCHED SAVANNAH DISAPPEAR INTO THE BATHROOM. HE made his way over to the bar where Dom and his wife sat. He noticed that when Sylvie saw him approach, she gave her husband a quick kiss and headed toward the bathroom, smiling at him as she passed him. He wondered if she sensed he needed a private moment with her husband. Even better would be if she could distract Savannah to buy him some more time.

"Drink?" Dom asked him as he motioned to the now empty stool next to him. The man was cool as a cucumber and seemed unsurprised at Shane's intrusion. Dom had willingly agreed to his plan without question when Shane had called earlier that day to see if he could bring Savannah in so she could work through everything that had happened last time. Shane considered himself to be a pretty good judge of character and had known from Dom's protective nature that night when Savannah freaked out that Dom would be the perfect one to dance with her. He was a big, physically imposing man who could easily take what he wanted, but also had a soft spot for women, as evidenced not only by the way he revered his wife, but by the way he had emptied out his own restaurant to save Savannah the embarrassment of having to face all those people when she'd fallen apart in the very public setting. He'd even gone so far as to break down a door in his own establishment to stop Savannah from hurting herself.

"No, I just have a minute," Shane said as he sat.

"You have a couple...Sylvie's good at small talk," the man said casually, knowingly.

Shane smiled briefly. "You're a very lucky man, Mr. Barretti."

Something dark passed through Dom's expression, but it was gone quickly. "Dom," was all he said.

"You're not just a restaurant owner, are you Dom?" Shane asked as he toyed with a cocktail napkin.

Dom slid his cool eyes towards Shane and then took a slow sip of his drink but didn't say anything. Shane ignored the intimidation tactic. "You own Barretti Security Group."

"Co-own, actually," Dom finally acknowledged.

"With your brother," Shane said.

"Brothers," Dom said, emphasizing the plural. Another flash of darkness. "What can I do for you Shane?"

Shane hadn't really given him permission to use his first name, but he supposed they were well past formality at this point. "I need you to do some digging for me."

"I don't know if you can afford me," Dom interjected. "Law students usually don't have a lot of pennies to spare, do they?" he quipped. "But then again, you're not like most law students either, are you?"

Shane straightened on the stool. The message was loud and clear – it appeared that Dom had already done some digging on his own.

Dom shrugged. "My wife is quite fond of your girl. She was worried about her after that night and I had your phone number..."

"So you decided to take a look behind the curtains, so to speak," Shane offered.

"I don't like for Sylvie to worry," was all Dom said.

"Right," Shane chuckled. "I think I'll take that drink now."

One wave of Dom's hand and the bartender appeared and poured a drink for Shane. He took a long sip and enjoyed the alcohol as it burned his throat and then settled in his stomach, warming it. Shane recognized the liquor as one of the more expensive brands.

"What is that you need dug up, my young friend?" Dom asked as he waited for the bartender to refill his drink.

"You've probably figured out that something happened to Savannah."

Dom nodded, anger clear in his features.

"She won't give me the details, but I've managed to figure out a few things from the little that she has told me." He had all of Dom's attention now, but the man remained mute. "I think it happened sometime after her parents died, but before she left for school. My guess is she knows the attacker."

He heard Dom draw in a breath. "But she won't give you a name."

Shane shook his head. "She's worried about telling her brother, but I think it's more than just knowing the guilt he'll feel for not having been able to protect her."

Dom's hand closed tightly around his glass and his body stiffened as if he were ready to strike. "You think the attacker was a friend of her brother's."

"She mentioned once that she shouldn't have opened the door that night." Shane chugged the rest of his drink as he felt his own anger mounting. "She wouldn't have opened the door to a stranger." He paused, then said, "It also could have been someone from her high school or something, but the way she's worked so hard to keep it from Logan makes me believe it's someone from his life – a college buddy maybe. Some of the guys would meet at his house for poker night throughout college. Savannah met them all at one point or another."

Dom mulled the words over as he nursed his drink and then nodded. "I'll have to dig into the brother's background – all of it. You realize that, right?"

Shane hesitated for only a moment before saying, "Do it." He knew Logan would understand and forgive the intrusion if it meant finding the monster that had taken Savannah's childhood. "Logan Bradshaw."

Dom nodded. Before either could say another word, the ladies were walking towards them, Sylvie saying something that made Savannah laugh. Shane vacated the bar stool he was sitting on.

"Honey, I was telling Savannah that she and Shane should join us one of these weekends up at the house. We could go out on the boat, maybe do some whale watching or island hopping," she said hopefully.

The difference in Dom's appearance was instant and dramatic. He smiled genuinely and his big hand instantly closed around his wife's tiny one as he drew her close. The woman automatically fit herself against his side as if she'd been born to be there and Dom's whole countenance relaxed once she was there. A pang of envy shot through Shane as he realized he wanted that same thing – he wanted Savannah to become an extension of him – like two halves that didn't truly work until they were together. Savannah seemed to notice Dom and Sylvie's connection too, because she looked up at him with those liquid blue eyes. But she made no move to sidle up against him because she knew, rightly so, that he was still keeping that last piece of himself apart from her.

"I would love that," Savannah said and Shane didn't miss that she'd said "I" and not "We."

"Are you ready to go?" Shane asked, suddenly needing to get as far away from this place as he could.

She nodded and he took her elbow. "Good night and thank you," he said to both Dom and his wife. As he led her away, he saw Savannah smile and silently mouth the words "thank you."

As they made their way to the front of the restaurant, Shane found his hand moving from her elbow down to her hand and then he was intertwining their fingers. He cursed himself for the intimate gesture, but his heart refused to allow his brain to release her. For every moment he spent with her, he kept pulling her closer instead of pushing her away. How was he ever supposed to give her up when he couldn't even tell his fucking hand to let hers go?

It made him a selfish bastard, but still his hand hung onto hers like a lifeline. And as they waited for the valet to get his car, he was drawing her closer to his body so she could benefit from his heat in the cool, damp Seattle air. People walked past them, cars honked in the busy intersection, but all he felt was her pressed against him. All he heard was her soft breathing. All he smelled was the floral scent of her shampoo along with that fragrance that was unique to her.

The ride home was silent and the only way he could keep his hand from grabbing hers again the way it demanded, was to hold on to the gearshift until his knuckles turned white. He pulled into his assigned spot and put the car in park. His nerves were frayed with a combination of lust and need, but just beyond that was a longing for something he knew he couldn't have and that was worse than anything. She'd made him feel more in the last month than he had in years. She'd seen things in him that he had tried so hard to bury, but instead of criticizing him or judging him for those weaknesses, she'd offered her strength and understanding.

He felt like his whole identity was crashing around him and panic needled at him. When he heard her unclick her seatbelt and reach for the door handle, he snaked out his hand and grabbed hers. She stilled but didn't say anything, as if somehow sensing the turmoil that was wreaking havoc on his soul. How had something as simple as a night out of dinner and dancing had this profound effect on him? And then he realized it hadn't. It hadn't been just tonight that had started this. It had started as a slow burn inside of him the moment she'd first touched him with those lips. He'd been blindfolded then, but something inside of him had known the woman leaning over him, her soft, sweet lips exploring his, was different. She hadn't even seen all the ugliness inside of him yet and she stayed. Even now as she sat next to him, she waited patiently for his next move.

"Why didn't you just walk away when you had the chance?" he muttered as he dragged her across the armrest in between them. His lips were on hers before she could even finish awkwardly straddling him. With the steering wheel behind her, it was a tight fit but she didn't seem to care because she was kissing him back. His mouth was demanding and hard, almost punishing. It was unfair to take his frustrations out on her for the confusing thoughts that were coursing through him, but he couldn't stop himself. She moaned as his tongue sought out hers and he felt her hands tighten in his hair. Her dress had ridden up so he could feel the softness of her thigh under his hand and he immediately began to seek out her warmth. The sound of a car door slamming was the only thing that kept him from slipping his fingers under the line of her panties.

He pulled back from her and ripped his mouth from hers. She cried out at the loss and tried to follow him. "Not here," he managed to get out, his voice sounding too guttural even for his own comfort. Getting out of the car was awkward as she scrambled off his lap and he nearly dragged her up the stairs two at a time. It was only sheer will that got them inside of the apartment and then he was stripping her as he hurried her towards the stairs.

Instead of trying to maneuver them up the spiral steps, he placed her hands on the thin metal bar that made up the top rail of the bannister and stepped behind her. Within seconds, his hard length was sheathed and pressing into her in one hard lunge. She cried out at his entry, but the slickness that welcomed him and her hips pushing back against him reassured him that his hurried methods were welcome. A few hard thrusts had her coming and he didn't even try to stop himself from following her over. His control was completely gone, replaced with the fiery hell of pleasure that he finally acknowledged he was never going to be able to let go.

CHAPTER 14

Savannah lay in Shane's bed and listened to him move around the kitchen. She'd felt him leave the bed a few minutes ago, but she'd been too exhausted and relaxed to even wake up enough to kiss him good morning. She was seriously hoping he was going to come back to bed, hopefully with coffee, because her muscles were too drained to do her body any good right now. He'd kept her up almost all night, his need suddenly insatiable. She'd lost count of the number of orgasms he'd given her and her body ached from his relentless lovemaking.

At some point, warning bells had gone off in her head that he was too desperate, too determined. It was like he couldn't stand to be away from her for too long and even after taking her, he'd stayed inside her for long periods of time as they each recovered. He'd pull out long enough to get a new condom and then he was working her body into a passion all over again. Hard and fast, slow and gentle. Shower, floor, wall – and he'd been there through it all. He hadn't just been fucking her to sate some physical need. No, she could see by the almost pained, hopeful look in his eyes that he was trying to vanquish some feeling inside.

She wanted to believe that maybe he was finally starting to feel a little bit of what she felt for him, but it was foolish to get her hopes up. He'd said some heart stopping things to her last night about how badly he needed her, the things he wanted to do to her body and some other dirty things that even now had her blushing, but had her body awakening with desire. But no words of love, no telling her they'd always be together. It was sex, she had to remind herself, phenomenal sex, but still just sex.

When she heard someone knocking at his front door, she glanced at the clock on his nightstand. It was early, just barely after six in the morning. She needed to get moving so she wouldn't be late for class. As it was, she barely had enough time to stop at home for a change of clothes. She couldn't help but stifle a laugh at the thought that she was glad their last time was in the shower so at least she wouldn't reek of sex when she got to work. She heard Shane open the door. Because of the open layout of the floor below, she could hear nearly every word being spoken as it drifted up into the loft.

"Mom. Dad. What are you doing here?"

Shit, shit, shit. Shane felt his mother's arms close around him as he stood there dumbly, spatula in hand. He'd been attempting an omelet and had been in mid-flip when someone had knocked on his door.

"Shane, honey, we've been so worried about you," his mom said as his father slapped him on the back in greeting. Linda Matthews reached out to pat her carefully coiffed, honey colored hair to make sure hugging her son hadn't messed it up. Fresh looking highlights suggested she'd been to the hair salon recently. She didn't look at all like her fifty-nine years and Shane knew she paid a lot of money to make sure that was the case. She was petite and slim, her five-foot frame encased in a purple pantsuit with absurdly high heeled gold, strappy shoes. Gold jewelry glittered on almost every visible body part and he couldn't help but wonder if the excessive jewelry physically slowed his mother down. Even with the early hour and the sun still hiding behind the horizon, she was in full makeup and had a fancy shawl draped around her shoulders.

"Paige called us," his father announced as he moved into the apartment and pulled off his heavy wool coat. Jonathan Matthews was wearing his typical go-to business suit and tie along with silver cuff links and the big gold watch he'd had before Shane had even been born. It was a Rolex that his father had received from his own father as a graduation gift when he followed in the family footsteps and graduated law school. Shane's grandfather had died before he was born so he'd never met the man, but his father always talked about how they'd planned to start their own firm one day. Shane supposed that was where his father's obsession with bringing his son into his practice had started. He'd just ended up with the wrong son since the first one refused to be forced into a life he didn't want.

Shane sucked in a breath when he suddenly understood what his brother had been trying to escape. Michael hadn't wanted any of it if it meant he had to someday give up the person he was meant to be with.

"She told us about the engagement," his mother said excitedly. "You should have told us you were finally going to make it official."

Shane couldn't really hear either of their voices anymore as realization slammed through him. He had literally taken his brother's place in every way, including falling in love with someone he wasn't supposed to want. He'd known it last night as he was making love to her and she returned his every touch and kiss, long after he'd sated her and himself. It had been like his body couldn't exist if it was disconnected from her for even a few minutes. He'd been rough at times, gentle at others. He'd made her laugh as he said naughty things to her and then had her screaming his name over and over as she begged him to give her release. Using everything in his arsenal, he'd tried to bind her further to him by owning her body, but all he'd done was give away more of his heart. He was in love with her.

Dizziness overcame him as his predicament kicked in and he leaned back against a small table near the front door. He wanted Savannah more than anything else in his life – more than his parents, more than the drugs. But how long would that last? At what point would he give in to that craving that was always burning the back of his tongue. That need for one more taste?

If he chose Savannah, he'd have to be willing to walk away from the only family he had left because they only wanted Shane, the soon to be lawyer and prodigal son, not Shane, the always on the edge, almost drug addict. He'd be rudderless, like Michael. He'd have Savannah, but she would be at risk everyday of losing him to the addiction that was always shimmering along the edge of his very being. She'd fight for him too, no matter what it cost her and then she'd have nothing. Even if it wasn't his intention, he would end up taking her love and using it against her to get what he wanted.

It was then that he realized how silent everything was. He looked up to see that his parents weren't watching him. Their eyes were on the young woman standing at the top of the stairs, her trembling body only covered by one of his dress shirts, her bright eyes shining with the tears of betrayal. His mind wandered back to his mother's last words and then he realized what Savannah had heard. Some complete and utter bullshit about an engagement that didn't exist.

"Savannah," he said but she turned and went back into his bedroom. His parents were standing like twin statues, their mouths comically open as they stared at the now empty space above them.

"Mom, Dad, can I meet you at your hotel in a little while?" he asked even as he was heading for the stairs, his mind racing. Could he even fix this? Should he?

"Who is that?" his mother asked dumbly. But he was already up the stairs by the time she finished her question and vaguely heard the front door snick closed at their departure. His eyes were on the woman who wasn't hastily dressing as he thought she'd be, but was sitting on the other side of the bed, the side she had seemingly claimed as hers after the first night she'd spent here with him. She was facing the wall, her back hunched, her black hair spread down her back and shoulders. Her arms were wrapped protectively around herself and she was rocking slowly back and forth. His gut clenched as he moved around to her side of the bed and he felt immediate relief when he didn't see any sharp objects in her grasp. The band was still on her wrist but she wasn't snapping it. He wasn't sure if that was a good or bad thing.

As he got closer, he could see silent tears running down her face. "I wasn't eavesdropping," she whispered. "The voices carry up here," she said.

Seeing her tears caused him physical pain and he knew this was exactly what their future would look like if he tried to make a life with her. She'd be hurting like this and he'd be off somewhere shooting up because the heroin meant more to him then she did.

He wanted to sit down next to her and wrap her in his arms, but he didn't. He leaned back against the wall so that he was facing her, but stayed closer to the foot of the bed. If he was within reach of her, he wouldn't be able to do what he needed to do.

"I know that."

"I couldn't keep my promise Shane," she said as more tears streamed steadily down. It was frightening how there was no sound to accompany them. He didn't want her to hold the pain inside because he knew what that would ultimately lead to.

"What promise?" he asked.

"You wanted me to keep my heart out of this so I would be able to walk away when it was over," she sniffed. "Our agreement. It was one of your conditions."

He nodded, his insides threatening to collapse in on themselves from the anguish he was feeling. "I remember."

"I knew I was in love with you that day but I agreed anyway."

He had already known she loved him because she wore her emotions on her sleeve, but it was both ecstasy and agony to actually hear the words. He wanted to say them back, to whisper them into her ear as he was buried inside of her, their bodies escaping from the harsh reality of the outside world.

"There's no engagement. Paige must have told my parents I had proposed to manipulate them into coming here. I told you the truth about not being with anyone else," he said quietly. No matter what, he couldn't let her leave here thinking he'd lied to her about that.

Savannah nodded and then used her sleeve to try and wipe some of the moisture from her face. She was a blotchy, beautiful mess and she was his. And he couldn't have her.

"I'll tell Logan everything about the attack tonight. He doesn't need to know about what happened between us." He hated how the word "us" barely made it out of her mouth and he hated it even more that she was using past tense to describe their relationship.

He knew he had to say the words to end this for good, but he couldn't make them leave his mouth. "Savannah," he began, not sure how to phrase his next statement. "I need to know that when you leave here, you won't hurt yourself."

She laughed harshly, the hurt in her tone ripping at his heart. "There's nothing to let out." She stripped the band off her wrist and dropped it to the floor. "I don't feel anything anymore."

He choked back his own sob at her words and stood to go to her but a shrill, piercing sound interrupted. He smelled burning and then remembered the omelet he'd been preparing. Had that only been a few minutes ago? Somehow between blending the ingredients and this moment – less than five actual minutes – he'd gone from discovering how in love with her he really was to how fucked up his entire life had become and finally to accepting that he couldn't have a future with her.

"Stay here please," he pleaded and then hurried downstairs. There were actual flames in the pan where the fluffy egg creation that he'd been increasingly proud of had once been. It took several minutes to find the fire extinguisher and put out the blaze and then silence the blaring alarm. By the time he got back to his room, she was gone.

Shane pulled away from Logan and Savannah's house and headed back towards the city. He'd left his apartment to go meet his parents, but ended up driving to her house to make sure Savannah had made it home okay. Her car hadn't been there, so he was hoping that meant she'd gone to work, but in her condition, that would have surprised him. As he neared downtown, he ignored the exit for the hotel he knew his parents would have been staying at – they were creatures of habit, after all – and headed towards the northwestern suburbs. The elementary school was busy with parents dropping off their children and long rows of buses depositing an endless line of kids on the curb. Shane drove around the employee parking lot, but her car was nowhere in sight. Frustrated, he sent her a text that said *I need to know you're safe*.

He began the trip back towards the city and then picked up the phone and called Gabe. When his friend answered he said, "Is she there?"

Gabe was silent for a long time before finally putting him out of his misery. "No, but she's at the gym. A friend of mine saw her come in a few minutes ago and called me to let me know. Apparently she's going at the bag pretty hard. I'm on my way there now."

He wasn't sure if Gabe heard his choked sound of relief and was too messed up to care. "Can you just keep an eye on her for me today?" he asked.

Another long silence. Then with a sigh, Gabe said, "Yeah." Shane hung up and pointed his car towards the city.

She just couldn't get the rhythm right. Her anger built as she jabbed at the small speed bag. It kept swinging wildly and nothing she did made it move in that clean, fluid motion that was somehow soothing and empowering at the same time. She threw another punch at it and missed. A few more hits connected and she could feel the burning in her shoulders start. It eased some of the raw pain that had begun leaching into her bloodstream after she'd walked out of Shane's apartment. She hadn't expected the pain because all she'd felt in his bedroom after hearing his mother talk about his supposed engagement had been emptiness. When he'd come into the room and she'd declared her love for him and he hadn't said the words back, it was like someone had removed all the blood from her body and injected her with ice water instead. She had nothing left – he'd broken her. She'd even discarded the band because you didn't need distraction from something you couldn't feel, right?

It had all come screaming back though and she'd somehow ended up steering her car towards the gym. She'd walked in and zoned in on the speed bag and now, as sweat ran down her in rivulets and her mass of hair clung to her, she put every ounce of her strength behind each swing. She didn't know she was sobbing with each punch or that the few early morning occupants of the gym had been and were still watching her with concern. And she didn't see Gabe until he stepped in front of the bag and gently caught her next throw.

She yanked her arm back from his hold and took a few steps back. She pushed some of the hair that was plastered around her face back and glared at him for the interruption. It was then that she noticed everyone watching her and then she realized why. She was wearing her pink dress from dinner last night. Her hair was loose and sticking to her sweat-drenched skin. Suspecting tears were running from her eyes too, she lifted her fingers to test the theory and sure enough, they came back with more than just sweat on them. Worse yet, she'd left her cardigan behind so her arms were exposed, the scars on the left one as plain as day.

"Oh God," she whispered as she felt all the eyes on her.

"Hey!" Gabe nearly yelled at her, but his deep, commanding voice did what he had intended and pulled her back out of the darkness she'd been ready to escape into. "None of these men are judging you Savannah," he said firmly as he motioned towards the room. "Every single one of them knows what you're feeling."

She looked around and sure enough, most of the men were nodding. She took a deep breath and watched them return to their workouts. Gabe used the distraction to grab her by the wrist. He pulled her a few short steps to the big weight bag in the corner.

"The speed bag is for precision and working on hand-eye coordination, but it's useless if you just want something to beat the shit out of," Gabe said as he worked some small boxing gloves onto her hands and then slapped the big bag. "If you really want to feel that burn, you use this."

How did he know that was what she was trying to do? He glanced at her arm, the scarred one, and said, "Everybody has a different way of getting the pain out Savannah. Alcohol, drugs, fighting, sex." He said the last one differently and then she remembered his previous profession. "There's no shame in doing what you need to do to survive."

She tested the weight of the bag by pushing against it. The thing barely moved, so she pushed it harder. Adrenaline flooded through her as she began striking the bag over and over. Within minutes her entire body ached, but she kept at it. The bag hardly swung, but the satisfaction that it did at all made her punch it harder. Dark, evil eyes looked back as she struck out. Cruel hands reached for her but she fought them off. That voice that told her to run and hide inside herself called out to her, but she smacked the shit out of it. Her body finally gave out on her and she stumbled to a halt and fell to her knees.

Gabe was there before she did a face plant and his big arm just held her as he settled behind her and eased the gloves off her hands. As her breathing finally began to slow, Gabe released her and she sank down on her ass and drew her knees up against her chest. She felt his presence next to her, but he let her settle for a few more minutes before he spoke again.

"When's your next appointment with Dr. Henderson?" he asked.

She was surprised that he knew who her doctor was and she answered, "Next week," automatically before realization sank in.

"He does emergency visits if you need to see him sooner. I can call him for you," Gabe said.

"Shane got his number from you?" she asked, a shot of pain kicking through her as Shane's name left her lips. Gabe nodded, then chuckled.

"I don't really fit the profile, do I?" he mused.

"What profile?"

"Victim," was all he said.

It took her a moment to understand what he was telling her and then she shook her head in denial. He couldn't be...

"I guess victim is what you feel like in the beginning, but somewhere along the way you start to think of yourself as a survivor. It took me a while to get that," Gabe mused.

"You were-" She couldn't get the word out because it was stuck in her head that such a thing could never happen to someone as big and strong and confident as Gabe.

"Raped," he finished for her.

Tears welled in her eyes and then they were falling. It was too much – it was just too much. She felt his big hand rub her back in comfort and realized that the touch felt exactly that way. There was no fear or shame. She trusted him one hundred percent now, like she did her brother and Shane. Another flash of pain, but she pushed it away.

"Does it get better the more you talk about it?" she asked.

"Yeah, it does. It sucked at first and it took me a long time to believe it really happened. I was ashamed to have to admit it to Riley especially. You don't want someone you love to have to suffer through something like that with you." She nodded because she knew exactly what he was talking about.

"I have to tell Logan," she finally said. "It's going to kill him," she whispered.

Gabe was silent for a moment. "It's going to hurt knowing that he wasn't able to protect you from that, that's true. But he'll see how strong you are and that will help."

"I'm not strong," she said softly. "I couldn't fight back...not even after," she muttered. "He destroyed my life and got to walk away and all I could do was this," she said angrily as she lifted her scarred arm.

"You did what you needed to do to survive. When was the last time you hurt yourself?" he asked.

"Almost a month ago," she answered. She'd had a couple of close calls but the last time she'd actually done it was the night of her disastrous date with Robert.

"So go another month, then another one after that. Come kick the shit out of this bag or call me and I'll let you throw me around a little bit," he joked as he referred to their self-defense training. "Or if you need something girly, call Riley and she can drag you shopping or go do some of that salon crap you girls seem to be so fond of." He waved his hand around as he spoke – she wasn't surprised that someone like him wasn't at all familiar with the goings on at a salon. "Don't let that asshole win. Don't let him take even another day."

They were both quiet for a long time and she wiped at her now dry, but sticky feeling face. God, she was a mess. She was like a raw, open wound and even breathing hurt. But she was also here instead of home in her room watching blood run down her arm.

"I'm in love with him," she finally said out loud.

"Did you tell him that?"

She nodded. "He doesn't feel the same. I'd hoped maybe things would change-"

Gabe sighed. "He called me a little while ago looking for you – he wanted to make sure you were okay." She looked up at that and she could tell Gabe was debating what else to say to her. "I heard something in his voice Savannah. If I didn't think it was something, I wouldn't tell you. But I've never heard that fear before – or the loss. Not even after his brother died."

She wanted to mash her hands over her ears because he was giving her the one thing that had sustained her all these weeks – hope.

"I want to protect you Savannah – I think of you more like a sister now than I ever have before and the last thing I want for you is more pain. But I've seen the way you look at him. It's the way I look at Riley."

She nodded, but emotion clogged her throat, making it impossible to speak. When she felt Gabe's arm go around her shoulder, she didn't hesitate to lean into him. Maybe if he just held her for a few minutes, she could find the strength she would need to fight for the future she wanted.

HIS PARENTS WERE ALREADY SEATED AT THE TABLE IN THE HOTEL restaurant when Shane arrived. He knew he stuck out like a sore thumb with his dirty jeans and faded T-shirt. He'd grabbed the nearest clothes when he'd discovered Savannah had left and hadn't had the energy to drive home and change. His mother looked at his clothes in distaste as he dropped into the chair next to her.

"Darling," she began but his father cut her off.

"Linda, we agreed," he reminded her and she fell silent. His father looked at him and then waved dismissively. "Son, we understand that sometimes a man's needs take over," he began as he reached for his coffee. "Just use some discretion in the future. Hotels," he suggested casually.

"What if it had been Paige who stopped by this morning?" his mother muttered.

Anger went through him at the way they insinuated Savannah was just some toy he was amusing himself with on the side. "Paige and I aren't together anymore, Mom."

Linda patted her hair and then stroked an imaginary wrinkle out of her blouse. "Shane, it was a fight – couples have them every day. It's okay to be nervous-"

"There's no fucking engagement!" he nearly yelled and his mother dropped her fork, the metal clattering against the fancy plate beneath it. His father was in the middle of taking a sip of coffee and froze, his fist tightening in anger on the delicate coffee cup.

"You will apologize to your mother," his father announced.

"Or what, you'll disown me too?" Shane watched the color leach from his mother's face and all of it seemed to transfer to his father's because the man's expression was thunderous.

"You ungrateful-"

"John!" his mother hissed.

His father fell silent and put his cup down. They were having a stare down when Shane felt his mother's hand close over his. He seethed with anger. It was like the past eight years of having his life decided for him and his acquiescing just so he could get a smattering of love, was catching up with him. His entire life was a joke. He'd bought and paid for their love with his very soul and he had no one to blame but himself. He'd sold his body to escape the shame of being owned by his parents and then he'd snorted drugs up his nose to try and overcome the self-disgust he'd felt at playing the role of whore to any woman who had a wad of cash to throw at him. He'd wrapped it all up in a neat little package and convinced himself it had been his choice and that he'd done it because he wanted to, that he'd enjoyed the rush.

But the truth was clear as day to him now - he'd done it all because it was all he was good at – being someone else. Being the better version of who he actually was. If he was a good enough son or a good enough fuck or a good enough piece of eye candy then he'd never be alone. His parents, the women, Paige – as long as he was exactly what they wanted him to be, they'd stay with him. Without them he was nothing, had nothing. A dead brother and a drug addiction that would consume him like it had Gabe's mom – that was who he would be when they walked away. And then Savannah had come into his life and blown it all to hell. He wanted her more than any of them, but she was the one thing he couldn't have.

"Shane, honey, what has gotten into you?" his mother asked as she patted his hand.

"Did you stop loving him when he told you who he really was?" Shane asked, his eyes now on his mother. She shifted uncomfortably.

"Who?" she asked with feigned lightness as she pretended not to know who he was talking about. She picked up the fork and poked at the food on her plate but didn't actually put anything in her mouth.

"Did you read the note he left?" She gasped and he saw his father tense. "If not, I still have it," he prodded. "Better yet, I can tell you what it said because after reading it a thousand fucking times, I pretty much have it memorized."

"Shane," his father uttered in warning.

"Dear Shane," Shane began. "I know this won't make sense to you and I'm sorry, but I don't know what else to do. Tell Mom and Dad that I'm sorry I let them down, but I just didn't know how to pretend to be something I wasn't anymore. Tell them I tried really hard."

He heard his mother let out a small sob, but he pressed on. "Tell them I love them and that I forgive them." His mother let out another strangled cry and covered her eyes with her hands. "Shane, don't lose yourself to them like I did. I love you, little brother. Please don't hate me."

He felt his own throat clog with unshed tears. "Love Michael," he finished and then there was only silence as his mother cried silent tears. For once, his father actually looked torn up and Shane felt pinpricks of guilt.

"I thought I could take his place for you. I thought that if I gave you everything you wanted for him that it would be enough. I thought I could find a way to live with it." He leaned forward and rubbed his hands over his face as if he could wipe the exhaustion away. "And you know what? If I hadn't met this incredible, funny, charming, strong, beautiful woman, I probably could have done it. I could have ignored the pain of being a substitute for my brother who turned out to be just a little less perfect then he was supposed to be. I probably could have found a way to live with a woman who only wanted me to be a matching accessory in the background of her next photo op. And I could have sat in the office next to my father and pretended to love defending the lowest of the low, all the while knowing I was putting people at risk every time I helped some son of a bitch get away with his crime."

Shane stood up. "But I fucked up just like Michael did and I went looking for that little piece of myself that was missing. Only, now I've found it but it's too late to do anything about it." He walked away and wasn't surprised when his parents did nothing to stop him.

CHAPTER 15

Savannah trudged into the dark house, every limb in her body rejecting even the simplest of moves like taking a step forward. After the drama of this morning, she was completely spent. She'd managed to call in to work sick at some point, but must have been on autopilot when she'd done it because the only evidence she'd even remembered that she was supposed to be in class was a text from the principal letting her know he'd found a substitute and asking her to let him know if she would need tomorrow off as well. Deciding to play it safe, she'd said yes even though she felt guilty for lying about being ill. But the truth was that she was just too wrung out to be of use to anyone.

Gabe had tried to talk her into spending the day with him, but she'd stood her ground and refused and he had reluctantly left her at the gym. She'd managed to get cleaned up in the women's locker room, but hadn't wanted to go home so she was still wearing the same dress and shoes that she'd put on with such care yesterday in preparation for her dinner date with Shane. It seemed like a lifetime ago. So instead of going home, she'd gotten in her car, filled up the gas tank and then pointed the car west. It was a short drive to the ferry and the wait wasn't long for a spot on the huge boat since it was a weekday morning and she was going in the opposite direction of rush hour traffic. The ferry ride had been short, but feeling that breeze caress her skin as she stood at the front end of the massive boat had felt like Shane was skimming his fingertips all over her.

As soon as the ferry docked, she just started driving. She went up and around the Olympic Peninsula. Her little car trudged up the side of a mountain so she could admire the endless view of the snow-capped Olympic mountain range and then it got her safely to the beach where she walked along the wet sand as the Pacific Ocean lapped at her toes. Hours passed as she put miles and miles behind her. The pain was still there though when she finally had to turn the car back north and make the long, slow drive back to the city. There was no big breakthrough or life-changing decision, but she'd made it through the day and that was what mattered. She'd make it through the next one too and each one after that.

There'd been no calls or texts from Shane after the one he'd sent this morning making sure she was safe. But there'd been several from Riley and Gabe and a few missed calls from her brother. It had taken her a good ten minutes to talk Riley out of coming over for a girl's night of ice cream and tears and she'd sent a text as soon as she pulled in the driveway letting Logan know she was home. No lights were on in the house, testament that her brother was working more long hours. She'd hoped to tell him the truth tonight about the attack, but it was nearing ten o'clock and she wasn't sure she had it in her to stay up long enough to wait for Logan, let alone have the emotional strength she would need to come clean.

After dumping her purse and jacket on the kitchen table, she made her way up the stairs of the quiet house, her mother's antique Grandfather clock the only sound to accompany her. She entered her room and kicked off her shoes. One of them hit the wall with a thump but she ignored it and made her way to the bed. She didn't even have the energy to remove her dress or pull back the covers so she just dropped down onto the bedspread and let her body sink into the soft bedding. But it hit her instantly that something was wrong – very wrong. Something cold and wet seeped into her dress and slid against the bare skin of her arms and legs and she instinctively scrambled from the bed. She fumbled for the lamp on her nightstand and then screamed at the sight before her. Blood was all over the pretty bedspread, the dark red stains now imprinted with where her body had lain. It covered her arms and legs too and likely the back of her dress. It was sticky and congealed but still fresh enough that is trickled down her skin in eerie streaks.

"Oh God," she cried as she leaned over and emptied the contents of her stomach on the floor. She retched for several seconds as the scent of blood wafted through her nose. She reached for her cell phone, but realized she'd left it in the kitchen. The cordless phone was on her dresser so she stumbled over to it and snatched it up and dialed 911. But when she pressed it to her ear there was nothing – no ringing, no dial tone. She desperately pressed buttons but nothing happened. Her eyes shifted to the bed once more, then the rest of the room. Everything was exactly as it should be except for the bed. A chill ran through her and she ran out of the room.

Her instinct was to get to her cell phone, but when she reached the top step she hesitated. Whoever had done this could be long gone or still in the house. She hadn't noticed anything off when she'd come inside, but she'd also been too tired to pay any attention. She grabbed the banister as she slowly started down the staircase, her ears listening for any sound. All she heard was the tick tock from the clock. Her slick, blood covered hand slipped along the wood as she began her descent. Her breath sound heavy to her own ears and it seemed to take hours to reach the bottom stair. She stilled again and listened, but there was nothing different.

She made it to entryway of the kitchen but froze when she heard what sounded like footsteps just outside the kitchen door. There was a shade on the upper portion of the door and since it was drawn, she couldn't see anything on the other side. Her phone was several feet away and as the doorknob rattled as someone tried it, she knew she wouldn't reach the phone in time. She grabbed a knife from the butcher block and watched in horror as the door swung open.

"SAVANNAH, WHAT THE HELL?" SHANE HEARD LOGAN SAY AS HIS friend flipped on the light after opening the kitchen door. He'd gotten a call earlier from Logan asking him for a ride home since his car wouldn't start. Sam was covering the bar for the rest of the night and Logan hadn't been able to reach Savannah to come get him. He had heard the fear niggling Logan's voice at being unable to reach his sister all day and he'd had to bite back his confession that he was the cause of his sister's silence. They'd both been relieved when Logan received a text just a few minutes ago from Savannah letting him know she was home safe and sound. He'd debated whether he should come in when Logan asked him if he wanted to stay for a quick drink, but had decided it was time to come clean to his friend. When he heard the surprise and shock in Logan's voice as he said his sister's name, Shane quickly pushed past him and ground to a halt at the sight before him.

She was standing in the entryway between the kitchen and the living room, still wearing the same dress from the day before. Blood ran down her arms and legs and she held a huge butcher knife in her hand, her arm stiff next to her body as if readying for an attack. Her eyes were wild with fear and she sobbed in relief when she saw them.

"Jesus, Savannah?" he said as he hurried to her and grabbed her by the upper arms, ignoring the blood that instantly stained his hands.

"I didn't," she stuttered, her voice broken and harsh with fear. "I didn't hurt myself," she stammered as the knife clattered to the floor. "I swear Shane, I didn't."

"I know sweetheart," he said instantly and he felt her relax marginally beneath him. "Tell me what happened," he ordered firmly.

"Upstairs. In my room. Blood on my bed." Her words were clipped and he felt her start to shake as the adrenaline started to wear off.

Logan was moving before he could even say anything and disappeared upstairs. Shane pulled her into his arms and said, "You're safe now. You're safe," He whispered it over and over as she began to sob against his chest. He used one hand to dig out his phone from his pants pocket. He called 911 and gave them the address.

"Logan?" he shouted as he hung up. "Cops are on the way!"

"It's all clear up here," his friend yelled back down.

Savannah was saying something against his chest and he pulled her back so he could understand her. "Mr. Pickles," she kept saying over and over. He realized then that she suspected the blood might be from her pet. He pulled her back against him and kissed her forehead as he told her it would be okay even though he couldn't guarantee that it would be.

Logan returned and he handed Savannah to him so he could go take a look at her room for himself. He hurried up the stairs and then stopped at the sight in her bedroom. He stared in shock at the blood that had soaked her bedding. Fear seeped through him as he imagined her lying there in it, her eyes closed, the blood seeping from her body. His hand clenched the doorframe at the image of her lifeless body and he forced it away. He focused on what was in front of him and then realized that there was too much blood to belong to a cat. Hope went through him and he began a slow, methodical search of the upstairs rooms. He found the animal in Logan's bedroom closet. He managed to grab the very freaked out cat and felt its nails rake into his chest as he cuddled it and tried to soothe the animal with his voice and hands. It finally settled down and he took the cat downstairs.

Savannah was still in Logan's arms when he returned to the kitchen and she cried out in joy at the sight of her pet.

"Mr. Pickles! Oh God, thank you, thank you," she whispered as she took the cat from him and clutched him against her chest. She reached up to kiss him on the cheek but the image of her body was still stuck in his head and he needed more so he settled his mouth over hers. It lasted just seconds, but gave him the reassurance that he needed that she was okay. Her brother's eyes flashed when Shane glanced at him, but the sound of sirens and flashing lights in the driveway bought him some time.

Savannah sat stiffly on the couch as more and more cops came and went. Mr. Pickles sat quietly in her arms, his soft breathing keeping her calm. He'd been clean when Shane handed him to her, but she'd been too relieved to see him alive and well to think about washing her hands before she grabbed her pet. As a result, his beautiful white fur was now stained red. Shane sat to one side of her, his thigh pressed against hers as his hand stroked her knee. Her brother sat on her other side, his hand supporting her back. The police had asked her endless questions, but she couldn't remember most of her answers. She kept seeing the blood and now she felt like she could taste it. Shane had used a washcloth to get most of it off her hands but at some point she must have touched her lips because the coppery taste lingered. She wished Shane would kiss her again so she could taste him instead.

"We should know what kind of blood it is by tomorrow," the police officer was saying. They had found the point of entry into the house. A broken window and popped out screen in the basement. A shudder ran through her that someone had been in her house, in her room and she knew she probably wouldn't be able to go back in there.

"You folks should find someplace else to stay tonight."

"We will," Logan said.

At the same time, Shane said, "They can stay with me."

It took another hour for the cops to finish asking their questions. Logan had tried to convince her that they should leave immediately but she had refused. She could live without her things, but she absolutely could not go another step without getting the blood off of her. He'd finally agreed to let her shower and had brought her some of her clothes that he'd found in the laundry room. When she looked in the mirror, she almost vomited again. Her skin was deathly white against the dark red of the smeared blood. Her beautiful pink dress was ruined. She turned the water on in the shower and then reached for the fastenings on her dress. That was when she heard the first crash.

LOGAN POUNCED THE SECOND SAVANNAH WAS SAFELY ENSCONCED IN the upstairs bathroom. He didn't struggle when Logan slammed him into a wall and said, "Did you touch her?"

Shane remained silent and Logan punched him. "My sister?" he screamed as he threw another punch. Instinct had Shane putting up his arm in defense, but he made no move to strike back. His friend threw him across the room and he stumbled hard against the coffee table. "You fucked my goddamn sister?" Logan's body slammed into his and they hit the coffee table which splintered beneath them. With the wind knocked out of him, he was defenseless against Logan's next blow.

"I trusted you!" Shane felt his lip split with the next punch and then saw stars as Logan slammed his head down against the floor. "You were like my brother!"

"Logan, stop it!" Shane heard her voice but it sounded like it was far away. Another vicious punch from Logan. "Stop it!" she shouted again and then he saw her standing in the middle of the stairs, still covered in blood. He wanted to tell her it was okay and to go back upstairs and get cleaned up, but he was having trouble forming the words. "Logan, stop it! He was helping me!"

Her words seemed to have no impact as he received another head slam. "I was raped!" she suddenly screamed at the top of her lungs. "Logan, I was raped!"

He felt Logan freeze above him. Seconds dragged by and then he heard Logan whisper, "No," as he scrambled off Shane and turned to face his sister who was still standing on the stairs, tears streaming down her cheeks. When she turned her eyes on him, she cried out and hurried down the stairs to his side.

"I'm all right," he managed to say as he pushed himself up. "Finish it," he said to her as she tried to help him sit up. She turned her attention back to her brother who stood in horrified shock above them.

"It happened when I was seventeen," she began.

"Why didn't you tell me?" Logan managed to utter as the harsh truth of what she was saying began to sink in.

She shook her head. The words seemed to be stuck in her throat so she fast forwarded. "I haven't been able to let anyone touch me since. I asked Shane to help me..." Her words dropped off and he saw Logan's turmoil-filled eyes flash briefly to him. She called her brother's name again and when he looked back at her she said, "Afterwards I started hurting myself."

Agony visibly went through Logan and a guttural sob escaped the man's throat. Savannah cried at her brother's expression so Shane grabbed her hand. "It's okay. Keep going," he said quietly.

"I started cutting myself with knives, then razor blades. I didn't know how else to deal with the pain. I was too ashamed to tell you."

Logan dropped to his knees in front of her and took her face into his hands. "Nothing you do could ever make me ashamed of you," he said firmly. "Tell me who it was." He was pleading with her and she finally dropped her head.

"It was Sam." Her voice was so quiet that Shane barely heard her. Logan was able to keep his hands from tightening on her face at her admission, but the rest of his body went taut with rage. Sam Reynolds, his business partner and friend.

"He came to the house one night looking for you. He said you guys were supposed to meet to talk about the bar he was helping you buy. I thought it was weird because you told me you were going to work that night, but he was your friend so I let him in."

Shane saw tears fall down Logan's face as his hands drifted down his sister's arms. The guilt and pain were a raw thing for his friend. His own gut churned at what Savannah was saying and he couldn't wait until he found the man and killed him.

"It happened by the door." She motioned with her head to the cold, hardwood entryway by the front door. "He was on me so fast. I begged him to stop but he just covered my mouth with his hand. I couldn't stop him," she sobbed.

"Shhhh, it's okay," Logan whispered as he pulled her against his chest. Her sobs turned to choking gasps and Logan stroked her back until she calmed.

"He told me that if I told you, he wouldn't help you buy the bar. He said he'd fire you and without a job we couldn't stay together. He said I was still a minor and they could take me away. I believed him." Logan held her for a long time and she finally settled, her body appearing drained.

"Honey, why don't you go upstairs and get cleaned up?" She drew back from her brother and then looked at Shane. Her eyes went back to Logan and Shane could tell by the stubborn tilt of her chin that she wasn't about to leave them alone again. "Shane and I are good," Logan said roughly but Shane knew that was far from the truth. Logan looked up at him and then said, "Can you take her upstairs and help her get cleaned up?"

Shane was surprised at the request since Logan had to know what helping Savannah meant. He eyed Logan suspiciously and then struggled to his feet. Savannah tried to help him and he winced as pain spread through his body. He wondered if his friend had managed to crack one of his ribs.

"Sweetheart, can you get me some ice?" Shane asked her and she nodded and disappeared into the kitchen.

Logan shot him a hard look and then tried to step past him, but Shane put out his hand. "Don't." His friend looked at him murderously and he wondered how much of that was for him and how much was directed at Sam. "I know what you want to do, but if you leave her now it will mess her up even more. Telling you was the hardest thing she's ever had to do and she needs you now." Logan stepped back from him, his need for revenge clearly warring with his need to protect his sister. "I'll go find him as soon as you and she are settled at Gabe's." Logan must have been surprised by the deadly conviction in his voice because he looked up and then finally nodded.

"I'll call Gabe and let him know what happened," Logan said, his voice hoarse.

Savannah returned and handed him an ice pack. He took it from her and then grabbed her hand and led her up the stairs.

"You'll be here when I come back down, right Logan?" she said worriedly.

"I'm not going anywhere," her brother said firmly and smiled at her. She hesitated and then finally allowed Shane to pull her the rest of the way up the stairs.

She was stiff as a board by the time he got her into the bathroom. Her eyes had glazed over and he could tell she was barely hanging on physically and emotionally. He turned the shower on and as steam filled the room, he gently worked the ruined dress off her. The blood had dried and the dress was stiff as he stuffed it into the garbage can. He removed her undergarments and tossed them in the garbage too. Her skin was cold against his hands as he worked and he began to wonder if she might be going into some kind of shock. Worry sifted through him and then he began stripping off his own clothes. She didn't seem to notice or care and that had him more concerned because he didn't want her retreating to that dark place that had held her prisoner for so long.

He lifted her over the lip of the tub and pulled her under the spray with him. The impact of the water didn't seem to have any effect on her. He grabbed the shower gel and dumped a liberal amount in his hand. He cleaned and massaged every inch of her, his fingers gentle but firm as he tried to soothe her tense muscles. Blood ran off her in waves and when he was satisfied it was all gone, he reached for the shampoo.

He felt her relax marginally as he began working her hair into a lather and by the time he was ready to rinse it, she was leaning back against him. Her back brushed his chest over and over as he maneuvered her hair to get it rinsed out completely. When he was satisfied that she was clean, he just held her like that and let the water soothe them both. He wrapped his forearm around her upper chest and used his other hand on her abdomen to pull her back against him so they touched everywhere. His tension eased when she let out a big sigh and her body relaxed completely against his.

It was only when the water started to run cold that he forced himself to move and get her dried off. There was a bathrobe hanging on the back of the bathroom door so he wrapped that around her, then helped her wrap a towel around her head. Within minutes, he had her dressed in the clothes Logan had left for her. She had yet to speak, but he guessed she was saving her energy so she could keep moving for a just a few more minutes. As they headed back downstairs and into the kitchen, he could see that Logan had been busy packing her and himself a bag and Mr. Pickles sat unhappily in a pet carrier, his tail twitching angrily as he let out some creepy mewling sounds that only cats knew how to make.

Shane drove the short distance to Gabe's apartment and Logan sat in the back with Savannah who had fallen asleep within two minutes. Shane's phone rang and he looked at the caller ID, then swiped the screen to answer.

"I have a name for you," Dom said. Shane could hear the distinct clicking of a keyboard in the background.

"Sam Reynolds," Shane said softly. Logan perked up when he said the name, but Savannah thankfully slept on.

Dom was silent, obviously caught off guard, but he recovered quickly. "Yeah. She gave you his name?"

"Yeah." Shane quickly told Dom what had happened that night.

He heard Dom curse and then sigh heavily. "He's a ghost Shane."

"What do you mean?" Shane asked.

"Sam Reynolds doesn't exist. His social security number's fake and the address he uses is an abandoned building on the south side that the city is tearing down in a few weeks."

"His business-" Shane began, remembering the sports bar Sam owned and that Logan once worked at.

"Smoke and mirrors – elaborate ones. Whoever he is, he's good at hiding."

"Shit."

"What is it?" Logan asked softly. Shane shook his head and Logan tensed.

"Thanks Dom, if you find anything else-" Shane began.

"Don't bother looking for him at your friend's bar," Dom said.

"Why?"

"I stopped by the place an hour ago when his name came up. The place was packed with people, but he was gone. Some drunk moron was behind the bar serving drinks for free. I kicked everyone out and closed the place down, but your friend lost a lot of inventory and the place is trashed. His cash register was emptied too, but that could have been Reynolds."

"Thanks Dom, I'll let him know."

"I'll keep looking." With that, Dom disconnected.

"What is it?" Logan asked.

"Let's talk at Gabe's. I don't want her to hear," he said softly as he looked in the rearview mirror at Savannah who was still out cold, her head leaning on her brother's shoulder. Logan nodded, tightened his arm around his sister and then stared out the window.

Shane stepped carefully over a pile of broken glass as he continued to survey the damage to the bar. It wasn't as bad as he expected, but he knew the loss of inventory alone would be devastating for Logan. His friend had worked himself to the bone to build this place up from nothing because he saw the potential that no one else did. Shane knew nothing about running a business, but even he could see that the location alone had been a smart move. Tourists littered the street and it was close enough to the stadium that football fans would come in droves celebrating before and after the games.

After reluctantly leaving Savannah with her brother at Gabe's apartment last night, he'd gone home to try and get some sleep. He had literally run the gamut of emotions yesterday and had been physically and emotionally drained, but the second his head hit the pillow, all he could see was Savannah covered in blood. He knew she was in good hands, but they weren't his and it made him crazy. When they'd arrived at Gabe and Riley's, Logan had carried her up to the apartment and into the guest room Riley had readied. Savannah never even stirred, not even when Shane released her cat from the carrier and he immediately scrambled up onto the bed to curl against his mistress. Logan had been hovering behind him so he couldn't even touch Savannah to reassure himself with her warmth.

Riley had stayed with Savannah in the room in case she woke while he and Logan had filled Gabe in on what had happened at the house. Shane shared Dom's information with both men and he saw what was left of Logan's composure shatter. When the man disappeared out onto the balcony to grieve for what had been done to his sister, Gabe followed and Shane took the opportunity to escape.

Less than twenty-four hours ago, he'd realized he was in love with Savannah. And in one day it was gone – he'd lost her as well as his parents and one of his best friends. And then he'd been tormented with visions of Savannah's lifeless body all night. His body was begging him to seek the relief that he needed, but only the idea of knowing Savannah was still in danger held him back from making that phone call to his dealer. Whoever Sam Reynolds really was, he had Savannah in his sights. There was no doubt that he was the one that had put the blood on her bed. In his conversation with Logan last night, Sam hadn't seemed to realize Savannah was back in town until the day he'd seen her bringing Logan's forgotten phone to the bar. It made sense now, why she'd avoided the place all these years.

More guilt had been piled on poor Logan when he remembered his conversation with Sam that day and realized he'd inadvertently told Savannah's rapist that she was dating someone. They'd contacted the police to let them know about Sam, but all three men knew there was little the cops could do if Sam had decided to disappear. But if he was as obsessed with Savannah as he appeared to be, she was and would be in danger until he was caught. And Shane was helpless to do anything. He couldn't even be there to keep her safe since he'd destroyed what remaining fragment was left of their relationship yesterday by not telling her the truth about how he felt about her. And if that wasn't enough, her brother was definitely going to have something to say about any future he may have wanted with her if he could ever manage to get his shit straightened out.

Shane searched the bar until he found the cleaning supplies he was looking for. He began sweeping up the remnants of bottles and glasses and dumped them into a garbage can.

"What are you doing here?"

Shane turned to see Logan standing in the doorframe that led to the back of the space where he had a small office and a closet with supplies and inventory.

"Couldn't sleep," was all Shane said.

"How'd you get in?"

"The friend I told you about found a spare key when he locked up last night. I got it from him this morning."

Logan looked around the bar, pain flashing briefly across his features as he saw what remained of all his hard work.

"I think once we get the glass and trash cleaned up, it'll look better," Shane offered as he worked. He waited for Logan to dismiss him but the man said nothing. He finally stepped carefully over the debris and made his way to the bar so he could see what was left. Only a few bottles on the top shelf remained intact.

"Five years," Logan whispered. "She kept this from me for five years." He turned and ran his hand over the old wood of the bar. "She thought this place meant more to me than she did." He slammed his fist down on the top of the bar and then scattered the few remaining glasses that were sitting there. Glass shattered around him, but he didn't seem to care and then he was turning his attention to the last bottles that had managed to remain untouched. He grabbed one and hurled it across the room. Glass and brown liquid sprayed all over the wall. "I trusted him!" he yelled as he flung the next bottle. "I trusted you!" More glass shattering. "I trusted everyone and you all lied to me!"

Shane realized that Logan must have figured out that Gabe and Riley had been hiding Savannah's secret as well. Shame went through him as he watched his enraged friend. When there were no bottles left, Logan braced his arms against the bar and struggled to catch his breath.

"She needed to be stronger to tell you Logan."

"So that's why you fucked her? To give her strength?" he snarled.

"Tell me what I was supposed to do Logan!"

"You should have come to me! I'm her brother!"

"She needed to be able to choose!" Shane shouted. "That fucker took that from her and she needed it back! Telling you had to be her choice! Allowing a man to touch her again had to be her choice!"

"Always the consummate professional, huh Shane?" Logan laughed coldly and shook his head. "Did you at least give her the friends and family discount?"

Shane was on him in three long strides. One swing and Logan hit the floor, blood spurting from his nose. "Fuck you, Logan," he said as he shook his hand to relieve the sting. "Fuck you." He reached into his pocket and tossed the spare key on the floor and then walked away.

Savannah picked her way past the headstones and paused to study the unique tree near the entrance to the cemetery. It looked old and dead, its gnarled branches twisted together at odd angles. There was something strangely familiar about the tree and then she realized where she'd seen it before. She looked back over her shoulder to where

Gabe was standing near the gates. He smiled at her look. The huge tattoo on his back looked exactly like this tree.

"Ask Riley to tell you the story," he called to her and then a wistful smile graced his lips. Like he was remembering something fondly. She shrugged it off and made her way down the aisle until she spotted her quarry. He hadn't noticed her coming, so Gabe's voice must not have carried when he had shouted at her. She was nearly on top of Shane before he looked up from the bench he was sitting on. He scrambled to his feet.

"What are you doing here?" he asked, clearly stunned to see her.

"You invited me to meet your brother," she said as she slid her arms around him. It felt good to have his solid body against hers again. He was tense at first, then returned her hug.

"How did you know I was here?" he asked but before she could answer he growled, "Riley." She smiled against his chest. "Please tell me you didn't come by yourself," Shane said.

"I made Gabe bring me. Or rather, Riley made Gabe bring me." She felt Shane pull back from her and look over her shoulder to where Gabe still hovered. The big man waved and then walked to his car.

"Looks like I'm going to need a ride home," she said as Gabe's car disappeared.

Poor Shane looked confused, so she tugged him down to the bench and leaned against him as she studied the big tombstone in front of her. They sat that way for several minutes.

"How have you been?" he finally asked. She hadn't seen him since the beginning of the week after he'd dropped her and Logan off at Gabe and Riley's. The last thing she actually remembered was how he'd taken care of her in the shower. She'd been cold all over, but he'd found a way to warm her up and bring her back. She'd slept for more than twelve hours straight and had only awakened long enough to use the bathroom and force down the sandwich Riley had handed her.

It wasn't until Thursday morning that she managed to feel human again, but the scene she stepped into was a nightmare. The tension between Gabe, Riley and Logan was palpable. When she left the bedroom, they were all sitting at the table eating breakfast in utter silence, Gabe and Riley on one end, Logan on the other. Her brother had looked haggard and bitter. He'd smiled at her when he had finally looked up from his plate, but his greeting felt hollow. Riley had quickly made her a plate of food and inquired how she was feeling, but everything about the scene felt awkward and forced.

"I really messed things up," she said.

She looked up at him and studied the purple and black bruises along his eye and cheekbone. There was a little bit of green along the edges indicating the injuries were slowly healing, but the damage Logan had inflicted was devastating. And knowing she was the cause of it broke her heart. It hadn't gone unnoticed that Logan was sporting a fresh bruise as well and she could only wonder at what terrible things had been said between him and Shane for Shane to finally lash out at her brother. Because the fight she had witnessed on that awful night had been one sided – Shane had only tried to protect his body from Logan's angry fists.

"It's not your fault," Shane began but she shook her head.

"Don't. Don't try to protect me from this. This is absolutely my fault." She leaned her head back against his shoulder. "I destroyed our family because I was a coward."

"No."

She ignored his protest. "Logan won't even talk to Riley and Gabe – he spent the last two nights at the bar."

"He needs time."

"I need him," she said. "I need you." He was silent and she figured that was his way of confirming she couldn't have the latter.

Before she could speak again, she heard someone call out Shane's name.

Savannah turned to look in the direction the high-pitched voice had come from. She felt Shane seize up next to her as they both watched his mother pick her way along the path directly towards them.

❧

SHANE WAS AMAZED NOT ONLY TO SEE HIS MOTHER, BUT BY HER appearance as well. Not only was she wearing a simple pair of Khakis and a cable knit sweater, but her hair was a windswept mess and she actually had sneakers on. There was not a lick of makeup on her face and her eyes looked red and puffy. She held what looked like a wadded up and very damp tissue in her hand, confirming his suspicion that she'd been crying recently. He stood and felt Savannah rise next to him, her hand automatically closing around his.

"Mom," he managed to get out before she saw his face.

"Shane, oh my God, what happened?" she said as she closed the distance between them and grabbed his face gently so she could inspect him up close. Although her touch was light, he still flinched as she skimmed her thumb over the sensitive bruises.

"It's nothing. A disagreement among friends." He pulled away from her. "What are you doing here?" He had assumed she and his father would have left Seattle earlier in the week after he'd gone off on them.

"I just wanted to come see your brother," she said as she looked over the grave. A frown crossed her features as she bent down to pull at a weed. "I pay the caretaker extra every month to get rid of these," she muttered as she tossed the weed aside. Her gaze fell on the less than fresh bouquet of flowers that were just beginning to show signs of rot. "And he's supposed to put fresh flowers out every week." She marched up to the tombstone and grabbed the flowers and threw them next to the grave.

"Mom," Shane said, a little worried and unnerved by her odd behavior. She looked up at him and then finally seemed to realize that he wasn't alone. "This is Savannah." He felt Savannah tense next to him and waited to see how his mother would react. If she showed Savannah any disrespect...

"Oh my dear, it's nice to finally meet you." His mother stunned them both by reaching out to pull Savannah into a warm embrace. "I'm so sorry we interrupted your morning the other day." She pulled back and patted Savannah's cheek. "Sometimes Shane's father and I forget that he's not our little boy anymore and that we need to respect his privacy." She clasped her hands together and Shane could only gape at her. Where was the condemnation, the disgust?

"It's nice to meet you Mrs. Matthews," Savannah said as she too seemed to struggle to find her words.

"Oh please, call me Linda."

"Mom," Shane began, growing more concerned by how flighty his mother was acting.

"Shane," she whispered in what sounded almost like a begging tone. She grew still as her gaze lifted to meet his. "Please, Shane, I'm trying. I wasn't expecting to see you here..." She looked around the cemetery. "I'm just a little nervous because I don't want to mess this up again," she said anxiously as tears flooded her eyes.

"I'll give you guys some privacy," Savannah said quietly and turned to leave. Before Shane could stop her, his mother was grabbing her hand.

"No, please stay." Savannah stopped and his mother held onto her. "I'm sorry for my careless words the other morning – I didn't know how my son felt about you and Paige made it sound like..." She waved her hands like she was dismissing the thought. "Please stay," she said again and smiled when Savannah nodded.

Her attention swung back to him. "I keep going back in my head to that night at dinner when Michael told us who he was. We were so caught off guard..." she explained as she began wringing her hands together. "Your father knew it was wrong the instant he did it – disowning Michael like that – but you know your father and his pride. He just needed time to cool off. By the time he reached out, it was too late," she said as a sob gripped her.

"You made me lie about how he died." Shane couldn't keep the accusatory tone from his voice.

"We were weak Shane. One second everything in our life was perfect – at least our messed up version of perfect – and then it wasn't. We didn't know how to deal with a gay son. And then to have to admit that we drove him to take his own life?" She shook her head. "We were cowards. All we had left was you and our reputation. It was selfish to ask you to take his place like that, but you just slipped so easily into the role that we never considered you might not want it."

It had been his own fault for playing the role so well, he realized. "I thought I could give you back the part of him you loved most."

"We didn't love Michael because he fit some ridiculous mold we had created in our heads for him. We loved him because he was our son. We love you because you're our son. Nothing you do or don't do will ever change that and I hope you'll give us the chance to prove it to you someday."

Shane was feeling raw and confused and not even Savannah's fingers stroking over his could ease the restlessness that hummed through him. "We need to go," he muttered and then politely kissed his mother on her cheek, ignoring the dampness there and the longing in her eyes.

"Of course," she said. "I'm just going to sit here for a little bit," she said as she took a few steps back.

He nodded once and then he was walking away, nearly dragging Savannah behind him. He heard her mumble a quick goodbye to his mother, but he didn't look back. She kept silent as he maintained the quick pace back to the car. He ripped open the passenger door for her and waited and then grunted as she grabbed his neck hard and pulled him down for a kiss. He let out all the anguish and torment he'd been feeling since the morning she'd left him. She had started the kiss but he quickly took it over. But for every harsh stroke of his tongue or rough nip from his teeth, she countered with softness. When his fingers bit into her hips, she skimmed his biceps, caressed his neck, stroked his face. His anger and frustration waned and he gentled his hold on her as the kiss turned warm and seeking.

He wasn't sure how many minutes they had stood there clinging to one another, but when he finally managed to pull back, she whispered, "You looked like you needed that." Calm enveloped him and he nodded. "Can you drop me off at the bar? I need to talk to Logan." He was still too wrung out to trust himself to speak so he nodded again and helped her into the car.

THE LITTLE BELL ON THE DOOR JINGLED AS SHE OPENED IT AND A rough, hoarse voice shouted, "We're closed!" The bar was nearly pitch black so it took her a minute to acclimate her eyes. She'd only been in the place a few times, but she guessed his voice had come from behind the huge wood bar. There was a little bit of light from the cabinets that usually held endless rows of various types of liquor, but there were no bottles anywhere in sight today. The place was a mess. Glass all over the floor, tables overturned, trash on the floor. Gabe had told her the bar had been vandalized when Sam ditched it, but she hadn't really comprehended what that meant. Her heart ached for Logan, knowing all the work he'd put into this place.

She found him sitting on the floor behind the bar, his legs drawn up, a half empty bottle at his side. Ironically, as a bar owner, Logan rarely drank, so to see him like this was difficult. He looked up at her with slightly bleary eyes but he was cognizant of her presence. "Don't sit," he said as he motioned to the floor. "There's glass everywhere." She didn't bother to mention he was probably sitting on glass himself. Instead, she grabbed a nearby chair and pulled it over.

She sat and drew her knees up to her chin and just watched him. "You shouldn't be here," he finally said. She had guessed correctly – he wasn't drunk, but he was starting to feel the loose tongue that just a little too much alcohol always seemed to bless people with. His buzz might actually help her get through his thick head.

"Why not?"

"Because you hate it here."

"I don't hate this place," she mused as she looked around.

"I do."

"No you don't," she countered.

"It took you from me," he said and she felt her insides clench.

"This place didn't do that. I did that." He shook his head viciously. "I took your friends too," she said.

"No! They're the ones that lied," he said.

"Because I asked them to."

"No!" he said again.

"They had to choose between us Logan because I put them in that position. They knew you were stronger than me – that you'd find a way to deal with their betrayal." She glanced down at her arm which she had finally stopped hiding with long-sleeved clothing. "They were worried about what I might do to myself if they told you the truth about the rape and the cutting."

He pressed his fists against his head as he considered her words.

"Why didn't you just come to me in the first place? I would have protected you. I wouldn't have let anyone take you from me."

"I couldn't risk losing you too, Logan." Tears stuck in her throat and she swallowed hard. "I should have had more faith in you, but you'd already given up so much for me. I didn't want to take your dream too."

"I'm going to kill him," he whispered coldly, his buzz seeming to fade.

"I need you in my life Logan. I need my brother back." He sighed and fell silent. It was like he knew what was coming, but she said it anyway. "I need Shane too," she said quietly, firmly.

"Savannah, you know what he is," he began.

"You mean what you are?" Logan looked up at her then and his expression went blank when he figured out that she knew the truth about him. "I'm not judging you Logan. I think I know why you did it, but the truth is, it doesn't matter to me. I love you."

"He's messed up, Savannah. I mean, really messed up," Logan said. "I don't know exactly what's going on with him, but he's changed since you left."

"I know that, but we don't get to pick who we fall in love with." Logan sighed at her admission. "He wouldn't give up on me, Logan. He was willing to give up his friendship with you to give me what I needed."

Savannah shifted in her seat. "Did you ever think that maybe he only shows you what you want to see?" At Logan's thoughtful silence, she continued. "His life is about conforming – being who the person he's with needs him to be. You see him as what? A guy who likes to fuck for money? A spoiled, rich kid who's had his whole life handed to him on a silver platter while you've had to work for everything you've got? Happy go lucky asshole without a care in the world? Shameless flirt? Whore?"

"Stop it!" Logan said, but he didn't deny it and she saw the color in his face drain.

"You pretend to be someone you're not for what, a couple hours a month? He has to do it every day, even with the friends he thinks of as family." She leaned back in her chair. "And he's so afraid you guys will reject him if you find out who he really is that he'd rather push you away first." She fell silent and watched her brother process her words. When he finally leaned his head back against the bar, there were tears in his eyes and she realized she had managed to get through that thick head of his after all.

CHAPTER 16

SHANE HURRIED THROUGH THE SLIDING DOORS OF THE HOSPITAL AND scanned the signs for the patient room numbers. He checked the text from Savannah again to confirm the room number and then rushed up the stairs. He hadn't heard from her since he'd dropped her off at her brother's bar. He'd watched her until he was sure she was safe inside and then he'd started driving. Between his mother's confession this morning and Savannah showing up, he was a jumbled mess. Everybody kept fucking with what he expected. Gabe and Riley refused to let him go even after he unleashed his cruelty on them, his mother had actually begged *him* to forgive *her* after he'd dumped all his shit on her and Savannah came back to him every time he needed her and pulled him back from the brink.

The text had come twenty minutes ago, but he hadn't seen it right away. When he finally did check his phone, his heart had caught in his throat at the message.

They found Gabe's Mom. It's bad.

A couple of minutes later she'd sent him the room number. He ached for Gabe, especially now that he knew how depraved Abby had become as a result of her addiction. He remembered her before the drugs too – she'd been fun and loving, a soccer mom type who adored her only son. She and Gabe had been a team and Shane had actually found himself envious of their relationship at times. But a handful of pills had changed all that and she had become a monster who destroyed everything in her path.

When he finally reached the room, he came to a crushing stop at the sight before him. Gabe stood by the head of the bed, Riley clutching his hand in both of hers. Logan and Savannah were on the side closer to where he stood in the doorway. But it was the woman in the bed that caused a shudder to do a slow crawl through his body. He hadn't seen her in years, but it didn't matter because he recognized nothing in the shell of a body lying under the white sheet. Tubes stuck out of her arms and another was down her throat, a machine nearby clearly pumping oxygen into her. She looked like a skeleton, her joints sticking out sharply against the material of her hospital gown. Her skin was gray in pallor, her closed eyes sunken into her head. Thin brown hair hung in clumps around her face. There were track marks up and down both her arms and between her fingers. Even her neck had several fresh lesions where she'd clearly used her jugular as an entry point for the heroin that had stolen her life.

He felt Savannah's hand close over his and he forced his gaze away from the horror in front of him. Gabe nodded at him briefly in silent greeting and he could tell that his friend was torn between hating the woman his mother had become and loving the one she'd once been.

Shane felt a doctor brush past him and he moved back out of the way as a nurse followed. The nurse handed Gabe a clipboard and he heard the doctor's gentle voice say, "After I turn off the ventilator, it will take a couple of minutes for her heart to slow and then it will stop completely. She won't feel any pain. You can hold her hand if you want to."

Bile rose in Shane's throat as he realized what he was witnessing. He watched Gabe sign the paperwork. The nurse placed two chairs next to the bed for Riley and Gabe and then he felt Savannah tugging his hand as she pulled him out of the room, Logan right behind them. His last glimpse before the door closed was of Gabe reaching out to take his mother's hand as the doctor switched a button on the breathing machine and then there was only the sound of the heart monitor as it tracked the last minutes of Abby Maddox's life.

SAVANNAH'S WORRY INCREASED AS SHE WATCHED SHANE'S AGITATION grow as he paced the small waiting room. She'd wanted to warn him about Abby's condition before he arrived, but there hadn't been enough time. She and Logan had spent most of the day cleaning up the bar after their talk. It had been nice to work alongside her brother, but he'd been distant and lost in thought. Not that she could blame him – she'd dumped a lot on him in the last few days. But it felt like they had a new place to start from and she was hopeful that he would find a way to start trusting those closest to him again. And she hoped he would start with Shane because choosing between them would be impossible. Somewhere along the way she had already decided she wouldn't let Shane walk away from her. Now she just had to convince him of that.

Several minutes had passed since they left Gabe and Riley and Shane showed no signs of awareness to her or Logan's presence. He was pale and his hands shook as he clenched and unclenched them. He looked like how she always felt when the urge to hurt herself overtook her. She finally got up and stood in his path. She was glad that he stopped before mowing her over – it meant that part of him was still there with them.

"Are you okay?" she asked. She was surprised when he shook his head almost violently.

"I can't do this," he said softly. "I'm sorry."

A chill went through her at the resignation in his voice. "Shane," she began but he grabbed her by the upper arms, his grip almost painful. She saw Logan rise out of his chair but he didn't intervene.

Shane pulled her into his arms and she felt his rapid breath on her neck as he clutched her almost desperately. He didn't kiss or caress her, just held on to her. His body was cold and she felt a tremor go through him. "Shane-" she said as panic seeped into her.

"I love you Savannah," he whispered against her ear. "I love you so much," he said in an agonized voice and then, just like that, he released her and left the room. She was so stunned by what he had said and the finality with which he had said it that it took her several precious moments to realize he was gone. She felt Logan's presence behind her, but she ignored the comforting hand he placed on her shoulder. Rushing to the waiting room door, she swung it open and searched the hallway but Shane was already gone.

She snatched her phone from her purse and dialed, but he didn't answer. She was about to tell Logan she was going after Shane, but then the door across the waiting room opened and a shaky looking Riley and pale Gabe stepped out, hands tightly intertwined. As much as she wanted to leave, her friends needed her too. So she closed the distance between her and the couple and wrapped her arms around them both. She felt Logan's arms there as well and then the tears began to fall.

BY THE TIME SAVANNAH CONVINCED THE LANDLORD THAT SHE WAS Shane's fiancé and had gotten locked out of their apartment, a full hour had passed since he'd left her standing in the hospital waiting room. She called and texted dozens of times, pleading with him to call her back, but there'd been nothing but silence. The words she had longed to hear scared the hell out of her now because of how he'd said them... final, permanent. Like he was leaving and didn't expect to be coming back.

She stayed by Gabe and Riley's side for as long as she could, but her instincts told her that she needed to get to Shane so she'd excused herself to go to the bathroom and left the hospital. She'd lucked out that Logan had given her the keys to his car to keep in her purse and she didn't feel even an ounce of guilt for taking it. As soon as she was safely out of the parking lot, she called her brother and told him where she was going. He had ordered her back to the safety of the hospital, but she'd hung up on him. When he called the second time and instantly started yelling at her, she hung up on him again. By the third call, he was noticeably calmer and nicely asked her to call him when she was at Shane's.

Savannah's fingers shook as she put the key in the lock and turned. She sighed in relief when the door didn't catch – she had worried that he might have secured the door further by using the chain above the lock. His apartment was dark and cold and eerily silent. If she hadn't seen his car out front, she would have guessed he wasn't home. She locked the door behind her and rushed up the stairs, her feet sounding heavy on the wood stairs.

A prayer of thanks went through her at the sight of him sitting on the edge of his bed. Her darkest thoughts had conjured up some truly horrible images of what she might find, so to see him upright brought instant relief. It was short-lived though, when her mind began to process what she was seeing. His head was hanging low, like he was studying his hands which were resting on his legs, palms down. He had removed his shirt at some point so she could clearly see that he had something tied around his left upper arm. The word "tourniquet" registered in her brain and she dropped her eyes to check for an injury, but there was none. That was when she saw the uncapped needle sitting on his nightstand, just inches away. A blackened spoon was next to it, a filthy looking brown substance coating the bottom. There was a lighter too and right next to that, a small bag with what looked like tiny white crystals in it.

She stepped closer to him, not sure if he was even aware of her presence. He didn't say a word, didn't look up at her. She dropped to her knees in front of him and put her hands on each side of his face and forced his head up. He was still cold, but his breathing was slow and even.

"I didn't do it," he whispered as he slowly covered one of her hands with his. At his words, she sucked in a breath and then looked at the syringe. Sure enough, it was full of the same substance that was in the spoon. A glance at his arm showed no needle marks.

She reached up to release the length of rubber he'd wrapped around his arm and he winced as the blood started flowing again. It made her wonder how long he'd been sitting there like that.

"I'm so proud of you Shane," she said as she fought back her tears.

"Get rid of it please," he asked, his eyes staring straight ahead as if he were afraid to look at the drugs. She snatched up the bag and spoon and then carefully capped the needle. She went into his bathroom and looked around, then grabbed the bottle of conditioner from his shower. After unscrewing the cap, she painstakingly emptied the contents of the bag into the half-full container, then squirted the contents of the syringe into it too before finally dropping the needle into the thick plastic bottle. She added some water to the container and then recapped it and dropped it into the trash.

Shane was sitting in the same position she'd left him in. She dropped back down in front of him and reached up to curl his unruly hair behind his ears.

"Tell me what's going on Shane," she said.

He was quiet for a long time, silent tears dripping down his face. "I've been fighting it for so long, but when I saw her tonight," he began but then stuttered to a halt.

"You mean Abby," she prodded.

He nodded. "I'm going to be like her one day. It's going to win."

"What is?" she asked gently.

"The heroin. I can still taste it even after eight years."

"Was that the last time you did it?"

"It was the only time," he confessed. "I did some cocaine off and on for a few years, but it doesn't have the same hold on me."

She did the math in her head. "So you would have been around sixteen?" She was trying to get some of the warmth back into him by rubbing his hands between hers.

"I let my brother shoot me up," he whispered.

She stilled at his words and then bit back the rage that went through her at the thought of his older brother doing that to him. "It's okay Shane, you can tell me."

"I found him using one day in his room. He was really high and he asked me if I wanted to know what it felt like. I let him do it Savannah. I wanted to know what could be worth so much that he would choose it over me, over everything else." He pulled his hands free of hers and rubbed them through his hair. "From the second it hit my system, I knew it would haunt me for the rest of my life. I loved it – the burn, the taste of it at the back of my throat."

"But you haven't done it since then?"

He shook his head. "Michael realized what he'd done and made me promise not to do it again. I saw what it had done to him and Gabe's mom and I fought it because I knew if I did it even one more time, I'd never be able to stop. When the cravings got too bad and everything would catch up with me, I'd snort some coke and be okay for a while." When he started to yank at his hair, she grabbed his hands in hers again and was grateful when he didn't fight her. "Then came the escorting. It was another rush that took the edge off, but it's always there, taunting me."

He pulled free of her and stood. He began moving around the room, much like he had been at the hospital. "I'm going to end up like her. There's going to be a day when I can't stop myself. When I choose it over everything else and it takes me and everyone around me down."

"You're strong Shane. You'll beat this thing," she said as she stood.

"Abby didn't! She chose this shit over her own fucking son! She was one of the best moms I had ever seen and it twisted her into a depraved monster. She raped her own son!"

Savannah gasped at that. She hadn't asked Gabe the details of his assault and had just automatically assumed it had been a man that had hurt him. She clutched her stomach.

"You can't stay with me Savannah. I love you, but there will come a day when I choose the drugs over you and it will destroy you. That will be you in that fucking hospital room watching me take my last breath! But not until I take everything else from you – your pride, your strength, your hope. I won't do that to you. Don't fucking ask me to," he shouted as he slammed his fist into the wall and then sank to the floor.

She was watching him slip away from her and the agony of it was tearing her apart. "No Shane," she said fiercely. "No! You don't get to decide this for me." She stormed into the bathroom, grabbed his razor from his sink and went back to the bedroom. Dropping down in front of him, her fingers tore at the housing of the razor as she worked the blade free.

Shane grabbed her hand and said, "No!"

"Why not?" she screamed as she yanked her arm from his hold. "If you get to the throw in the towel then so do I!" She popped the blade out.

"Savannah, please don't," he said quietly.

"If I do it, will you stop loving me?" she asked.

"No."

"Will you walk away from me?"

"No."

"Even if I tell you to go?"

"No."

"If I beg you to go?"

"No." He shook his head. "No, no, no."

"Then why are you asking me to?"

She dropped the blade to the floor and wrapped her arms around him as he dragged her closer. "I'm sorry," he said against her neck, but she shook her head, too overwhelmed to tell him she didn't need an apology, she just needed him. He must have gotten the message because his arms tightened even farther around her and the only words she heard after that were the ones telling her how much he loved her.

CHAPTER 17

SHANE STROKED THE ARM THAT LAY ACROSS HIS CHEST AS HE STARED at the ceiling. She had started off snuggled against him after he carried her to his bed, but this morning she was lying on her stomach, her face turned away from him. But even in sleep, she refused to let go of him entirely, thus the arm that still kept them connected. Having her here was both joyful and terrifying. He'd known in his gut last night at the hospital as he pushed her away that she would come for him, but he figured once she saw him in the throes of his addiction, she wouldn't even bother looking back as she walked out of his life forever.

The heroin had been easy to score from the dealer who'd sold him cocaine in the past and the guy had even tossed in some extra as a welcome back present. Not once during the ride home or as he prepared the drug had he even thought about stopping himself. He'd made up his mind after seeing Gabe's mother lying lifeless in that bed, her tormented son signing away his last hope of ever getting back the woman that had raised him. He'd known in that instant that that was his future too and he was tired of fighting the inevitable. He was tired of pretending he was anything other than an addict. He was just plain tired.

Tourniquet wrapped, drugs prepared, syringe filled – it had been the easiest thing he'd ever done in his life – like he'd been born to it. But when he had touched the tip of that needle against his bulging vein, he heard her voice in his head as she apologized for falling in love with him. He felt her lips against his as she pulled him back from the darkness over and over. And then he heard her tell him that she wanted to take away the pain he felt inside. She'd seen through every wall he built up and knocked them down as if they were matchsticks. She wanted him, the real him, even if he didn't really know himself who that was.

So he sat there as the minutes ticked by and waited for that tingling at the back of his throat to take over like it always did – to shove Savannah out of his head and replace her with the promise of relief. But all he heard was her, so he put the needle down and just listened and remembered how she tasted, how she felt. And then she was there, her touch real. She had won this time – he'd been able to choose her. But he had to find a way to make sure she was always his first choice.

He felt her stir against him and then sensed her eyes on him. He looked down to see her smiling sleepily at him and he couldn't help but smile back. He shifted so that he was leaning over her and she instantly wrapped her arms around his back. He kissed her long and deep and heard her sigh. She had probably expected another battle this morning, but he was done fighting. She was his now.

"You have too many clothes on," he muttered.

"You should probably do something about that," she responded and then rubbed her hips against his growing erection.

He stilled and grew serious, his eyes capturing hers. "I love you, Savannah. More than you'll ever know," he managed before he was kissing her again and then doing something about the clothes like she'd told him to.

"LOOK, THERE'S A SHELL RIGHT THERE," SHE SAID, POINTING TO A white speck in the middle of the six eggs he'd cracked into the glass bowl."

"I don't see anything."

"It's right there," she said again as she reached for the fork in his hand.

"It'll give the omelet a little something extra. Your job is the toast," he said briskly as he began whipping the mixture with the fork. She gave him a disgusted frown. She was sitting on the kitchen counter, her slim legs on full display, but she had once again snagged one of his shirts to cover the rest of herself with after they'd managed to drag themselves out of bed for sustenance. He wondered if she knew that seeing her dressed in his clothes like this turned him on almost as much as seeing her naked.

He searched for a pan in the cabinet and placed it on the stove. Before he could light it, he heard her say "Oops, Shane, I spilled." He turned around and sucked in his breath at the sight of her. She was holding the jar of strawberry jam in one hand and was sucking a finger from the other hand in her mouth. A big glob of the jam was on her bare thigh and there was a clear swipe through it where she had run her finger through it – the finger she was now licking clean. "Can you help me clean it up?" she asked innocently as she slid her finger through the jam on her leg once more. If he hadn't turned painfully hard instantly at the sight of her, he would have enjoyed playing out her little game. He loved that she embraced her sexuality; it was something he never would have guessed about her in a million years, but getting to watch it unfold as her confidence grew was going to be a lot of fun.

She squeaked in surprise as he bypassed her lips all together and latched on to her thigh and sucked the jam off. He lapped at the skin until the sweet, red substance was gone and then he dipped his finger into the jam and yanked her further off the counter, spreading her legs open so he could reach her core. She leaned back on her elbows so she could watch as he spread the jam over her clit. He heard her cry out as he sucked it from her, taking her flesh between his lips. She came hard and fast.

"Are you still on the pill?" he muttered as he shoved his sweats down.

She nodded, her eyes lighting up as she realized what the question meant.

"I got tested right after our first time in the hotel and again a few days ago. I'm clean," he said as his cock sprang free.

"Yes," was all she said and then he was pulling her down as he thrust into her. He put his arm between her and the sharp edge of the counter as she rode him. Their coupling was frantic and they came at the same time. Once he caught his breath, he kissed her slow and languidly and then told her he got to wear the jam next time. She blushed, but agreed and then disappeared up the stairs to jump in the shower while he finished the omelet. But as soon as he went to try and light the stove for the second time, there was a knock at his door.

He muttered a few colorful curses and then went to answer it.

"Dad," he said, shocked both to see his father there and by his condition. It was like he had aged ten years in just the few days since their disastrous breakfast. His slacks were wrinkled and there was no jacket or tie to accompany his dress shirt.

"Can I come in son?" Even his voice sounded more aged. Was that even possible?

Shane opened the door and looked up towards the loft. Savannah stood there. She'd managed to pull pants on, but she was still flushed from their lovemaking. A worried look passed over her and he wasn't sure if it was for him or herself. "Come meet my father, sweetheart," he said. He shot a warning look at his father as Savannah navigated the stairs.

He clasped her hand when she reached the bottom and told her with his eyes and touch that nothing would change between them. He saw her smile shakily and then an almost imperceptible nod. "Dad, this is Savannah. Savannah, this is my father, John Matthews."

Savannah held out her hand and Shane breathed a silent sigh of relief when his father respectfully took it. "It's nice to meet you Savannah."

"What are you doing here? Is mom okay?" Shane asked. He'd seen her just yesterday and aside from her stunning words and jittery behavior, she'd otherwise seemed okay.

"Yes, she's fine." His father was having trouble making eye contact with him. It was like the confident, almost arrogant person he knew had left the building and in his place was a shaky, fearful old man.

"I came to ask you if you would join your mother and me for dinner tonight – both of you," he nodded at Savannah. "We'd love to get to know you better Savannah," his father said.

"I'd love to Mr. Matthews."

He nodded. "It's John." He turned to look at Shane. "What do you say, son?"

Shane was flummoxed and finally realized he had been silent for too long when Savannah tightened her hand on his. "Um, yeah, sure," he finally stuttered. "But Savannah and I need to check with some friends today...you remember Gabe Maddox, right?"

"Of course," his father responded. "Nice young man."

"His mom died last night. We need to see if he and his girlfriend need anything so we might need to cancel-"

"Yes, yes," his father said, nodding thoughtfully. "Tell Gabe we're really sorry for his loss. She was a nice woman before..." his voice trailed off awkwardly.

"I'll call you later," Shane said. Suddenly his father's arms were around him, almost clinging to him. Shock went through him and he automatically released Savannah's hand so he could return the embrace. He couldn't remember the last time his father held him and tears stung his eyes at the instant comfort he felt. Would this actually all work out? Would he be able to keep his parents after all this ended?

"Love you Shane," his father whispered brokenly and then he was gone, pulling the door closed behind him. He felt Savannah's arms close around him.

"You okay?" she asked.

He nodded dumbly, still off kilter from his father's display of emotion and declaration.

"Come take a shower with me," she said gently. "Then you can kick that omelet's ass." He was still mute with shock so he just took her hand and trusted her to lead him where he needed to go.

"How are you?" Shane asked as Gabe handed him a bottle of water and he followed his friend out onto the balcony. Savannah was inside with Riley helping to coordinate funeral arrangements. He and Savannah had only arrived a few minutes earlier, but Riley used their presence to give Gabe the break he looked like he needed and had ushered them both outside.

"It's tough," Gabe admitted. "I kept thinking I had prepared myself in case it ended this way but I guess you never really can."

"I'm sorry I took off last night – and that I hadn't gotten there sooner," Shane said as Gabe dropped down into a deck chair.

"It's okay. Things happened so fast between getting the call from the police that she'd been found and making the decision to let her go. They actually found her a couple days ago, but it took them a while to figure out who she was and track me down. She was in an abandoned warehouse and paramedics were able to get her heart beating, but the doctors said there was no brain activity after that." Gabe took a long drink of water. "Afterwards, Riley and I just wanted to get out of there."

"Yeah," Shane muttered.

"You can tell me, you know." Shane looked up at Gabe in confusion. "Whatever it is you've been hiding for so long." Gabe leaned forward in his chair. "You looked like you saw a ghost last night when you saw my mother. I thought maybe it was because of Michael, but it's more than that, isn't it?"

Shane nodded hard.

"It won't change anything between us," Gabe insisted.

"It doesn't seem fair," Shane said quietly.

"What doesn't?"

"That I'm the one that has a chance to beat this." Shane leaned against the railing of the balcony and studied the big pond below them. "Your mother, my brother – they were both so strong but it took them anyway. Why do I get to be the one that walks away from it?"

"Maybe because you have something worth fighting for?" Gabe said evenly, seemingly unsurprised by Shane's indirect admission.

"Your mother had you. What's worth fighting for if not your own kid?" Shane asked desperately.

Gabe was thoughtful for a moment. "A year ago I would have agreed with you, but things are different now." He glanced through the glass doors at the two women and smiled when Riley immediately lifted her eyes as if she sensed he was watching her. There was no wave or blowing of kisses – just a look between lovers, a silent message. "You remember what you said to me? That day in the construction yard that you knocked me on my ass?"

"I said a lot of shit that day," Shane said, smiling slightly at the memory of the stunned expression on Gabe's face when Shane had sucker punched him.

Gabe laughed, but then sobered. "You told me she was like my drug. That didn't make sense at first, but I started to realize you were right. I'd become so used to automatically trying to save her, I never really asked her to fight for me. In my head, I just assumed it would be an easy and automatic choice but it's not, is it?"

Shane sucked in his breath at the pointed question, more confirmation that Gabe had figured out the truth on his own somehow. "No, it's not."

"She didn't really have anyone to fight for her when it all started. I was just a kid – I took care of her when she couldn't take of herself. I protected her secret because I thought that was what I was supposed to do. I didn't know how to fight for her, beside her."

Gabe stood and looked around the quiet complex. "I can play the maybe game for the rest of my life but it won't really solve anything. Here's what I do know," he said as he turned to look Shane in the eye. "I'll fight for you Shane. Riley will fight for you. Savannah, Logan, we'll all fight for you. All you have to do is ask and I swear, you'll never have to do it on your own again."

Shane forced some air into his lungs and then closed his eyes. "I need help Gabe."

❧

Savannah saw Shane and Gabe hug and felt a sigh of relief go through her. There'd been no doubt that Gabe would be there for Shane no matter what, but she knew how hard it was for Shane to have to admit the truth about himself to his best friend whose own life had been devastated by the very drug that Shane craved day in and day out.

She felt Riley take her hand and give it a quick squeeze. Her friend was watching the two men as well. "He'll be okay," Riley said as she released Savannah. Savannah nodded and blinked back a stubborn tear.

There was a knock at the door and Riley went to answer it.

"Hey," Logan said as he entered and gave Riley a quick kiss on the cheek. He pulled Savannah into his arms and said, "They got him." She was confused at first but then he said, "Sam. The police have him." She felt Logan wave over her shoulder and heard Gabe and Shane come back inside.

"What is it?" Shane asked as he appeared at her side. Her knees felt shaky as she realized it was finally over.

"The cops caught Sam trying to get past border security in Canada. They're extraditing him back here tomorrow."

"Thank God," Riley said as Gabe pulled her against him.

Savannah choked back tears as she looked around the small room. Logan had his arm around her shoulders and Shane was gripping her hand. Everyone was smiling and relaxed for the first time in weeks and Savannah couldn't help but wonder if they had finally started putting the broken pieces of their little family back together again.

❧

"GABE HELPED ME FIND A PLACE THAT HAS AN NA MEETING tonight," Shane said as he pulled her into the apartment. "I'm gonna ask my parents if we can meet them tomorrow night instead, if that works for you," he said.

"Definitely," she said. Tomorrow was Monday and now that Sam was behind bars, she was free to return to work. There'd been little doubt that he'd been the person who vandalized her room with the blood, which had luckily turned out to be pig's blood, not human. Shane had suspected he was behind her flat tire that day at the school too and one look at the gaping hole in the tread had confirmed that it hadn't been a stray nail or just wear and tear. She'd always been afraid of Sam for the obvious reasons, but she'd never guessed he might come after her or toy with her the way he had. And when Shane said his name was an alias and no one really knew who he was, a chill had gone through her. What evil things was he hiding in his past that made him take on a new identity?

It was almost four o'clock and all the anxiety and excitement of the past week were starting to catch up with her. She was about to suggest they go take a nap together when she heard her phone ding.

She read the text and then said, "Logan wants me to come to the bar. He needs my help with something."

"With what?" Shane asked as he grabbed two sodas from the fridge and handed her one.

"Didn't say, but he mentioned earlier that he was getting some deliveries this afternoon. I told him I'd help him unpack stuff. It gives us a chance to get caught up on things," she said with a smile. Things between Logan and Shane were still tense, but her brother seemed to have accepted that her future was with Shane because when she told him earlier that day that she'd be spending the night with Shane again tonight, he had just nodded.

"You want me to drive you?" Shane asked.

"No, I have to switch cars with him anyway. I kind of commandeered his car last night," she said sheepishly.

"That's my girl," Shane said proudly and kissed her. "Call me when you get there."

CHAPTER 18

SHANE FELT LIGHTER THAN HE HAD IN YEARS AS HE CLIMBED INTO his car. He was nervous about getting up in front of a group of people and admitting he was an addict, but when it was over, he'd be able to come home to Savannah. And tomorrow, he'd do it all over again. If it meant meetings and sponsors for the rest of his life, he'd do it. His family was counting on him. He was counting on himself.

His phone rang and he looked down to see *Dominic Barretti* appear on the screen.

"Hey Dom."

"It's not him."

Shane stilled. "What?"

"I heard about the arrest so I tapped into security footage taken at the border crossing. It was his truck, but the guy isn't Reynolds."

Ice went through his veins and he jammed the key into the ignition. "How do you know?" he asked, even as he backed out of the parking space and tore down the street.

"I did some surveillance on Logan after you asked me to check out his friends. I saw Reynolds at the bar. I never forget a face." The man sounded desperate and concerned and that had Shane even more freaked out.

"Savannah's at the bar. She got a text from Logan a little while ago asking her to meet him down there."

"Hang on," Dom said and he heard what sounded like Dom putting him on speaker and then clicking on a keypad. Shane ran a red light and veered around a corner, barely missing a truck going through the intersection.

"Her phone's at the bar. But there's no signal for Logan's. It's probably turned off."

"Jesus," Shane whispered.

"I'm ten minutes away," Dom said quickly and the line was disconnected.

Shane dialed Savannah's number and waited, praying to hear her voice. He did, but only because her voicemail picked up. He dialed again as his foot pressed harder on the accelerator.

SAVANNAH WAS REACHING INTO HER PURSE TO ANSWER HER PHONE as she opened the door to the bar. She'd missed the first call because she'd been in the process of parallel parking the car when it started ringing. Her hand finally closed around the phone that was at the bottom of her bag, but she hesitated when a strong odor permeated the air as she swung the door open with her free hand. The stench was so strong it nearly knocked her backwards. It was gasoline, she realized as she stepped inside the dark room. Had there been some kind of spill nearby?

"Logan," she said, pinching her nose.

Her phone rang again. She began reaching for it once more, but stopped when she saw a dark shape on the floor next to the bar. "Logan!" she screamed as she recognized her brother's scuffed work boots. She dropped her purse as she fell to her knees next to him. She shouted his name again and then shook him hard. It was too dark to see clearly, but she recognized the sticky substance on her hands instantly. Blood. On his chest. "Oh God," she whispered. She dropped one hand back to his chest and searched the floor for her purse. She cried out in relief when she felt his chest rise and fall beneath one hand as her other hand closed around the strap of her bag. It took her only a second to dig out her phone.

"Drop it or I'll put a hole in his head right now."

Savannah froze at that familiar voice, the one that had starred in her nightmares for years. She released the phone and raised her hand to show she wasn't holding it. She felt his presence behind her and fear held her in place as he moved around to her side. She slowly turned her head and found herself staring at his demented eyes behind the barrel of a gun that was pointed not at her, but at her brother.

"Get up," he said. She didn't move right away, but when she saw him draw back on the hammer of the gun, she struggled to her feet. "Over there," he said, motioning to the corner of the bar. She stepped over Logan's legs and stopped in the place he had pointed. Her back hit the unforgiving wood behind her as he closed the distance between them.

"Did you know you were the most expensive piece of ass I ever paid for?" he muttered as he stuck the gun against her temple. "Twenty percent," he said harshly. "That fucker charges me an arm and a leg for twenty fucking percent." He kicked one of Logan's legs. "Ungrateful piece of shit!"

The cold metal bit into her skin and she closed her eyes and waited for one of his jerky movements to cause the gun to go off and end her life. He finally turned his full attention back on her, his thick fingers closing around her neck before drifting down her chest. "But you...you were worth every fucking penny." He lowered the gun slightly and then trailed his fingers over her left breast. "Do you still carry my mark?" His fingers pinched her hard and she bit back a scream. Somewhere behind her, she heard her phone ring again.

"What do you want?" she finally asked. She needed to figure out a way to get Logan help. There'd been a lot of blood and her brother still hadn't stirred. He might not have much time left.

Sam's fetid breath washed over her as he laughed in her face. He didn't answer her. Instead, he pulled what looked like a lighter from his pants pocket. She remembered the gas, but before she could stop him, he locked the flame and then flicked the lighter across the room. Flames shot up the wall and then pools of gas lit up as one fed the other until the whole room was surrounded by fire. He'd left only the opening to the back hallway as an escape route. Pockets of fire were all around Logan but blessedly, Sam hadn't appeared to have doused him as well.

"Let's go," Sam said as he gripped her upper arm in a vise-like grip. He began pulling her towards the back exit, his intent to leave Logan behind to die clear. She struggled against him and managed to pull free for a second but then he put her in an arm lock from behind, his thick, beefy limb cutting off her air as he dragged her with him.

"Logan," she screamed as she watched the flames creep closer to him. If Sam got her out of this room, Logan would die for sure. She began to struggle harder, but as he cut off more of her air, her vision began to dim. And then she heard Gabe's voice in her ear as he explained the hold he was going to put on her before he actually touched her. As he spoke, he explained each step of what her response should be and then she was doing it. Relaxing her body, jabbing her elbow, grabbing a finger and twisting.

Her surprise attack caused Sam to drop his arm and she spun around and kneed him in the groin as hard as she could, then stabbed her fingers into his eye sockets. He screamed and pushed away from her and fell backwards over some boxes. His huge body disappeared behind the wall of flame and she heard his scream of agony. Losing her own balance, she hit the floor hard and tried to suck in some air but all she got was smoke.

Tears ran down her cheeks as the intense heat enveloped her. She crawled forward through the blackness and felt for Logan's body. It felt like hours before her fingers finally brushed his jeans.

"Savannah!"

"Shane!" she screamed but she couldn't see him. The fire was loud and she thought she heard glass shattering but she wasn't sure. She tried to drag Logan towards the back exit but he was too big. "Shane!" she screamed again, not even sure if her imagination had conjured up him calling her name. But then he was there, his arms enfolding her, pulling her back as flames roared around them. "Logan!"

"I got him!" another voice called and she saw a huge man grab Logan and haul him over his shoulder. He had Gabe's build but the nearly bald head told her it was Dom. Shane grabbed her under the legs and lifted her into his arms. Dom was right behind them as they worked past the last of the flames and escaped into the alley behind the building. She choked and sputtered as oxygen warred with the soot in her lungs and the bright light hurt, but she ignored it all and crawled over to where Logan lay lifeless on the ground, blood still seeping from the bullet wound in the center of his chest.

"He's not breathing," Dom said as he began CPR, his big hands compressing Logan's damaged chest before stopping to blow air into his lungs.

"No!" she screamed. She couldn't lose him now. She felt Shane's arms circle her from behind as she watched Dom work to save her brother. Paramedics appeared and then firefighters were there with hoses.

"We've got a pulse," one of the paramedics said as he checked Logan. Dom eased back to let them work, his relief evident.

Within minutes she was in the ambulance, her brother's limp hand in hers. There hadn't been room for Shane, but he told her to go with her brother and that he'd be right behind them. The paramedic had put an oxygen mask over her face, but otherwise focused all his attention on Logan. She heard the cool, calm voices of the paramedics as they told the hospital what to expect, but everything faded to the background as she focused on Logan and told him she was there. She kept talking, even when his heart stopped again.

SHANE WATCHED SAVANNAH IN GROWING CONCERN AS SHE FORCED herself to stay upright in the waiting room chair. He'd managed to stay behind the ambulance the entire way to the hospital and had paled when he saw CPR being performed on Logan once again. Savannah had stumbled out of the ambulance as they lowered her brother's gurney, a blanket wrapped around her shoulders and an oxygen mask dangling from her hand. She refused to release her brother's hand and Shane finally had to pry her hand loose so the medical staff could get Logan into the hospital. After that she'd gone eerily silent. A doctor had checked her out in the ER and she was cleared by the time Gabe and Riley arrived. His parents were there too, even though they'd never met Logan. To Shane's surprise, Dom lingered as well, though he stayed on the fringes of the group.

They'd both arrived at the bar at the same time. It had been Dom who had broken the glass on one of the front windows near the corner where there were fewer flames. His relief at finding Savannah and Logan alive had been short-lived when he saw the condition his friend was in and felt the anguish of Savannah's sobs as she watched her brother's life seep out of him. The ER staff had managed to get his heart going again and he'd been rushed into surgery nearly four hours ago. Riley had managed to talk Savannah into going into the bathroom to help her clean some of the soot off her face, but she refused to eat or drink anything.

Feeling helpless, Shane finally stood and plucked Savannah from the chair and pulled her into his lap. He couldn't make her talk, but he could let her feel that he was there. She could take his heat and strength and use that to sustain her. She was stiff at first, but then finally curled against him, her arm wrapping around his neck as she buried her face against him. They stayed that way for another hour and then finally a doctor came out.

"Miss Bradshaw?"

Shane helped her stand and saw her lip quivering as she tried to prepare herself for the worst.

"The bullet nicked his heart, but we got the bleeding to stop and were able to repair the damage. He lost a lot of blood but we're giving him transfusions. It's going to be a long recovery, but he should be okay." Savannah sobbed in relief and crumbled against him as she nodded her understanding.

"Give us about an hour to get him up to ICU, then you can see him."

"Thank you," Shane said to the doctor. Gabe and Riley huddled around them as relief swept through the group and he felt his father's arm patting his back. He saw Dom near the door, his dark eyes watching them and then he left, a quick nod in Shane's direction. He didn't even have time to nod back at the man before he was gone.

EPILOGUE

Logan was a terrible patient, Shane thought to himself. Yes, Savannah was definitely the hovering type, but Logan clearly wasn't someone who was good at taking orders. It had been less than a week since he'd been shot, nearly burned to death and had his heart stop not once, but twice and yet he wanted to know when he could go home.

"If you try to force one more spoonful of that crap down my throat Savannah..." he threatened as she shoved a mouthful of orange gelatin at him.

"God, no wonder the nurses are so sick of you!" she huffed as she put the food down and then went to fluff his pillow for the fourth time.

"Shane, can you do something here?" he asked.

Shane put up his hands. He knew better than to try and intervene. He'd done that on the second day when he tried to tell Savannah she needed a real meal and a shower. Somehow that had turned into her yelling at him because she thought he was telling her she smelled bad. Logan had still been out of it and Savannah was sick with fear so her shouting had quickly turned to tears and in the end, Riley took over, putting on her "mom" hat and dragging Savannah to her and Gabe's place for a scrub down and a hot meal. And that was only after Shane had promised to stay with Logan and call her if there was any change.

"Savannah, please," Logan said, a little more gently. "Would you do me a favor and get me some real food from the cafeteria? Something greasy?"

She mulled it over and then finally said, "Only if the nurse says it's okay." She grabbed her purse off the chair, planted a kiss on Shane's lips as she passed and then left the room. Shane smiled and then pulled up a chair so he could sit next to Logan. His friend looked a lot better than a few days ago and he couldn't help but reach out and grab his hand.

"Too close," Shane muttered before releasing Logan's hand.

"Is it all gone?" Logan asked.

"The firemen got most of the fire out before it did too much structural damage, but the inside is gutted."

A dejected look came over Logan and Shane couldn't blame him. His friend had poured everything into the place and it was nearly all gone.

"You gonna start over?" Shane asked.

Logan shrugged. "It's insured, but the deductible is huge. Maybe it's a sign to let it go."

Shane was quiet for a moment. "If I've learned anything over these past couple of months Logan, you don't let your dreams go. You might have to fight harder than you thought for them, but you don't just let them go." Logan fell silent and he knew his friend had a long road ahead of him to gain his health and his future back.

"Do you remember any of it?" Shane asked.

Logan shook his head. "I went there to meet the delivery guys. I walked in and then everything went dark. I don't even remember him shooting me," he said, clearly flabbergasted by the events that had put him in this bed.

"They found a body, but the damage is pretty significant. They'll do DNA testing to confirm it's him, but Savannah saw him fall into the fire."

"Is she okay? Really?"

Shane knew Logan was asking if Savannah had resorted to hurting herself again to deal with the stress.

"She's okay Logan. She's really strong. It's just been hard for her. She watched you die. Twice. It's going to take her a while to deal with that. I wouldn't expect her to stop hovering anytime soon."

Logan laughed. "Yeah, I guess." The men fell silent for a moment. "I'm sorry Shane – I said some stuff to you that I didn't mean. My big brother instincts kicked in..."

"It's okay-"

"No, it's not," Logan said. "I'm glad you were there for her – that you saw what she needed. She knew in her heart that she could trust you. I should have seen that too, instead of assuming you were just messing around with her."

"It's not like I gave you a reason to think anything else. I played the part because it's all I know how to do."

"So, where do you go from here?" Logan asked.

Shane leaned back in the chair. "Not sure. I haven't officially dropped out of law school yet but that's probably what'll happen."

"And your folks? They're okay with that?"

He nodded slowly, mulling it over. "They might actually be. I dropped them off at the airport last night and told them I wasn't going to be joining my dad's firm. I expected this big blow up, but my mom told me to just come to Chicago for a visit then. My dad told me to bring Savannah with me."

Logan whistled. "That's it?"

"Yeah, it's pretty fucked up. I guess we're both starting over, huh?"

"Yeah, I guess so," Logan said and then watched with appreciation as his sister swept back into the room, a huge cheeseburger on the tray in her hands. "Now we're talking," Logan said as he dug in.

"WILL YOU MOVE IN WITH ME?"

Savannah froze at the question as she reached the top stair of the loft. He was already in bed, his shirt off. He was lying flat on his back, his eyes watching her as she moved further into the room. She went to him and straddled his lap. His hands spread out over her thighs as his intense gaze held hers.

"Yes," she said simply even though her insides were screaming with joy.

"We'll need to get a smaller place – something more affordable," he said.

"Yes," she said again.

"I don't know what I'm going to do for a living."

"Yes."

He smiled and then finally seemed to notice she held her hands behind her back.

"What's behind your back?" he asked as he leaned up on his elbows. She could already see the lust building along with the anticipation of whatever she had planned.

"I love you," she said.

"I love you too," he responded automatically. "Show me," he said, motioning to the arms she had behind her.

She finally showed him what she'd gone down to the kitchen for. "I brought the jam," she said as she showed him the jar. His eyes lit up as he recalled their conversation about it being his turn to wear the jam next time.

"Shit," he moaned as he flopped back down on the bed. "You better get the ties too."

The End

ABOUT THE AUTHOR

Dear Reader,

As an independent author, I am always grateful for feedback so if you have the time and desire, please leave a review, good or bad, so I can continue to find out what my readers like and don't like. You can also send me feedback via email at sloane@sloanekennedy.com

Join my Facebook Fan Group: Sloane's Secret Sinners

Connect with me:

www.sloanekennedy.com

sloane@sloanekennedy.com

ALSO BY SLOANE KENNEDY

(Note: Not all titles will be available on all retail sites)

The Escort Series

Gabriel's Rule (M/F)

Shane's Fall (M/F)

Logan's Need (M/M)

Barretti Security Series

Loving Vin (M/F)

Redeeming Rafe (M/M)

Saving Ren (M/M/M)

Freeing Zane (M/M)

Finding Series

Finding Home (M/M/M)

Finding Trust (M/M)

Finding Peace (M/M)

Finding Forgiveness (M/M)

Finding Hope (M/M/M)

Love in Eden

Always Mine (M/M)

Pelican Bay Series

Locked in Silence (M/M)

Sanctuary Found (M/M)

The Truth Within (M/M)

The Protectors

Absolution (M/M/M)

Salvation (M/M)

Retribution (M/M)

Forsaken (M/M)

Vengeance (M/M/M)

A Protectors Family Christmas

Atonement (M/M)

Revelation (M/M)

Redemption (M/M)

Defiance (M/M)

Unexpected (M/M/M)

Shattered (M/M)

Unbroken (M/M)

Protecting Elliot: A Protectors Novella (M/M)

Discovering Daisy: A Protectors Novella (M/M/F)

Pretend You're Mine: A Protectors Short Story (M/M)

Non-Series

Four Ever (M/M/M/M)

Letting Go (M/F)

Short Stories

A Touch of Color

Catching Orion

Twist of Fate Series (co-writing with Lucy Lennox)

Lost and Found (M/M)

Safe and Sound (M/M)

Body and Soul (M/M)

Crossover Books with Lucy Lennox

Made Mine: A Protectors/Made Marian Crossover (M/M)

The following titles are available in audiobook format with more on the way:

Locked in Silence

Sanctuary Found

The Truth Within

Absolution

Salvation

Retribution

Logan's Need

Redeeming Rafe

Saving Ren

Freeing Zane

Forsaken

Vengeance

Finding Home

Finding Trust

Finding Peace

Four Ever

Lost and Found

Safe and Sound

Body and Soul

Made Mine